It was meant to be

"I couldn't leave you," John finally murmured, the kiss broken, their faces touching. "I stood outside your door for the longest time. All I could think of was holding you in my arms . . . the baffling rightness of it."

"I'm glad you came back," Karin said softly, trembling.

He didn't tell her of the voices in his head that whispered that what he was contemplating did not belong outside marriage. His need for Karin—as natural as sunlight and rain and the changing seasons—came from his very core.

"I want to make love with you," he said clearly, urgently.

With. Not *to*. She liked that. And his shining eyes seemed to promise her a night to treasure, no matter what happened tomorrow. . . .

Raising her hand to his cheek, she confessed, "I want that, too."

ABOUT THE AUTHOR

Lauren Bauman knows all about transition. After working for six years as a Harlequin editor, she left to pursue her first love—writing. Her new job title of "author" was swiftly followed by "mother." Laurie and her husband had their first child, a son, shortly after her Superromance was finished. The happy family live in Kitchener-Waterloo—Mennonite country—where *Seasons* is set. Laurie is currently working on her next book.

Seasons

LAUREN BAUMAN

Harlequin Books

TORONTO • NEW YORK • LONDON
AMSTERDAM • PARIS • SYDNEY • HAMBURG
STOCKHOLM • ATHENS • TOKYO • MILAN

FORTY YEARS OF
Romance

Published May 1989

First printing March 1989

ISBN 0-373-70354-6

To Larry and our Jason,
with love

CHAPTER ONE

AFTER HE LED THE HORSE into the stall, John Martin lingered in the barn, glad to be sheltered from the bitterly cold gusts outdoors. His arm rested against the strong warm flank of Wicked, whom he'd raised from a colt. The rebellious streak that had earned the horse his name had long been subdued, but John still saw traces of that same wild spirit in the eyes and gait of the animal who faithfully pulled the family buggy, season after season.

"We're two of a kind, fellow," he murmured, affectionately slapping the mahogany-brown haunches, then inhaling deeply. The barn's fresh, earthy scent of straw and livestock was as familiar to him as the chores he carried out there daily.

"Hello, John," a soft voice said from the doorway behind him.

"Elizabeth," he acknowledged more sharply than he intended, giving the animal a final pat before turning.

"Your mother sent me for you. Dinner is ready," she explained quietly, apologetically.

She was always a little afraid of him, and he regretted the brusqueness of his tone. But he'd felt instant irritation at his mother's unsubtle attempt at matchmaking. According to Anna Martin, the hardworking and good-hearted Elizabeth Snyder would make the perfect Mennonite wife for her son. And since Elizabeth was also a member of the same Old Order group, a union would be acceptable, uncomplicated.

But being matched to anyone at this difficult time in his life was out of the question for John.

"I'll be along shortly," he said, hoping the direction of his thoughts had been well hidden.

"I'll wait." Her hands buried in her black cape, she watched as he threw an old blanket around the horse, then drew some sugar cubes from his pocket. "Ah, so we are not the only ones who get special treats on a Sunday," she said, her dark eyes sparkling.

John smiled at her. "True."

He opened the barn door for her, then fell into step beside her as they headed toward the Martins' large, sandy-colored brick house. Jutting out from a small driving shed to the left of the stone driveway were the wheels of two black buggies. From inside the shelter came the whinny of one of the visiting Snyders' horses, the only sound of life in the frozen white landscape.

The Martins prided themselves on the orderly appearance of their home and yard, as all Mennonites tended to do. Alongside the tidy corncribs, stacked to the brim with ample livestock feed, stood neat piles of the firewood that would see the family well through the winter. At the front of the yard rose perfectly lined rows of bare apple trees, their crooked branches silhouetted against the adjoining snow-covered field from which only a few dried stubbles protruded as evidence of last year's corn crop.

"Are you going to the fellowship meeting this evening?" Elizabeth asked, sounding breathless.

John looked over at his young companion. Although she kept her head down, he could see that her cheeks were flushed, not only from the cutting wind, but also with a high coloring of another sort. Her long black hair was center parted and pulled back from her face beneath the dark bonnet she wore. She was pretty, he supposed, aware of her looks in an objective way. He had known her for many years because they belonged to the same church, but only recently had Elizabeth started seeking him out, shyly and self-consciously, despite his lack of encouragement.

"How old are you, Elizabeth?" he asked suddenly, stopping by the snow-dusted, green gate that bordered the yard.

"Eighteen."

"Well, I'm thirty-one."

"That doesn't matter to me. The difference in our ages, that is . . ." she replied, holding his stare boldly for a few seconds, then looking down again.

He didn't reply directly to what she was telling him. "I feel as if I don't belong at the meetings anymore. I'm the oldest there."

What he couldn't say was that the Sunday ritual of barn games, square dancing to harmonica music and hymn singing, well loved by the Mennonite youth as permissible social activities, not to mention courting grounds, away from the watchful eyes of parents, now seemed frivolous and juvenile to him. It was another painful reminder of how much he had changed.

He'd tried hard, for a while, though. He'd pretended to be having fun. He'd managed to fool everyone but himself.

He looked directly at her. "I'm sorry, Elizabeth. I just can't go back to all that anymore. Things are different now."

A long moment passed before she spoke in a clear, determined voice that surprised him. "It's not just because of Emma anymore, is it? At first we all thought you just needed time, after she died. But it's more than that, isn't it?" She drew a deep breath. "Is it me? I know I may seem . . . awkward, at times. But I can learn. I can be whatever you—"

"No." Reaching over, he stroked her cheek with the backs of his red, roughened fingers, struggling for the right words, the words that would hurt her as little as possible.

"Elizabeth, you are very sweet, and I do care for you. But . . ."

"'But . . .'" she echoed, her eyes filling, turning from his touch.

"It's not you . . . it's me. Please understand." His dark brown eyes pleaded with her.

"It's natural to feel confused when your wife dies, especially at Emma's young age. Of course, your thoughts will seem upside-down for a while, but then your life will settle back into the old patterns."

"I'm not sure I want the old patterns anymore, Elizabeth. That's what I'm telling you. I may have to leave the farm, the Old Order."

Her eyes widened in shock. "B-but you can't do that. What would your parents do? You're the only son—"

"It will all work out," he said with more reassurance than he felt. "Let's go in. No one will be happy with either of us if we make them wait any longer 'to eat themselves full,' as Mother says."

Taking her by the elbow, he directed her into the warm kitchen. Elizabeth stood unmoving, disoriented, just inside the doorway for a few seconds. Before John closed the door behind them, his gaze was drawn to the whitened, sunlit rolling hills that stretched far beyond what his eyes could see.

KARIN SHERWOOD LEANED BACK against the wooden rail of the bridge and gazed out at the view both man and nature had provided for her on the late afternoon of a golden winter day. To the south towered the outlines of a huge old barn, silos and a farmhouse with a picture-perfect gray wisp of smoke curling from its chimney top. How good a crackling fire would feel after her walk in the subfreezing temperatures, she thought wistfully, but her small apartment in Kitchener had no such luxury.

All around, open fields and cedar bush were parted by the Conestogo River, an ivory mass of ice and snow, except for two dark pools churning determinedly just below her. And to the north stood a plain white Mennonite church. Nearby, rows of simple headstones marked the graves of the pioneers and their descendants who had come to Waterloo County from Pennsylvania as early as 1800.

As if the past was suddenly coming alive, Karin could hear the clop-clop of a horse-drawn buggy drawing near. Four dark bundles huddled under blankets in the carriage—a man, woman and two children, their faces ruddy with the cold. Karin pushed herself against the bridge as the vehicle passed, its modern, orange yield sign incongruous with the buggy's old-fashioned appearance.

Only the younger two glanced back at her curiously. The parents looked straight ahead with that same aloofness she'd noticed many Mennonites held toward outsiders to their close-knit community. Or maybe the couple had been afraid that Karin would snap their picture with the camera dangling around her neck, a practice they shunned, associating it with vanity.

Karin was surprised at how intrigued she was by these simple, plainly clothed folk whom she'd seen at the local farmers' markets or along the country roads since she'd moved to the area a few months ago. She, who needed to change her life-style and home with the regularity with which others tackled spring-cleaning, found it hard to comprehend the static nature of the Old Order Mennonite community. But because their way of life was so different from her own, she was tantalized by it—and perplexed by her strong interest. She'd even visited the Meetingplace, an information center about the Mennonites in the nearby town of St. Jacob's.

Karin couldn't imagine a day without her modern conveniences—her stereo, her new microwave oven and VCR, her blow dryer for her long thick hair—but some of the most conservative Mennonite orders still functioned without phones, electricity or cars, let alone zippers on their clothing. They quietly worked their farms and managed to stay self-sufficient. They paid all taxes and had their own schools, but many refused insurance, medicare and old-age pensions, relying on each other in times of trouble. They wouldn't go to court or war. It was really quite amazing.

Their numbers had surprised her, too. There were about forty thousand Mennonites living in Ontario, with Waterloo County having the heaviest concentration. Their forefathers all had one thing in common—they had either fled or been exiled from their homelands in Germany, Switzerland, France or Russia because of their unpopular religious practices during the Protestant Reformation in the sixteenth century.

Karin couldn't help but admire their determination to preserve their heritage, their strong sense of family and community—elusive qualities to her. She lived alone, by choice. Her family ties were minimal, by circumstance. Actually, her time-consuming job and scattered friendships constituted most of her life.

So far she was enjoying the challenge of managing a new fitness club. And the novelty of living in Kitchener's small-town atmosphere, as compared to the bustle of cosmopolitan Toronto, where she'd last stayed for a while, hadn't worn off yet. But, judging by her track record, she knew the inevitable moment would come when she'd want to start all over again someplace else.

And for the first time in her life that prospect disturbed her. Greatly.

Maybe there was nothing out there that could hold her, fulfill her, stave off the stark empty feeling she'd been experiencing more and more lately. She'd tried telling herself her panic was escalating because a milestone, her thirtieth birthday, was approaching at the end of the summer. Still, she couldn't help but wonder if her constant need for change meant there was something wrong with her.

But dwelling on such melancholy thoughts was pointless, uncharacteristic of the bubbly, confident self she presented to the world. She was *determined* to conquer her emptiness. A good brisk walk was what she needed, why she'd driven out to the country earlier, abandoning the laundry, bill paying and letter writing that she should be doing on a Sunday afternoon, when the health club was closed.

Pulling her ski jacket over her jean-clad hips and stuffing her gloved hands into her pockets, she decided not to waste any more time, and set out along the path beside the river.

She had a sudden craving for a hearty homemade stew after the walk that was sure to be invigorating, but she'd have to settle for whatever frozen meal-in-a-bag she had on hand. Unless she went out for dinner...but Sunday was such a family day at the local restaurants that eating out alone just didn't appeal to her....

TEN HEADS BOWED for a silent grace around the long kitchen table. On any one Sunday, Anna Martin never knew exactly who would drop by for a visit or a meal, but she was always prepared for the possibility of company—she'd provided for up to fifty people on occasion—with plenty of food on hand. She and her only daughter, Mary, had been busy all afternoon Friday baking loaves of bread and homemade pies in their cast-iron, wood-fueled stove. Saturdays were always spent selling preserves, pies and summer sausage at the local market.

While the family had attended service that morning, a pork roast had been cooking and cabbage rolls simmering, filling the large kitchen with a rich, inviting aroma.

Today the Martins were joined by Joseph and Ada Snyder and their three children—Elizabeth and her two younger brothers. Facing each other at opposite ends of the long table were John's spry, white-haired grandfather, Erwin Martin, and his father, Jacob. Both men were quiet and serious by nature, so household meals were generally solemn affairs, which was why John always enjoyed the livelier Sunday gatherings with visitors.

Smiling to himself, he watched the enthusiasm with which plates were piled high with the tasty food. Although strict discipline was practiced in many aspects of Mennonite life, eating plentifully had always been encouraged. John had a healthy appetite, one of the few pleasures he felt no qualms about satisfying to the utmost, and he was lucky to have inherited the Martins' tall leanness. With gusto, he topped his brimming plate with a fluffy mound of mashed potatoes, dousing them in hot gravy.

"Have you heard how your brother Samuel is coming along?" Jacob Martin asked of his longtime neighbor.

Joseph Snyder nodded, his bushy brows knitting in concern. "We have prayed hard for him. He's sixty-three, a strong man, but still . . . he lost one arm. Fortunately, the doctors were able to save his leg with surgery."

"He is a lucky man to be alive," murmured Joseph's wife, Ada, giving him a warning look as she glanced at Daniel, her eleven-year-old. "I still don't understand how the attack could have happened. Samuel tended boars all his life."

"They can turn on you at any time," Jacob said, shaking his head. "I heard that Samuel grabbed a short stick instead of his sturdy one to lead the boars into their pens. He is paying dearly for that carelessness. A wild animal knows when a human is defenseless, especially one weighing four hundred pounds with ten-inch tusks that can rip a man apart."

Elizabeth had set down her fork and was staring at her plate when she asked quietly, "What did they do with...the boar?"

"He was put to sleep, then tested for rabies, but he was not contaminated," Ada Snyder told her gently.

Gerald, the middle Snyder boy, piped up, "Did they eat him for Sunday dinner?"

"Of course not. Boar meat is too tough," his mother admonished.

"Regardless, no one should eat the meat of an animal that has turned into a mean fighter. It's not right. No violence ever is." Anna Martin adroitly changed the unpleasant subject then. "Now who will have more pickled beets or candied carrots? I always say it is better to eat more than less!"

"And she certainly practices what she preaches," her husband said fondly, his eyes lingering on her well-rounded shape beneath the long apron and simple print dress. Her lightly graying brown hair, wound into a bun, was tucked into the obligatory white organdy prayer veil she wore constantly, because in the Bible, St. Paul said that women should cover their heads when they pray, and she might pray at any time.

Anna playfully punched her husband in the arm. "Ach, we all need a little extra meat to keep our bodies warm, especially in this brisk February weather."

Ada Snyder nodded. "When we were driving here in the buggy after service, all that kept me from being chilled to the bone was the thought of your cozy kitchen."

"I hear the Webers from Woolwich Road have bought a car," John announced matter-of-factly, instantly realizing his mistake as silence fell upon the table.

Jacob Martin cleared his throat. "Yes, and it has brought much heartache into their family. Never has there been a car in the family, through generations of Webers." Jacob's weathered face creased in disapproval. "Now Glen and his new wife attend a different church in which cars are allowed, he has electricity in his home and he does not speak to his own parents."

"I understand his father will not speak to him," John could not resist clarifying.

Anna Martin glanced at him anxiously. "His father is only concerned that by taking on the material things of the world, Glen will soon lose all that he has been taught."

"If he truly believes what he has been taught, he will not lose anything," John said defiantly.

Once more the room grew quiet.

"I have always been taught that we must tolerate the choices of others," Elizabeth said at last, her cheeks pinkening as John threw her a grateful look.

"Which is all fine, until one must bear the crosses of one's own flesh and blood," Jacob muttered.

"This is not the place for such a discussion," the elderly Erwin Martin interjected sternly, glancing from his son to grandson, who were eyeing each other in a private challenge.

After a few moments of halting conversation, the meal proceeded with idle chatter—some friendly gossip among the women about the latest births and deaths in the community and plans for the next quilting bee, and a businesslike exchange among the men about the low market prices cattle had brought at the last public auction. The Snyder boys listened respectfully.

As John ate the rest of his meal in silence, he began to reflect on the many hours he had spent in this very kitchen: his quiet contentment after a long day's work in the fields; listening to his sister, Mary, hum as she sewed by the window light; watching his mother clean the old stove; seeing his father bent over the kitchen table, tallying the farm's monthly cost of supplies, ignoring John's arguments for a second tractor. Jacob Martin rarely listened to reason when it came to matters of change.

The kitchen had witnessed John's carefree boyhood, his care-filled maturity. But the room itself had changed little throughout the years. The well-constructed wooden table and straight-back chairs had seated three generations of Martins to date. The only splashes of color in the room came from a blue-and-white checkered tablecloth and the bright purple bloom of some African violets, sharing the sill of the big curtainless window with a row of lush green houseplants.

Everything else in the room was functional—a sturdy pendulum clock, a calendar, wooden pegs for coats, the hanging well-worn kitchen utensils. The indoor hand water pump, gas lantern and step-stove with a pipe leading to the upper rooms had served the family well for many years.

The house had been the only home John had ever known. When he had married six years ago, he and his bride had been given sleeping quarters on the second story. His parents had expected to move into the adjoining *gross-daddy* house with his widowed grandfather when John's family had grown large enough to need additional space. By that time his sister, Mary, would likely have married and moved onto her husband's farm property. But things had turned out quite differently. John's wife, Emma, had died of cancer two years ago, and there had been no off-spring—a deep disappointment not only to the young couple, but to Jacob and Anna Martin, who wanted grandchildren and also recognized the economic necessity of having as many family members as possible help run the farm.

To say they would not take kindly either to John's desire to leave the farm, would be a huge understatement. He forced back his thoughts to the meal....

Plates were being wiped clean with thick slices of fresh bread while the serving bowls were being cleared away, then a lavish assortment of homemade pies and cakes appeared, and once again the same plates were filled and emptied.

Taking their pipes and mugs, the men ambled into the living room, while the women stayed in the kitchen to clean up. John lingered at the table over a second cup of coffee. The lively chatter of the women and the clankety collision of dishes, pots, cutlery and glasses were a pleasant diversion from the dark direction of his wandering thoughts. Drifting into his consciousness were the men's voices, growing heated as they discussed whether to add growth hormones to their cattle, a practice that they disagreed with, but one that they might have to adopt if they were to stay competitive.

"Out you get, John! We can't work around you," his mother finally scolded.

"How about some help?" he asked impulsively.

"That'll be the day," said Anna. "I've seen the way you chop wood. I won't have my china at your mercy."

"John used to break less chicken eggs than I did in our rounds," Mary pointed out, smiling coyly and handing him her towel.

"Don't be foolish, Mary. Dishes aren't a man's work. Come on, John, off with you."

He threw up his hands in mock helplessness and got to his feet. "Let it be known that I tried to help, but I've been rejected."

His mother's full face broke into a wide grin. "'Rejected'! Go with the men, where you belong, lad, and have a good chin with them!"

But the prospect of debating the same dry, joyless topics that had been covered Sunday after Sunday just did not appeal to John. Nor did biting his tongue about such controversial issues as the Webers' new car. So much more inviting was the fresh, invigorating air outdoors. "No, I think I'll go for a walk, instead."

Anna Martin's smile faded. "But we have guests. Your father would not—"

"I'd like some time alone," he said firmly, pulling on his heavy black coat and work boots and grabbing his wide-brimmed hat. His hand slipped into the coat's oversize pocket to check for the forbidden camera he'd placed there earlier.

He did not have to look back at the women's faces to know they all wore somber expressions. Solitude was not something his people understood, especially on a Sunday, the one day set aside for visiting. But solitude was what he needed most these days.

He walked with purpose along the deserted road, relishing the wide open space. Most of the morning his restless spirit had been confined in the austere meeting house, listening to words that had lost their meaning to him, not only because they were in the traditional Pennsylvanian Dutch dialect, an unwritten German with a mixture of English, but because his intellect was questioning everything and finding few answers. The rigid ceremony allowed for no individual expression, and he kept restraining himself from jumping up and telling the solemn-faced members that his anguished soul found no peace there.

Today he had decided he could not return.

The only moments of tranquillity he knew of late came from the cold wind as it caressed his face, penetrating his numbed feelings, and the sight of the frozen river valley, crisscrossed with sunlight and shadow. He headed there to piece together the fragments of the most important decision of his life.

CHAPTER TWO

ONCE KARIN had started following the route carved by countless anonymous footsteps in the sheltered valley, she'd warmed up considerably. Still, she snuggled into the fur-lined collar of her coat, not bothering to wear the pink earmuffs she'd bought on a whim yesterday. The crunch of her boot soles on the hard-packed snow and the occasional creak of a tree were the only sounds as she slowly made her way, curious to see where the path led.

Squinting against the bright glare of the sun, she didn't notice the man on the hill overlooking the riverbed, until she was about fifty feet away. He was looking off in the other direction, so he hadn't seen her. Her heart quickened because of her isolation, then she recognized the familiar Mennonite hat and baggy black garb. As a probable pacifist who refused to fight wars or own weapons, chances were he would do her no harm.

He was leaning against a wide gnarled tree, one knee up. His lone dark figure, outlined in the sunlight and surrounded by a sweep of alabasterlike field, created the perfect subject for a photograph. Fumbling with the new camera as she walked forward, she convinced herself there was no harm in taking one little picture, especially if she was quick enough that he'd never notice her boldness.

But just before the camera clicked, he turned and stared at her. In that instant, she caught a look of profound sadness radiating from eyes dark and weary and brooding.

And she felt that more than her camera had invaded this stranger's private moments.

Slowly she walked toward the man. When she stood just below him, she called up, "I'm sorry. I didn't mean to disturb you."

To her amazement, he smiled, causing a dazzling transformation to his former morose look. "You needn't apologize. It's a free world. Sometimes, that is," he added with a trace of bitterness. "Are you a professional photographer?"

"No. Not by a long shot." They both grimaced at her unintentional pun. "I'm still at the instruction-manual stage. This was a Christmas gift from someone," she said, pointing to the shiny 35-mm, remembering with a stab of pain the day the package had arrived instead of the father she'd expected after several years of being apart. But he'd had a chance for a big gig in Los Angeles, he'd written....

The Mennonite stranger looked down at her, and she was drawn into warm dark depths the color of rich walnut. Small creases around his eyes and a rugged, browned complexion indicated long hours spent working outdoors and the kind of natural vitality that didn't come from attending health clubs.

"Would you mind if I took your photograph, too? On my camera, that is...." From his pocket he pulled out a well-worn black leather camera case.

She looked from him to the case and back, twice. "Ah, sure...."

"You're surprised that a Mennonite owns a camera. Granted, I bought it secondhand, or thirdhand, maybe. Who knows?"

"Well, since most Mennonites don't seem to like having their picture taken, I assumed..."

"You're perfectly right. But, fortunately or unfortunately, depending on your perspective, I'm not like everyone else. Wait there, I'll be right down."

Taken aback by this unexpected encounter, Karin watched him scramble down the steep embankment with strong, sure steps. He was a tall, solid-looking man, his wide shoulders apparent even in the loose-fitting heavy overcoat he wore. Short wavy hair, a darker shade of brown than his eyes, poked out from beneath his hat. About him she sensed a restrained intensity.

"You really don't mind?" he asked when he was by her side, stuffing his gloves into his pockets.

"Of course not. I, ah, owe you one."

"If you'd just leave your camera here with me then, and I'll get a picture of *you* by that black walnut tree, but you don't have to climb the bank. I'll take it from here. Did you know that black walnut trees always grow by water? The Mennonites consider them a symbol of fertility. Lovely...." The camera clicked and he smiled at her. "Now if you wouldn't mind standing by the river there, looking off...that way, so I can catch the sun reflecting off those icicles...."

She obeyed his deeply melodious voice as he proceeded to tell her how and where to stand, making her tilt her head ever so slightly so he could capture her profile. Following his strangely hypnotic voice in the otherworldly winter wonderland, she felt herself relaxing. She looked out to the river with a grand hope, because she knew instinctively that was the feeling he wanted from her.

After he'd snapped a few different angles, he murmured, "Thank you. It's not often I even have a subject."

Karin turned, aware of a sudden awkwardness between them. "What will you do with the pictures?" she asked, her

stomach somersaulting after meeting those warm penetrating eyes again.

"Oh, it's just something I started about a year or so ago,
for my own enjoyment. I've been to this very place many
times during my life. Every time there is something different in the way the light, the river, the seasons all change,
intermix. I like to capture such special moments. And today you have come here."

*With a beauty that took his breath away... the largest,
bluest eyes he'd ever seen, framed by long golden hair, the
combination making him think of sky and sunshine on a
brilliant summer's day. Her face was round, her lips full,
made for smiling... and other delights.* But of course, he
would not speak of such fancies.

Instead, he asked, "What is your name?"

"Karin Sherwood," she said softly.

"Hello, Karin."

"Hello—"

"John. John Martin."

His name was like him—solid, strong, with no harsh-
ness to the sound of it. "You must live close by... John?"
she asked, wanting to prolong this meeting, telling herself
her interest was only because he was the first Mennonite
she'd had a chance to converse with.

He nodded, pointing to some buildings just peeking over
the horizon. "That farm by the road. We have about one
hundred acres, enough for some corn, mixed grain and
wheat, some grazing land for our beef and dairy cattle, a
maple bush and an apple orchard. It's a small operation by
some standards, but plenty for us to manage."

"That sounds like a lot of land to someone like me who's
used to a few square feet of balcony space or a yard shared
by a houseful of renters. Do you come from a large family?"

"No, there's just my sister and myself. I know my parents would have liked more, particularly my father to help out with the farm work, and now—" a dark look crossed his face, then disappeared just as rapidly "—but it wasn't meant to be. What about you, though? Are you from around here?"

"No. I moved from Toronto to Kitchener a few months ago. I invested in some new appliances and houseplants to make myself believe I'm going to stay for a while, and I even brought old Rocky. But who knows what'll happen?"

"Rocky?"

"Oh," she said, laughing, and he was mesmerized by her large, dancing, sky-blue eyes. Her brows and long lashes were dark, most attractive against the fairness of her hair and the natural golden color of her skin. "Rocky is this wonderful antique rocking chair—big and scratched, but real sturdy. I inherited it from my grandmother, and it's the only piece of furniture I can't seem to part with. I've hauled it with me almost every time I've moved, which is more often than I care to remember. I've also had to store it with friends, which has not made me too popular. It's been kept in some of the most unlikely places...even a bathtub once...."

His chuckle was strong and deep, and it made his eyes light up most disarmingly. Suddenly a great gust of wind blew, and Karin shivered. "I'm getting cold standing here. Would you care to walk for a bit?" she ventured.

He glanced toward the house, knowing his long absence would not go unnoticed, but he was drawn to her refreshing company. "Yes, I'd like that," he said quietly, surprising himself, wondering if she suspected how few women he'd ever talked to outside Mennonite circles.

"I hope I'm not taking you from any work," Karin said, noting his quick look toward the farm.

"Oh, no, we do only the essentials on a Sunday. It's the day set aside for visiting and for attending service, every second week, that is."

"Every second week?" she echoed, wondering when was the last time she'd been in a church. Maybe it was at her friend Carol's second marriage a year and a half ago, a marriage that had only lasted eight months.

Falling into step beside her on the narrow, uneven path, John explained, "We share the meeting house with another Mennonite order, the Markham Mennonites. Unlike the Old Order, they choose to drive cars, but the chrome must be painted black. Just one of the differences that caused the Mennonites to split into so many separate groups—about seventeen in Ontario alone."

She nodded. "Before I came here I thought all Mennonites were the same, wearing black hats or bonnets and driving buggies. I was surprised to learn of all the distinctions between groups."

"From foot washing at service to fenders to fashion, as I've often thought but never dared to say aloud."

Karin stole a glance at him. His eyes were twinkling, and she sensed that he was as surprised by his sudden irreverence as she was.

She pressed on, her curiosity piqued. "Most people still associate the Mennonites with the more conservative orders, even though they are the minority. Because of their rather... unique style of dress. I mean—"

"I know precisely what you mean. Unfortunately the original intent of wearing simple clothing was to be inconspicuous, but that has had an opposite effect."

"I hope I haven't offended you...."

"No, somehow, I don't think you're like some of the tourists who gawk at us as if we're some kind of religious freaks, who treat us as objects of curiosity, instead of real people."

"I'm not sure why, but I'm interested in you . . . in your Mennonite background, how you think . . . if you don't mind talking about that. . . ."

Their shoulders bumped as they maneuvered their way over the icy mounds. "Sorry," he mumbled, thinking how much he liked her candor. "No, I don't mind, as long as you remember I'm probably not a typical Mennonite."

"Who's typical of anything?"

"True enough, but my father for example, strives to be the perfect Old Order Mennonite. He'll never allow electricity in our home, but he finally relented to having a line run into the barn—only when approved by the church. Now we have light at all hours—emergencies tend to happen in the middle of the night for some obscure reason— and we have electrical milking devices. We also own a tractor. However, my father still won't allow a telephone in the barn to be used for business, even though some Old Order members have one there." He grinned conspiratorially. "I've caught my mother chatting on her sister's phone, though. Of course, I'd never tell my father. Although he says he respects the different practices of others, he is not a flexible man with his own family."

"Particularly you?"

"Particularly me."

"So how do you fit into the whole picture? You go to the Old Order church, so you must have chosen to be baptized there. All Mennonites practice voluntary adult baptism, don't they?"

He pushed aside a hanging branch for her, then dropped behind her and waited for a long moment before he spoke.

"Yes, but I didn't take my vows until I was twenty-five, which was considered late. I just wasn't . . . ready earlier. Then, when I did finally join the church, my reasons were all wrong. I've since realized that I was only trying to do what was expected of me." He paused. "I should have listened to my own heart."

Karin stopped and turned to face him, because the tightness in his voice was as real as the chill in the air. "Is it too late to change?" she asked tentatively.

His words were weighed very carefully as he answered slowly, "No, but I can take many paths. Next time I want to be sure I follow the right one. Whatever I choose won't be easy. Others will suffer. Right now I'm considering a job offer from an old friend."

A light snow was starting to fall, and the wind was picking up. They were standing by a grove of cedars, but the river path beyond led to a wide stretch of unprotected field. "Do you want to turn back?" John asked. "When the sun sets, the temperature will drop even more."

"Then we should return," Karin admitted reluctantly, not wanting their talk to end, but realizing for the first time how cold she was.

They walked in silence for a few minutes before Karin spoke. "Perhaps you would be happier in one of the more progressive orders, with less restrictions. . . ."

"No, I think I'll have to find my own way in the world."

How different the boundaries of the "world" were for each individual, Karin thought. What she took for granted was probably foreign to him, and many like him. "Maybe you've just inherited the same itchy heel that drove the first Mennonites up to Canada from Pennsylvania," she said. "They had to be mighty determined to come hundreds of miles by wagon."

"True, but more than an itchy heel was behind their migration. They weren't too popular during the Civil War because they refused to fight, so the prospect of starting a new life where the farmland was ideal was worth the trek, I'm sure. Even the isolation in the unpopulated North was appealing, since they wouldn't have to conform to any set ways." He paused reflectively. "If anything, I've probably inherited my ancestors' tendency toward nonconformity."

"But you don't want to be like other Mennonites."

"So whatever way you look at it, I'm a misfit!" He grinned at her, strangely feeling better about himself than he had in a long time.

"What you're going through must be common, though," she was saying. "Aren't more younger Mennonites joining 'the world,' as you call it, than staying with their various orders?"

"You mean, will we become an endangered species? No, the numbers are growing, in fact, as more outsiders join the progressive orders. And some Mennonites are even switching back to the stricter orders, because they don't like the looser attitudes of some groups. Families continue to be large, too."

"Hmm..." Karin barely heard his answer, focusing instead on the deep resonance of his voice, wondering why it had such a calming effect on her. "It must be hard to think of leaving something you've known your whole life," she said after a moment.

He nodded and his eyes were drawn to the distant house. "Much is good about the Mennonite ways, especially in times of trouble. Everyone helps each other. And there's love, a strict but kind love. But I found little freedom. Perhaps I need that more than others."

"There's a price for freedom," Karin said softly.

"Ah, but that's what I must discover for myself."

Without speaking they walked to the place where they had met, below the sprawling black walnut tree that overlooked the river. They both stopped, knowing they must part.

They were standing close, their breath coming in frosty bursts. Karin's eyes dropped involuntarily to John's lips just as he happened to lick them. Nervously she stepped back and began fumbling in her pocket to retrieve her forgotten bright pink earmuffs. She put them on, her numbed ears welcoming the warmth as she fluffed the layered strands of her bangs and hair around the muffs.

His mouth was twitching when she dared to look up again. "We're not the only ones who dress unusually," he quipped.

She laughed. "My ears will never forgive me if I don't put vanity aside."

"Ah, vanity. The greatest evil, or so they say."

"And what do you say, John Martin?" she asked, unable to keep a playful note from her voice.

"I say you look very fetching, with or without the bunny ears," he returned, matching the lightness of her tone.

Suddenly the air between them was highly charged, filled with endless possibilities, sweet nameless possibilities.

Directness and impulsiveness had always been traits of Karin's, and at this moment they were tugging at her, refusing to be ignored. "Shall we talk again?" she asked, meeting his dark eyes with more braveness than she felt as her pulse started racing.

"You could be very dangerous for a man who is facing some difficult choices."

"Maybe I could help—"

"But," he interrupted, "another part of me is sorely tempted, very eager to learn more about Rocky's nomadic life."

Her heart seemed to kick over. "And who's winning?"

His feet shifted as he looked toward the frozen river, then back at her, saying nothing. Suddenly he reached out and caught a few snowflakes on his dark wool glove. He brought his hand close to her. "See. Each snowflake has a six-sided symmetry, but no two are alike. Out of the trillions that fall in a single storm, each is uniquely beautiful."

"Yes, but what—"

"Did you know that scientists have recently unlocked the secret of a snowflake?" he went on enigmatically. "I've spent much time at the library, since we have so few books at home, and—"

"I don't think I want to know," Karin interjected with a smile. "You'll destroy one of life's charming mysteries."

"Please hear me out," he said, his eyes flickering unfathomably, his gloved hand lightly taking hers as they watched the gathering starlike shapes. "All snowflakes are different, because as they fall thousands of feet, floating for an hour or two, each branches out according to constantly changing temperatures, humidity and wind patterns. So, beginning from a speck of dust that gathers swirling particles in the atmosphere, each snowflake grows from the inside out."

His hand released hers. "I'm like a falling snowflake, Karin, and I don't know where I'll land or what I'll become. It wouldn't be right to ask anyone to share my journey right now." He smiled with a great sadness. "I have enjoyed meeting you, though. Goodbye."

He was thinking that it had been far easier to discourage the familiar Elizabeth than it was to turn away from the woman he'd met so briefly. Still, his stride was determined as he walked off, a dark figure dominating a canvas of hazy winter-white.

CHAPTER THREE

"FOUR MORE, THREE MORE...keep those tummies tucked. Last one. Now, side lunge, leading with one arm. Count with me. Eight, seven—I can't hear you, ladies—six, that's better. And don't forget to smile. Did I hear a groan? Come on, work! It's all worth it, believe me...."

From her seat at the reception desk, Karin watched Cindy MacLeod, one of her four fitness instructors, lead the low-impact aerobics class. *She's really good,* Karin thought, pleased that she'd been able to persuade the small but well-muscled dynamo to quit her job at a rival health club and join her own team.

Karin had been surprised to learn that Cindy was raising two teenagers on her own and that she was thirty-nine years old—she could pass for at least fifteen years younger. A real fireball, Cindy generated that same energy and enthusiasm in her classes, which was exactly what Karin wanted. She believed exercise should be fun, and she tried hard to create a lively, spontaneous atmosphere at her club.

Once more, Karin scanned the computer listing in front of her. Two hundred members after the first three months of operation. Not bad. But she needed to add five times that number by July, and the past two weeks had been slow. In her usual blindly optimistic way, she'd promised the Supreme Fitness owners back in Toronto that she could easily meet the steep quota. And if there was anything Karin hated, it was to know she'd failed or that she'd let down those who were counting on her—particularly Carol.

Carol Levine, the vice president of the Canadian-wide Supreme Fitness operation and a good friend of Karin's, had fought hard to convince the two owners that Karin possessed the drive, leadership and innovativeness to turn the expansion club into a profitable enterprise in record time. Since Karin had only been a certified instructor at the Executive Club in downtown Toronto for less than a year and had been temporarily in charge of a suburban club for two months while the regular manager underwent minor surgery, the owners had been skeptical about Karin's managerial capabilities. But finally they'd agreed to give her the job, on the condition that they see results in short order. If not, she would be replaced by a more experienced manager.

That had been in October. Because the Kitchener location had been scheduled to open in December, traditionally the most popular month for health clubs, Karin had been rushed through the required management and updated fitness training courses, but she had surprised everyone with her quick learning, versatility and calmness under pressure. She'd even stood her ground when the owners had asked her to accept a lower commission rate for each member she signed up. Frankly, she'd never expected them to back down, but they had. She'd told them she would give the job one hundred percent effort, and she wasn't going to accept less than her worth. She had four more months to prove that worth.

Cindy called out to her to lower the taped music for the cool-down and stretching portion of the hour-long workout. Karin obliged, staring idly at the familiar rows of flushed faces and glistening skin, the many different bodies sheathed in leotards and sweat suits of all colors, shapes and sizes. Cindy was as flexible as a licorice stick as she bent into a long stretch, and the women followed to the best of their abilities.

What Karin liked most about working at the exclusive women's club was the fact that they all shared the goal of good health and fitness. A certain closeness formed in the casual setting. Even though she didn't get to know anyone too deeply, she thought of her friendly staff and members as family, or the closest thing to family that she had in her life right now.

But she needed to do some serious brainstorming to further increase the size of this so-called family....

When the class was over, the women all headed in different directions—some to the exercise machines that lined the room, some to the pool and whirlpool area, and the majority to the changing room to quickly shower before rushing off to other commitments. One of her other full-time assistants, Kim Chong, was working the floor to help women through their various fitness programs. Sandra and Heather, who made up the rest of her staff, both had the day off.

"Great workout," Karin enthused as Cindy flopped down beside her, a towel draped around her neck, her short auburn curls damp.

"Easy for you to say," Cindy retorted, smiling as she rubbed her spandex-covered calves. "Busy pushing paper around again, are you?" The two women had struck up an easy rapport from the start.

"I did my bit earlier—two classes this morning as well as a taxing marketing report. And I'll have you know that I'm expending great mental energy trying to come up with creative ways to attract more members. What do you think of placing clowns on the street to lure passersby in for a free prize, or inviting Jane Fonda here, on the off chance that she's always wanted to visit lovely Kitchener...?''

"Right! What about the tried-and-true method of door-to-door flyers or ads in the paper with wonderful introductory offers—''

"We've done all that already. Besides, my promotional budget is shot. I've even had to reorder more free guest passes, since we seem to have given out a zillion already to members. No, I need something really unique and big—and cheap—or I'm not going to make my quota."

Cindy shook her head. "I think all you need is more patience, Karin. You're doing a fantastic job. Those who've joined rave about the club. It just takes time for word to get around."

"Unfortunately time is at a premium. And since the length and terms of prepaid memberships have been limited, I have so little scope for bargaining."

"Yeah, but I'm sure that'll keep working in your favor. Potential members are shopping around for service and facilities now, not just price. And you give more individual attention than both of the other clubs I've worked for in town. With your new equipment, that great lounge and the cleanest locker rooms I've ever seen, you've got your competition beat cold. Wait until memberships start expiring at the other clubs. You'll be overwhelmed...."

"I hope you're right," Karin said, smiling at the woman who always seemed to be filled with reassuring common sense. Maybe that came from being a mother. "Thanks for the pep talk, anyway. You wouldn't consider hanging around the locker room of your last employer and spreading the good word about us, would you?"

"I, ah, don't think I'd be too welcome there," Cindy said dryly. "What if you talked to the Toronto brass and told

them their initial expectations may have been a little un-
realistic, just to relieve some of your pressure?''

"That's a last resort. For now, I said I could do it, and I
will. Somehow.''

"Maybe the great marketing powers-that-be forgot to
take into account the strong German heritage of the Kitchener-Waterloo area. We're talking Oktoberfest celebra-
tions with kegs of beer, greasy sausages and heavy rye
bread—I mean, this is hearty fare. The locals love to eat,
and newcomers soon learn the joys of indulgence. And then
there's the thousands of farmers and Mennonites with all
their foods that really 'schmeck,' as we say. We're not
talking about a lean-and-mean mentality here. . . .''

"All the more reason to be fitness-conscious," Karin returned, an image of one particular, very healthy-looking
Mennonite flashing through her mind. "My market isn't
the rural farm folk who generally get plenty of daily exercise. I'm trying to lure the sedentary urbanites as more flock
to the area with all the industrial growth that's been happening.''

A noisy group of women suddenly filed out from the
dressing room. After a chorus of thank yous, goodbyes and
have-a-good-days, Karin turned back to her assistant and
asked casually, "Have you ever known any Mennonites
well?'' Cindy had lived in the region most of her life, so she
had been an invaluable help when Karin was first finding
her way around the adjacent twin cities of Kitchener and
Waterloo.

"The Mennonites? A few. They tend to stick to themselves, except for the most progressive orders who dress like
us, go to the local colleges and such. One of our new club
members comes from a Mennonite background, in fact—
Janice Schmidt.''

"Really?''

"Don't look so surprised. They're not all social misfits or that much different than we are. Janice was telling me about some huge international Mennonite conference she went to in France a few years back. She's also her church's representative for the Mennonite Disaster Service—the organization with voluntary members across North America. They all pitch in if supplies, people or money are needed in any emergency. Most recently they helped with that terrible flood out in the Prairies."

"Yes, I read about that. You have to admire people who undertake that kind of volunteer work. I always have great intentions, but..."

"And I have two girls at home who complain they don't see enough of me as it is." Cindy bent to loosen her well-padded, soft leather Reeboks and wiggled her ankles. "What's the sudden interest in the Mennonites, anyway?"

"Oh...I don't know. Well I do, actually. I met a man last week while walking by the river. One of the Old Order Mennonites, apparently. He seemed nice, in a genuine way. Intriguing."

"Forget it! Didn't you see *Witness* years ago? Harrison Ford knew he had to walk away from a good thing."

"Wasn't his girlfriend Amish, though?" Karin countered, wishing she'd kept the meeting to herself.

"Amish...Mennonite...a few differences in their origins and day-to-day practices—I think the Amish men wear beards, while the Mennonites don't, for example—but any romance with outsiders is shaky from the start. The Old Order are the least flexible of all the Mennonites when it comes to outsiders."

"Slow down," Karin said, laughing at Cindy's strong reaction. "Who said anything about romance? I just said he was interesting."

Cindy searched her face suspiciously. "But it was the *way* you said it. How old was he, anyway?"

"Early thirties, maybe."

"Then he's married, for sure. The Old Order still marry young."

Karin blinked. For some reason she'd never even thought of the possibility—John Martin had looked so alone. "He wore gloves most of the time, so I didn't give him the old ring test."

"Uh, they don't wear rings or any jewelry, for that matter."

"Oh. Anyway, he seemed kind of mixed-up. Was talking about breaking away and such. The last thing I need right now, if I had any romantic aspirations, which I don't, is someone who's as unstable as I am." She blocked out thoughts of her embarrassing, impulsive behavior with him.

Cindy stood up and glanced at the big wall clock. "I wish I'd realized that before I got tied up with my ex and all his vices. But then I wouldn't have grown up so fast into the strong, mature woman you see before you today. And I wouldn't have my two infuriating but amazing daughters, who are probably wondering where I am. It's getting late— I gotta run."

"Sure. I'm going to work on a few ideas to boost membership. Hey, what do you say we hire a male stripper for the Saturday afternoon class?"

"If I find an eligible one, I'm sure not going to share him with everyone else," Cindy called back, grinning impishly before disappearing behind the swinging door that led into the staff quarters.

Suddenly Karin had an acute mental image of a scantily clothed, muscular John Martin, alone with her in the well-mirrored exercise room. Phew! What was the matter with her, anyway? Fantasizing about a decent, pleasant stranger she'd probably never see again. Maybe she had been working too hard lately, but at least she was thinking of Eric less and less.

Her concentration problem was solved a few minutes later when one of the regulars walked in with two guests—two potential new members—and she was soon busy showing them around the club and demonstrating the state-of-the-art Nautilus equipment.

JOHN RAISED HIS ARM and brought the ax down in one powerful sweep. The stubborn log finally broke apart—a good clean split. He tossed the pieces into the pile he'd accumulated on the gray March afternoon and saw his father watching him.

"You've been going at that wood with a vengeance," the older man said, glancing at his own smaller stack. "But I'm not complaining. During that cold February snap, we used a lot more kindling than usual."

John straightened and wedged his ax into the next stump. He knew he'd only been delaying the inevitable for the past few hours, trying to rehearse the right words in his mind. There was no easy way to say what had to be said.

"I have to talk to you, Father."

Jacob Martin bent to gather his freshly cut wood, which he began adding to the fortresslike wall that surrounded the farmyard. "So, talk," he said suspiciously.

John knew his father had been aware of his discontent for a long time, but his way of dealing with the problem was to ignore it and to hope that time and prayer would solve the matter. He had not even questioned John about his many mysterious absences from home of late or his refusal to attend Sunday service.

"I have decided to leave the farm. And the Old Order. I have found a job." The words, spoken aloud at last,

sounded blunt, carrying none of the torment, the excitement that was in John's heart.

Jacob slowly set down the logs he was carrying, then
stood motionlessly, his back to John.

"You must not be hasty, son. You cannot walk away
from your people. We are blessed with a good life—food on
the table, a roof over our heads...."

"I am grateful for what I have," John said with difficulty. "But I want to be freer, learning from my mistakes,
following my own path. And if that means I must join
the...world, then that is the way it must be."

Jacob faced him then, and he was fighting anger, his
brow deeply lined, his color rising. "You are wrong to think
that owning a car or a radio or wearing store-bought new
clothes will bring you peace. Such instruments of worldli-
ness will only take you further from the way of the Lord,
from humility and goodness."

"I don't seek material possessions for their own sake,"
John said quietly, "although I no longer feel threatened by
them, and I'll use what I need."

"The world lures you in other ways that will slowly destroy you. I have seen—" He stopped and his eyes were
filled with a deep anxiety. "Only by disciplining the self can
you not fall prey to the greed that has caused wars and violence and other forms of human weakness."

"My conscience is what I must live by. You have shown
me that it's honorable to work hard, to contribute something worthwhile to the world, to be a good neighbor. But
I no longer want to be separate from the world. I want to
know about its realities, its many people beyond this community, this farm...."

"But someday this land will be yours, John," his father
said, gesturing with a look of pride to the cultivated acres,
the large family garden, the orchard, all blanketed by a

slow-melting snow. "The land has been in the Martin family since our forefathers cleared the forest, making it possible for our family to have a home here. You must preserve what they have given us and pass it along to your children, as I have done."

"I love the land, but farming isn't in my blood as it is in yours, Father. The days stretch ahead for me, and there has been no luster for a long time. Someone who is better suited to this life should work the land for you. I want to work more with people."

Jacob leaned against the woodpile, as if to support himself, and he studied the strong-willed set of his son's face. He was not as tall as John, and the way he propped himself made him seem even shorter. Long moments passed before he said, his voice strained, "Perhaps you could serve on the Mennonite Central Committee as a volunteer. You could choose a missionary program in a different country, then you could return to your home—"

"I've considered that, but I've found a community-type job that excites me a great deal. It's in a group home for troubled teenage boys. I'll be working with Henry Gingrich—you remember him from years ago at market, don't you?"

Jacob nodded, his eyes narrowing. He had never approved of his son's friendship with the former Old Order Mennonite.

"I ran into him a month or so ago and discovered he has been looking for an assistant for some time while his wife is away furthering her education. I'm lucky to have landed such a job with so little experience." *And just at the time I was contemplating making a break, but was afraid to without a specific plan,* he thought but did not say aloud. "Henry believes in me as much as I believe in myself."

John did not add what a difficult time Henry had had in convincing the officials from the Ministry of Community and Social Services to hire him as a temporary replacement while his wife took her sabbatical. But finally, after numerous meetings with John and Henry at Greenbank, the group home on the outskirts of Waterloo, the supervisors had approved the appointment. What helped sway the decision in John's favor was the fact that a female childcare worker would visit the premises frequently. She could provide the balanced care that this group home—a family-model type—strove for.

"You are a fine one to help others with problems," Jacob said in a low tight voice.

"But don't you see? I, too, have questioned everything in my life. I can help others who need guidance find what is right for them. But I know you'll need help with the farm, too," he added, drawing a deep breath. His father was a strong, able man, but the farm required at least two workers for its constant upkeep. "If you will consider selling some acres—"

"No."

"Then, perhaps you could hire one of the Brubacher boys. With four of them, they have more hands than they need. And if you ever need help, I'll see what I can do...."

But Jacob wasn't listening. Meeting his son's eyes challengingly, he said, "You need to take another wife, John, and then you will be happy again. Emma is gone and you must fill the emptiness she left with another. There is Elizabeth..."

John shook his head sadly. "I wish it was so simple. But it's not."

Father and son stared at each other in silence. Finally Jacob spoke, his head held high, his eyes flickering with resignation. "Your leaving will hurt your mother and sister very much."

"They are not losing a son or brother unless you choose to shun me."

The words hung in the windless air between them, becoming a question.

"I cannot disown my only son, no matter how disappointed I am in him," Jacob said at last, with great effort. "This will always be your home, if you choose to return. I shall pray that you will and that the world will not make the son that I have raised a lesser man." His voice broke. Reaching quickly for his ax, he went back to his chopping with slow steady strokes.

Jacob Martin did not raise the subject of his son's decision again. He fell into a bleak silence that John could not penetrate during the week in which he prepared to leave.

His mother had taken the news hard, too, but when her husband wasn't around, she asked John question after question, trying hard to understand his reasons and to learn about his plans. That he would be unwelcome at their church's service because of his defection was an unspoken fact between them. But she urged him to join a more progressive order, suggesting the Red Brick Mennonites, so-called because they worshiped in a red brick meeting house instead of the white clapboard building used by the Old Order. John had told his concerned mother that he no longer wished to belong to any formal church, because his heart and head were at such odds with each other.

When he'd informed her that he would be renting a small apartment in town, though spending most of his time at the group home, she'd just shaken her head knowingly.

"John, you will feel like a caged animal," she'd warned. "You were always a child who liked to run, and you are a man who needs much space around himself."

He'd assured her that he would make the best of the situation. Having his own place, however small, meant the world to him. Besides, it was all he could afford on his new salary, and he wanted to keep what he'd saved from the modest monthly payments his father had been giving him since he was eighteen, as a future reserve.

Anna Martin finally accepted his decision as much as it frightened and baffled her, and set about, in her diligent, practical way, of getting him ready.

She washed his few articles of clothing; she mended his worn trousers and shirts; she started baking pans of cookies and squares with a surprising fervor, then found secret places for them in the cold cellar, never mentioning what she was about to her husband.

John's sister had seen the strain between him and his parents, but she had been reluctant to interfere. Finally John had told her of the recent developments while they were alone, walking along the creek bank where they'd played boisterously as children—swimming on hot summer days; swinging from a rubber tire across the shallow waters to the other side; skating on the frozen ice, bundled up against the cold winter winds.

Mary had cried softly at the news, and the sight of her wounded wet eyes had finally broken through the wall that John had built around himself as he took each step that would lead to his new life.

"What will I do when you're gone?" Mary had asked dolefully. "It will be so quiet. Father and Granddaddy say so little. At least Emma and I used to have fun, and now—"

"You'll have to look after Wicked for me," John had said quickly, and she'd just sniffed, unpacified. He'd taken her in his arms then, squeezing her through their thick coats. "You will marry someday, little one," he'd said, feeling an overwhelming sense of protectiveness toward his nineteen-year-old sister.

"I know," she'd murmured spiritlessly.

"And I'll visit you whenever I can," he'd promised.

"Maybe I can come see you at Greenbank or your new place, if Father would allow that...."

"You must speak to him about it, then do whatever you feel is right. He hasn't closed the door to me, as I feared he might, and for that I'm grateful. But he hasn't forgiven me, either."

Mary had pulled away then and with a determined effort wiped the tears from her face and smiled at him. "Hey, let's get our skates," she'd challenged. Her eyes were still glistening, but a familiar quiet merriment was evident.

And they'd gone skating, as they had done so many times before, the ice firm but thin.

On the day he was to leave home, John felt a strange calm. At dawn the sun had broken through the mid-March sky, raising outdoor temperatures, softening the snow and exposing patches of the rich, dark earth.

A soft sunlight streamed through the window of the room he had shared with his young wife, the green shades rolled up for daytime. Sitting on the bed one last time, he remembered their gentle love, how it had brightened the plain surroundings, how it had added a pleasant dimension to the daily ritual of hard physical work.

Emma had died in this bed, too. He had respected her wish to come home at the end, but a long time had passed before the image of her pale suffering face had faded... before he could remember the other Emma, the sweet delicate girl he'd married. He'd wanted to care for her, protect her from all harm, but he'd been powerless against the force of the disease that had overtaken her young body.

As Emma had fought back, he'd seen a strength of spirit emerging, a glimpse of the person she would have become, and he'd known he had loved the girl, not the woman, and that he was losing both.

He'd been appalled at the deep sense of indignation and injustice he'd felt at her premature death. But releasing such strong black emotions, casting blame, had gone against everything he'd ever been taught. So he'd retreated into a bearable state of numbness, going through the motions of his life, but unconnected to it. When he'd slowly started to feel again, the pain had dulled and the rage subsided. He didn't know who he had become, only that he had changed. At some indefinable point, he had lost the innocence that had tied him to the Mennonite way.

Outwardly he looked the same, but he felt differently, he thought differently, and the time had finally come to be honest with himself and his family.

All his clothes had fit into one worn leather suitcase, the only one his family owned. Tucked into one of its corners was a friendship bracelet, made of bright shiny buttons—a gift Emma had shyly presented to him while they were courting. He also packed the full-sleeved wedding shirt she'd sewn for him. Under the opening of the collar was a heart worked in tiny white knots. The sight of the handmade presents made his throat tighten.

Downstairs he had already collected several boxes of books and wedding gifts—some china, a colorful quilt that had been lovingly made in his and Emma's honor, some other bedding. He also knew his mother had gathered extra kitchenware for him and secretly filled a small box with baked goods, away from the reproachful eye of her husband, who would interpret her goodwill as an act of condonation.

His bedroom furniture and a few odd other pieces would also provide a measure of continuity between his old and new lives. Still, there would be plenty of room in the van when Henry came to drive him away.

"Well, it won't be the same without you around here. It seems like only yesterday you were a young lad being punished for your mischief, and now—"

"And now you think I'm heading into even bigger mischief," John said, smiling as his grandfather shuffled into the room, his suspenders hanging from his shoulders as they always did. So far Erwin Martin had said little about his grandson's departure. He had rarely meddled in John's upbringing, although John had been aware of his chagrin on many occasions. Somehow the two had managed to share a quiet respect through it all.

"I know it hasn't been easy for you the past few years. We all wanted to help, but—"

"There was nothing you or anyone could do, Grandfather."

"Ach, someday you'll let someone get close again. Maybe it's best you wander on your own a bit. You may find whatever you're looking for."

John threw him a startled look, the sentiments expressed uncharacteristic of his stern grandparent.

"Age does strange things to even the most iron-willed man," Erwin said, chuckling.

"I wish I didn't have to hurt others," John admitted, his dark eyes meeting those of the relative he knew he resembled. Their faces were cut of the same strong, angular cast. Their bodies were rangy, well-muscled, although Erwin's shoulders had taken on the slope of age.

"You are thinking of your father. He is not taking this well, I am afraid. But you must not think he is a cold man. He has his own demons to fight."

At John's questioning look, Erwin tucked his hands into the pockets of his trousers, his customary pose before he launched into a story, usually about the early days on the farm.

"When your father was a teenage lad, he had a wild streak, like yours, like most of ours, I suppose, before we learn the wisdom of self-control. Jacob was fascinated by cars, but in those days they were strictly forbidden to us. They were seen as vehicles of the Devil himself. There was not the tolerance that has come today because of the new Mennonite orders. Well, Jacob had become friends with an English boy who lived a few farms over, and secretly he learned to drive."

"My father?" John sputtered.

Erwin nodded, his eyes going to the window. "One day there was an accident—the roads were slippery. Young Jacob was driving. The car spun and slid into a Mennonite buggy with two passengers, a man and woman. They were both members of our church. Unfortunately, the woman was badly injured. To this day, I am sure Jacob is still trying to atone for those ill-fated moments. He is very frightened of the dangers of the world, of progress."

John could only stare at his grandfather, shocked at what he'd heard, a new understanding of his father ricocheting within. "Thank you for telling me, Grandfather," he murmured.

"You must not repeat this."

"You have my word."

John picked up his suitcase then and rested his arm across the older man's shoulders as they walked out of the room together.

He did not look back.

CHAPTER FOUR

KARIN HAD A NEW SATURDAY-morning ritual. Before opening the club at nine o'clock, two hours later than during the weekdays, she liked to stroll through the lively Waterloo Farmers' Market, which started as early as 6:00 a.m.

Hundreds of vendors, both Mennonites and non-Mennonites, sold a wide assortment of wares—homemade bread, baked goods, jam, fruits and vegetables, cheeses and meats, as well as such handicrafts as quilts, knitted clothing and wooden puzzles. In the winter months the market was held indoors, but in other seasons, trucks were set up outdoors, offering an even wider variety of fresh garden produce.

As much as Karin occasionally missed the sophisticated city of Toronto, with its cornucopia of fine restaurants, boutiques and gourmet food shops, she liked the quaint country charm of this busy market. She even preferred its folksy, less commercialized atmosphere to such city markets she'd visited as the St. Lawrence in Toronto or the one on Vancouver's Granville Street.

Because she'd arrived even earlier than usual today, Karin leisurely wandered from stall to stall. She bought some cooked cheese, for which she'd only acquired a taste since moving to the area, and a chunk of spicy summer sausage. She was deciding whether to indulge herself with some thimbleberry jam, when she caught sight of a bin of dark-colored, thick sauce. A small Mennonite woman, dressed in a long black frock covered by an old white sweater, approached her.

"Would you like to try some? It's apple butter. Very good on bread."

"Sure."

The woman scooped a dollop onto a small wooden spoon and offered it to Karin. Her smile was genuine as her customer licked her lips in satisfaction.

"Tasty," Karin marveled, savoring the light cinnamon-and-molasses flavor. She decided to splurge and buy a small container with some fresh whole-wheat buns. "For the days I cheat on my diet," she said to the woman.

"Bah, you don't need to diet. You are very thin."

"I make my living helping others stay thin, so I have to look the part." Fortunately Karin had a high metabolism that kept her weight low, so she mainly exercised for toning, stamina and muscle strength.

"What do you do?" the Mennonite woman asked as she bagged Karin's purchases and took her money.

"I run a health and fitness club, lead aerobics classes and such...."

"Oh," the woman murmured politely, staring blankly at her, as if Karin were speaking a foreign language.

"The fitness boom is catching on everywhere," she said weakly, but the woman had excused herself to serve another customer. Karin was surprised to see her eyes narrow, her expression turn cool.

"Hello, John Martin," she heard her say in a clipped voice to the man towering over her.

In contrast to the other woman's frostiness, Karin felt a warmth spread through herself as she turned and echoed, "Hello, John Martin," her tone decidedly more pleasant.

"Mrs. Snyder...Karin...." He acknowledged them one at a time, quickly recovering from his momentary surprise. "I came for some of the best doughnuts in the county," he said brightly to Mrs. Snyder.

"How many?" she asked quietly, remaining aloof.

"Half a dozen. Your family is well?"

"Yes."

"Elizabeth?"

"Fine."

"That's good, that's good."

Drawing a deep breath, Mrs. Snyder said in a low voice, "I must speak out to you, John. Your mother is deeply hurt by your actions. Your father is also gravely worried about his farm, come spring. You have walked away from your responsibilities."

"Change is not always easy," he answered, his eyes never wavering from hers, his back held tall and erect.

"Have you spoken to your mother and Mary today at their booth?"

"Briefly," he said, adding with a forced brightness, "Have a good day and give my regards to your family."

Mrs. Snyder said nothing as he touched Karin's arm and led her away. They wove a serpentine path through the crowds until they reached a relatively quiet corner by a fast-food stand. The steamed hot dogs and iced soft drinks seemed out of place to Karin amid the other homemade and homegrown fare.

"So you left your home," she began, thinking how good he looked. His dark brown hair had grown, falling just below his ears in a disarray she found attractive because of its imperfection. The same long black coat he'd worn at their last meeting hung loosely around his broad shoulders. A slightly wrinkled, checkered flannel shirt in golds and browns that set off the rich color of his eyes was tucked into dark navy jeans.

"Hmm," he answered distractedly. "Several weeks ago."

"You have new clothes."

"Some, for purely practical reasons," he said, smiling, and Karin's heart lurched as she experienced the incredible power those eyes held over her. "I don't do the laundry as often as my mother did. Nor have I ever ironed," he added, glancing down at his creased shirt. "I have a lot to learn. The boys tease me...."

"Oh. How many boys do you have?"

"Four." At her startled look, he explained, "But they're not mine. Heavens! No, I'm...not married. I work at a group home for troubled youth. I'm supposedly taking the place of my co-worker's wife, who's researching her doctorate in social work at UBC in Vancouver."

"Why 'supposedly'?" Karin asked, intrigued and undeniably relieved at the revelation of his single status.

"Well, Henry's particular group home operates as a family-model type, which means it's usually run by a married couple. He tried carrying it without Melissa, his wife, since she left last September, but found it all too much to handle. He finally got approval from the Ministry to hire me until the fall, when Melissa returns. After that I hope to have enough experience to work in the same field elsewhere."

"You like it, then?" Karin asked, although she already knew the answer by the way his eyes were shining.

"Yeah, I really do. Henry calls us 'the odd couple,' but we get along. He understands what I went through leaving the Old Order, because he did the same himself. And the boys, well, they're a handful, but they're great kids."

"How old are they?"

"Fifteen, sixteen. It's a relatively small group, but each boy needs a lot of individual attention. All in all, though, they're a tough bunch of survivors, despite their problems. We're helping them find their strengths so they can eventually make it on their own in the community.''

Karin saw the genuine concern he brought to his new endeavor and knew that he had found an occupation to which he was well suited. ''It sounds like very difficult but satisfying work. Do you still see your own family...or is that not possible considering...?''

A shadow crossed his ruggedly attractive face. ''I've chosen not to return as yet. It's difficult for all of us.''

Suddenly they were jostled by passersby as the arenalike room was quickly filling to capacity. Caught unawares, they were pressed against each other, one side of Karin's face resting just below John's shoulder so that she could feel his warm breath on her neck. She tried turning away from him, but instead was pushed even closer, becoming more conscious of his solid muscular frame and their complimenting heights. A tumultuous spiral began deep in the pit of her stomach and sent little shock waves through her.

When the crowd cleared, she eased herself back and saw that John was holding up a bag of squished doughnuts.

''Oops,'' she said, suddenly feeling as if she were floating on air.

''Neither the doughnuts or I are complaining,'' he murmured, reddening.

His embarrassment and the innocent quality behind it suddenly made her remember the thrills and anguishes of her adolescence, those all-absorbing crushes that always ended in heartbreak, which was probably why they were called crushes.

''I should go,'' she said quickly, ''or I'll have a riot of enraged exercise enthusiasts on my hands.'' His eyebrows lifted quizzically. ''Oh, I manage a women's health and fitness club in downtown Kitchener.''

"Ah, so that's why you look so... fit," he said, his eyes drawn self-consciously to the snug lines of the two-piece red nylon jogging suit she wore under her unzipped jacket.

Their eyes met in a collision of blue and brown, and neither could look away.

As if compelled, John finally said, "I think it's time I learned more about Rocky and his owner. If you'll give me a second chance, that is."

A dagger of imminent peril stabbed at her, for reasons she could not fathom at the moment, but Karin ignored the warning. He looked as scared as she felt, and that helped. "Okay," she answered in a voice unlike her own.

And with a strange breathless mix of awkwardness and anticipation, they arranged to meet outside her club later that afternoon.

THE LAST EXERCISE CLASS of the day had finished, and slowly the club was emptying. Karin was giving a fitness test to a new member who had arrived late for her appointment. Gently pinching the skin under the women's upper arm with a caliper, she noted the reading, consulted her chart and calculated the amount of body fat.

"Thirty-two percent," she announced cheerily. "Not bad, but the average for your age group is between twenty-four and thirty-one percent. We can get yours down if you adhere to your fitness program at least three times a week."

"Nothing *too* strenuous, I hope," said Cheryl Johnson, an attractive accountant in her early thirties with short, streaked blond hair. "It's been a while since these muscles have worked harder than carrying a few groceries, the contents of which I dare not mention in present company."

Karin laughed. "Don't worry. Your program will be geared to your individual level of fitness. I'll be giving you your very own computerized fitness analysis. We'll start off easy, then adjust your exercises from time to time. Now let's check the efficiency of your heart and lungs. Hop on this computerized cycling machine for a twelve-minute workout. Your pulse will be checked at various stages—after you've reached your target range, then after you've cooled down.''

Cheryl climbed awkwardly onto the bike and watched apprehensively while Karin adjusted the seat and dials. "I tried to quit smoking as a New Year's resolution, but I'm sort of back at it now," she confessed.

"You might want to stop by on Tuesday evenings, then," said Karin. "Start pedaling. Good. I've set the tension nice and low to start. How is it?"

"Fine. What's this about Tuesdays?"

"We offer a support group for club members who are trying to kick the smoking habit. And on Thursdays we have a series of speakers on various topics—nutrition, exercise during and after pregnancy, family fitness activities and so forth. Both nights are becoming very popular." *And slowly drawing valuable new members,* she was proud to add silently.

"I'll think about it . . ." Cheryl muttered, her breath already coming in short gasps.

"When you're ready, just let me know. For now, carry on pedaling, keeping the tension reading—here—at about seventy. I'll see you in a few minutes."

She walked away, then smiled at Kim, who was manning the front desk—watching the phones and signing members in and out. "Could you check Cheryl's pulse for me? I'll be in my office, gathering up some paperwork in case I get bored at home on Sunday."

"Did anyone ever tell you you're a workaholic, putting the rest of us to shame? Some people actually like to spend their day off just vegging in front of the TV...."

"Hey, when I'm filling out the forms for a record forty new members in one week, I don't mind at all."

"Good stuff!" At eighteen, Kim Chong, a striking, raven-haired Oriental beauty, was the youngest member of Karin's fitness team. Even though Kim was not her most punctual employee, her zany but ever-cheerful personality endeared her to the rest of the staff and club members.

Karin ducked into her office and quickly began sorting through files. She had a long way to go to meet her quota, but the results for that particular week had been encouraging. One evening she'd hosted an open house that had brought good *free* media coverage and dozens of interested new guest members. Persuading them all to sign up for an annual membership and following up by phone or letter to the ones who couldn't make up their minds were her main concerns right now.

Suddenly her eyes flew to the clock, and her stomach knotted. She was to meet John in half an hour! During the day she had started to feel grave doubts about the date that they'd arranged so impulsively.

He was a nice person, but was the former Old Order Mennonite her type? He was certainly less sophisticated than the ideal man she'd concocted in her imagination. She'd decided that the perfect man would be sure of himself and of his direction in life. He'd be well established in some solid profession, a lawyer perhaps, someone like the sexy and sensitive Harry Hamlin on TV's *L.A. Law*. Most importantly, he'd be crazy about her, wanting to indulge her every whim, and she'd be the one in complete control of the relationship, caring for him, but only enough that he would never be able to devastate her. Nothing was worth that, she'd discovered.

Whether such a man existed outside of her fantasies or beyond the television screen was another matter, and she was in no real hurry to find out. She was determined not to be one of those desperate women who panicked when they turned thirty and married the first likable, eligible soul who lasted more than a few dates.

In the meantime, she would consider her hastily planned meeting with John as merely one of those experiences that made life interesting. And she *had* found him intriguing, before she started thinking about an actual date so much. So, enough thinking. Right now she had to locate a certain blasted folder, buried somewhere in the paper madness on her desk.

Just when she found it on top of her filing cabinet, where she must have put it several hours ago, the door opened and Kim poked her head in. "I think you should console our friend Cheryl. She only lasted six minutes on the bike. I took her pulse anyway."

"Thanks, Kim. Tuesday night, here she comes," Karin said, rushing out.

Forty minutes later, the main door finally closed on Cheryl, who had lingered to discuss the personalities of her three Persian cats. Kim had already left, and Karin was scurrying around, turning off the whirlpool, gathering items that had been abandoned, checking that the club was indeed empty of members.

She stepped out of the changing room and came face-to-face with John Martin.

"Hi," she said, thrown off guard by his commanding masculine presence in a club that saw few males, except for the occasional maintenance man. She pulled off her sweatband, then quickly brushed back her hair from her forehead and neck with a few deft strokes. "As you can see, I'm running a bit late. I'm glad you came in out of the cold, though."

"I wasn't sure if I missed you. I was a little late myself...."

"I'll be out in a second. Just have to pick up a few things in my office. You can sit in the lounge over there or explore the workout areas." Dashing into the adjoining room, she thought how very uncomfortable he looked.

John stood rooted to the spot, coat in hand, wondering what on earth he was doing here. When he'd met the interesting stranger along the river and at the market, places he was familiar with, he just hadn't thought how vastly different their two worlds were. He felt like a country bumpkin in this ultramodern room of mirrors and high-tech equipment, meeting a beautiful, svelte woman in her form-fitting black leotard with a bright red sash at the waist. Even such an insignificant detail as the baggy red woollen things she wore on her legs took him aback.

His eyes were drawn to the bold burgundy lettering above each of the twelve contraptions of steel and leather that lined one side of the large room. Posture. Weak Stomach. Arm Flab. He stared at the next two and couldn't resist a puzzled smile.

"What's so amusing?" Karin asked, emerging with an armload of binders and folders. She was wearing her red nylon suit again, presumably over the leotard.

"I have to plead ignorance and inquire what on earth you mean by Saddlebags and Cottage Cheese?"

"Cellulite on the inner and outer thighs, of course," she replied smartly. "The ladies find the signs inspirational as they are counting down their leg lifts on the machines that work at those problems."

"I see," he muttered. "And does the equipment really help? Does the, er, 'cottage cheese' disappear?"

"For those who work steadily, it can." She suddenly felt as if she were talking to one of her new clients, but she didn't know how else to answer his question. "Most of the women report all kinds of benefits as they grow more physically fit—increased mental energy, a greater self-esteem, even financial savings as the cost of chocolate eclairs rises—you name it! It's a fun place to work, and rewarding when you see the highly motivated ones feeling so much better about themselves. The others, well, that's why I'm here, to give them that push they need. Everyone wants to look and feel their best, but they're not willing to put in the extra effort."

"What motivates you, I wonder?" he asked, and his warm intimate gaze had a way of making the question intensely personal.

"My paycheck," she joked, thinking he probably wouldn't consider her answer any better if she told him simply that she liked the club for now, but that she had never found anything that absorbed her, heart and soul. "Have you thought about where you want to go? Coffee? A drink? If you're hungry, we could grab some dinner somewhere."

"I'm not that familiar with the restaurants around here. Or restaurants, period, for that matter. We never—" He stopped. "We'll go wherever you wish. Or at least anywhere that I'd be dressed appropriately for," he added, glancing down at the same jeans and shirt he'd worn earlier.

Suddenly Karin knew that the evening would be an absolute disaster if they went to a crowded restaurant or bar, making polite conversation across the table from each other.

"Actually, I'm beat. Why don't we just go to my apartment and I'll make a pot of spaghetti. I haven't had a feed of good ol' complex carbohydrates in a while. You like spaghetti?"

"I'll try it," he said sheepishly.

Incredible! "Why do I feel as if I'm in an early rerun of *Mork and Mindy*, when Mork has just landed on earth from some other planet?"

"I beg your pardon?"

"An old TV series, but you didn't watch... Never mind," she said, breaking into a grin. "Let's go."

KARIN'S LEGS WERE CROSSED comfortably as she leaned back on the large floor cushions that surrounded the window nook and sipped from her wineglass. She'd changed into an oversize blue sweater and stonewashed denim jeans.

John sprawled across from her, his own wine goblet in hand. He'd seemed to relax once they arrived at Karin's small apartment in an old, low-rise building several blocks from the club facilities.

The main living area was simply decorated with a secondhand off-white sectional couch, some colorfully woven wall hangings and several large floor plants, miraculously alive despite her neglect. John had called her place "charming" when he'd walked in and had solemnly allowed himself to be introduced to Rocky, the huge solid oak rocker as much of a homey monstrosity as he'd imagined, he'd admitted.

He'd been fascinated with her multipiece stereo system, asking question after question. Karin had decided to play her *Graceland* album by Paul Simon, hoping John would like the combination of melodious soft rock and traditional South African rhythm. He was listening intently to a cappella song, a haunting melody of voices crying out in both English and Zulu.

"Beautiful but melancholy at the same time," he commented. "What's the song called?"

"'Homeless,'" Karin answered lazily. Her first glass of wine was already making her feel languorous.

"Where was home for you before moving here?"

"Toronto. I shared a house with a bunch of people—an unemployed poet, an insomniac, a recent divorcée and a chain-smoker. Needless to say, I'm currently enjoying my solitude. I especially don't miss finding mysterious scratches on my records."

"But where was your first home—the one with your parents?"

She shrugged. "That's a tough one. My folks split when I was about six. One of those cases where opposites attract, but they should never have married. Satch—that's what we call my father—was a part-time jazz musician, and he was always out late or away, not the domestic sort, while Mom was a homebody, content to putter around the house, garden, bake, that sort of thing. She liked everything orderly, and Satch was full of... surprises, unreliable. Neither would change or even bend a little. He finally left with one of his lady friends."

In her faraway look was both the hurt little girl and the rational woman who had tried to understand the human frailties of adults.

"So you lived with your mother?"

Karin nodded. "In Vancouver. We had to move into an apartment, and Mom wasn't very happy there. She went back to nursing, shift work, so I stayed with neighbors a lot."

"And your dad, did you see him?"

"Sometimes. He left his office job to become a full-time saxophonist with various bands. He was really quite good. During the holidays I used to travel with him—across Canada, New York a few times, Munich once, the Caribbean...that was my favorite place. He played from hotel to hotel, island to island, during the evenings in exchange for free lodging and meals and lazy days lounging in the sun. Satch was a crazy fellow—we had lots of fun." She laughed softly, her eyes bright with fond memories.

"'Had'? Is he—"

"Oh, no! He's alive and well, somewhere, I'm sure. We just don't see each other anymore. Haven't for a few years. When I was twelve or so he just stopped asking me to accompany him. When I finally saw him again, he told me he wanted me to be more independent. Me! I couldn't believe it. Anyway, I tried not to bug him too much after that." She stopped, bit her lip. "As it turned out, I did strike out on my own soon after I finished high school. Mom was marrying a retired dentist, and they were moving to Florida, so I thought it was a good time to get my own place. Mom and I weren't getting along very well—actually we never had. I was always a contrary child, or so she said. Probably too much like Satch."

The chantlike beat of the song ended, and John's voice seemed to echo in the suddenly quiet room. "So where did you go?"

"You'll have to read my memoirs someday for all of that," she said evasively.

"Briefly, then." And there was a gentle command in his voice.

"*Briefly,*" she repeated, "I worked as a window dresser, then in a vintage-clothing boutique. With the money I saved, I headed to Europe, worked on a kibbutz in Israel for a while, then did some waitressing in a London pub.

Eventually I returned to Canada to learn that Mom had...
I was happy that she found someone before—" She drew a
deep breath. "Mom died in a car accident while I was God
knows where."

John's head was whirling, trying to keep up with her
story, to imagine the kind of life she'd had, so much more
versatile than his own, but with the same lonely, almost
desperate quality of someone who wasn't sure where he or
she belonged. His eyes told her he was sorry about her
mother, that he thought he understood about the rest, but
she looked away uncomfortably, determined to get her history over with as expediently as possible.

"Anyway, I ended up in Toronto and went back to
school. Got a physical education degree, but no job. I knew
I wanted to work with people, and I'd always liked sports,
so I finally started working at one of the fitness clubs I used
to belong to. One thing led to another, and I ended up at
Supreme Fitness. In my early fitness zeal, I even tried con-
verting my father into a health nut, telling him to cut down
on his drinking, red meats and greasy foods, but he let me
know what he thought of such common sense. Maybe
that's why he hasn't called in a long while. He did send me
a guilt offering at Christmas—my camera. But that came
via one of his girlfriends, Joanna, who'd picked it out for
him. Luckily for me, she has more expensive tastes than my
dear father." Her tone was light, too light.

She reached over to the Chablis chilling in a clay cooler
beside her and poured more of the light fruity wine into
each of their glasses.

"So you've never married?" John asked, fascinated by
the graceful movements of her long slender hands and the
elegant line of her neck, which added a soft dimension to
her strong earthiness.

"What makes you think that?" She lifted her chin, her pose suddenly defensive and ready to do battle at the same time.

"I'm not sure. I just don't think so."

"Well, you're right. But don't get psychoanalytical on me. I've read all that stuff on broken families and the effects on the poor kids. For a while I even used it as an excuse for all the problems I had as a teenager. But, actually, I think I did a wonderful job of raising myself when my role models weren't around, don't you agree?" she asked, showing him her profile in a mock pose. Her guest wasn't smiling. "Okay, maybe I did have some shaky times, but I got through them, and I'm damn proud of that. I know I can handle anything. Anything," she repeated with a flourish. "And I'll start by whipping up some of my Spaghetti Sauce Super-Plus." She jumped up.

He looked up at her pensively for a few seconds, then asked, "What can I do to help?"

"How are you at chopping vegetables?"

"I'm a fast learner," he said, standing and following her into the tiny kitchen, the counters covered by a potpourri of cookbooks, dishes, bills and jars that were filled with a colorful assortment of dried ingredients.

"Just give me a second to get organized," she said, pushing everything into a corner.

"Do you have a special man anywhere...in Toronto, maybe?" John inquired, knowing his timing was off and that he sounded presumptuous, but it was suddenly imperative that he know the answer.

Karin was pulling food from a well-aged fridge and setting it on the tiny space she'd cleared on the counter. She only stopped moving for a fraction of a second. "Oh, there was a guy. But we broke up when I took the job here. We worked together at the Executive Club, which is usually bad news for couples, anyway."

"Are you, ah, still friends?"

"No," she answered sharply. She made a great show of searching for something in the fridge. "We may have to use garlic powder—oh, there's the bulb. Do you like spicy food...? I tend to get carried away."

She turned toward him. He was leaning in the doorway, his fingers tucked casually into the back pockets of his jeans, watching her with lazy narrowed eyes.

"Well, do you?" she asked, wishing she wasn't so aware of his well-proportioned body. She had to keep a clear head until she had a chance to assess the situation.

"Sure. Go ahead and get carried away," he said slowly, thinking her candor had limits. He'd have to pay close attention to what she *didn't* say about herself if he was ever to understand her, if he *wanted* to understand her, that was.

Her life had been filled with such an intriguing mixture of caprice and caution, though, that he could not resist wanting to know more....

THE MEAL PASSED PLEASANTLY, the two at knee-bumping distance from each other at Karin's small kitchen table. By the time John had finished his second helping, he was adept at twirling the spaghetti around his fork in one smooth motion, although his tomato-stained chin was evidence of his efforts. Karin had also concocted her special Caesar salad, which he loved.

"We could certainly use your culinary expertise at Greenbank," John said when he'd finished, leaning back in his chair contentedly. "Unfortunately, Henry and I fall short in that area. The boys are starting to demand we order out for pizzas every second night, but that doesn't look too well on the records of our food budget!"

"How's the home funded, anyway?" Karin asked, her hand idly moving along the stem of her empty wineglass.

"Mainly through the Children's Aid Society and some donations from churches and other charitable organizations. Children's Aid works out a per diem rate for each boy, covering the house rent, clothes, our salaries, transportation, food—especially food, with the appetites those fellows have."

"Don't give up on cooking—some of the best cooks I've known have been men. No recipes, lots of herbs and whatever else happens to be on hand."

"In my case, that involves a lot of trial and error, mostly error."

Karin smirked. "Well, then, you have nothing to lose by letting the boys experiment with their own creations."

"You know, that's a wonderful idea.... I bet the guys would really enjoy it. We assign certain household duties, of course, but the cooking has always fallen into the group parents' domain. I can't believe I never thought of this before."

"Probably because you come from a patriarchal family with traditional male/female roles," Karin teased.

"Meaning I was the one to get aching muscles and calluses! Some days, what I wouldn't have given to trade the fields for the kitchen."

"And I'm sure your womenfolk would have cooperated gladly on some of their worst days, too!"

"Likely so...." he admitted, grinning warmly back at her.

"What's your sister like?" Karin suddenly asked on a more serious note.

"Mary? She's the perfect Mennonite daughter. She will probably marry an Old Order Mennonite, raise her children in the old ways and never question what's expected of her.''

''And you were never tempted to take that path of least resistance—to marry, have your own family?''

John's eyes wandered to an out-of-date wall calendar hanging beside him, but he wasn't focusing on the dozens of names and phone numbers scribbled upon it. ''As a matter of fact, I was married at one time to a Mennonite.''

''You're not divorced? I didn't think—''

''No, Mennonites do not allow divorce. Emma died of cancer, two years ago.''

''Oh....'' Karin had not expected to hear that. ''You must miss her very much,'' she said gently.

His eyes met hers. ''I did at first. But, strangely, it was her death that finally released me from myself, from my own self-made prison.'' He stopped because he'd never spoken to anyone about this. But Karin was looking at him in such a nonjudgmental way, and so many other new things were happening to him that he found himself willing to open up to her.

''I married her,'' he went on, ''thinking she could be a sanctuary from the rebellious thoughts that plagued me, hoping that by marriage I could fit into the life that was expected of me, but she couldn't make all that possible. We both knew it, although we never discussed it. I honestly don't know what would have happened if she hadn't got sick. I would probably still be on the farm, but a very unhappy man....''

''Still, it must have been very difficult to watch someone you care for suffer and...die.''

He nodded, his eyes staring at some faraway place that did not seem to be a part of the room. When he spoke again, the words were barely audible, torn from somewhere deep within. ''I've never felt such rage...at...at the unfairness of it all, not solely for my sake, but for Emma's. She was so young. And I was shocked at the anger I carried inside. That's not a time I wish to remember. Thankfully, acceptance came at last, much later than it had for Emma. She proved to be a strong, courageous woman."

"What you endured then and afterward has taken much courage, too," Karin murmured, feeling the raw edges of his sorrow. "Did you have any children?"

"No," he said with a transparently forced indifference. "I used to wonder whether that would have made a difference to my unhappiness, and now..." Suddenly he got to his feet, radiating a restless energy. He went into the living room and stood by the window that overlooked the busy street.

"Would you like some coffee?" Karin called to him after a few moments.

"Okay."

When she entered the room carrying two mugs of coffee, she said, "I'm sorry if I made you remember unpleasant events."

"Actually, I was thinking how much more vivid now are the pleasant memories. Amazingly, the...other ones do fade with time. Our psyches can be our friends."

Karin folded her legs under her as she sank into a corner of the plush sofa. "What were the pleasant times like, if you don't mind talking about them, that is?"

He joined her, one arm sliding along the top of the small couch, the other holding the handle of his mug. "Why?" he asked, looking at her sideways. "Those years now seem as if they happened to another man."

"But they didn't," she countered, waiting.

So he began to tell her, haltingly, smiling crookedly from time to time, that he'd started noticing Emma at the Sunday evening fellowship meetings. She had been painfully shy, set apart from the rest, and he'd been drawn to her because of that. As was the custom, he had sent her a note, asking if he could drive her home, and she'd accepted by way of another note. Their quiet courtship had begun.

They had been married the following November, after harvesttime, when fieldwork was not demanding. The simple, four-hour ceremony had taken place in Emma's home, followed by a lavish dinner, then singing and visiting by the many guests.

He had not taken a honeymoon with his new bride. Instead, they'd spent weekends throughout the winter calling on their large families and receiving gifts. In the meantime they'd lived at the Martin homestead with his parents, since John was the only son. Otherwise the youngest male would have inherited the property and Jacob Martin would have purchased another farm for his older son.

John had had little time alone with his wife. All meals were shared with the family, and their days were filled with different tasks, but that was the way it had always been.

As Karin listened, she kept imagining cozy family scenes around big tables, everyone knowing they belonged there, not feeling as if they were a temporary guest in someone else's home, as she'd so often been. And she thought it one of life's ironies that John had recently walked away from the family haven she'd never really had, trading it for the solitary starkness that had been thrust upon her....

He had stopped talking and was watching her closely. "What is it, Karin?"

"Oh," she said with a light laugh, embarrassed that he'd noticed her mind had strayed. "I...I was just comparing your simple wedding with some of the elaborate arrangements friends of mine have had—costly receptions with photographers, florists, the whole bit, following the etiquette bible to a T, and nearly suffering a nervous breakdown in the process. Then, afterward, mortgage payments for a house they can barely afford in today's crazy real estate market...."

"Is that what you were really thinking?" His eyes challenged hers, as if he saw right through her nervous babble.

"No."

"Tell me."

"You don't give up, do you?" His eyes would not release hers, and she heard herself admit, "I was thinking that independence and belonging seem to be mutually exclusive for some of us...."

"Is that what you'd like, Karin? To belong? To marry and have your own family?" he persisted, placing his coffee mug on a painted milk crate that acted as a side table.

She tore her eyes away, breaking the spell he was weaving around her. She thought briefly of her fantasy man, but he was certainly not a conversation piece. Her mouth hardened into a tight line. "Oh, I lost my naiveté about that kind of 'belonging' a long time ago. Or maybe I never had much. The only responsibility I've ever had is to myself, which has taken me long enough to master. Why upset a good thing? Besides, I'd never know what I'd be missing if I settled down. It's a big world out there." She took one last gulp from her cup, then set it on the floor beside her, her manner breezy, indifferent.

Never had she looked as vulnerable as at that moment, John thought. She was unaware of the wistfulness in her lovely blue eyes and the tensing of her shoulders and fists, as if she was gearing up to take on the world and to prove she didn't need anyone.

John stared at her mouth, such a sweet inviting mouth, and he experienced an incredible urge to feel those lips against his. But with all his will, he fought the inappropriate desire and looked away. The room was filled with a strained silence.

"Why didn't you kiss me?" Karin finally asked quietly.

He could not meet her gaze. How could he tell her that he didn't know what she expected from him and that he no longer knew what he expected from himself? The old John, whom he had lived with for more than thirty years, and the new John, who was still a chrysalis bursting out of his shell, were not living together very compatibly at the moment.

"Did you want me to?" He bought time by answering her question with another.

Karin had been wondering about that since she'd met him. "Yes... and no," she answered with a light laugh. "See, you're not alone in your indecision."

"You're very beautiful," he said slowly, still not looking at her. "Many men must have tried to... court you."

His use of the old-fashioned term was endearing to her. "Not in the gallant... and true way you mean," she said softly.

"I've only been with Emma," he admitted, staring down at his hands. "And that was after... after we were married."

"I've only been—in that sense—with one man I *thought* I was going to marry, but he... we didn't, after all. Does that bother you?" Karin asked gently.

He did not answer right away. "No, I don't think so. Not if you did what was right for you at the time."

"But you believe—"

"I don't know what I believe anymore," he said simply, raising his eyes to look directly at her. "Sometimes I just *feel*."

And suddenly, as if it could not escape the power of suggestion, the burning pull of desire was there once more between them, stronger than ever.

"It seems inevitable that I kiss you tonight, Karin," he said on a deeply expelled breath.

And then he was leaning toward her to cup her chin in his hand and brush his lips against her waiting mouth. Karin grew still as he pulled back, ever so slightly. Their lips met again, less tentatively, the warm moistness blending and deepening for a sweet suspended moment.

They drew away together in a slow motion that prolonged the kiss even more, their foreheads touching before Karin eased her head back to stare uncertainly at him. She'd sensed a restrained intensity about him from almost the first moment they'd met, and it was there again, but magnified to a startling degree.

His hand reached up to gently lift a strand of her hair that had fallen forward, lingering along her neck before reluctantly easing away.

"We should say good-night now...before we spoil anything," Karin whispered, her voice shaky as his intensity coiled through her, becoming part of her own.

"It has been a good night," he murmured with difficulty, his own breathing as uneven as hers. "I was terrified. I've never been on a date."

"It didn't feel like a *date*," she said, smiling raggedly. She was going to add, "until our first kiss," but decided not to as she glimpsed a shadow cross his face.

"Karin, I—" He stopped, began again. "Although you have asked for nothing, I have to tell you that I can promise you nothing. I—"

"I don't trust promises—just reality," she returned, her nerves taut from the kiss, his nearness and the warm dark eyes that seemed so trustworthy, the most dangerous kind...

He stood and pulled her up from the couch, watching his hand slowly release hers, his expression troubled. He thanked her for the meal with a strained politeness. The easy comfort between them had disappeared, to be replaced by a different awareness, a complex one that Karin did not yet understand. She murmured something equally civil but distant, and then suddenly he was gone.

FILLED WITH A FEVERED ENERGY, Karin sat on the carpeted floor and attempted some deep breathing and then a few stretching exercises in order to relax herself. But her brain was operating on two different levels, the mechanics of her movements separate from the free-floating turmoil inside.

Finally, she curled up in her rocking chair, setting it in motion with one foot. The soothing action soon brought order to her scattered thoughts, and one vivid emotion stood out from all the rest: she was scared as hell. And there was still time to avoid the pain she'd walked into so blindly with Eric Lester....

Carol had tried warning her about Eric, but her friend and colleague hadn't told her anything about him that Karin hadn't known. Sure, Eric exuded virility and he'd dated lots of different women, but Karin had met a lot of different men, too, and she'd never fallen in love before. Eric had been charming, adventurous; he'd made her laugh and feel special. He'd showered her with gifts and funny cards and proclamations of love. He'd sworn how much he'd missed her when they'd only been apart a day or two.

At first it had all been a wonderful flirtatious game to Karin. No man had ever been quite so ardent in his affection, and slowly, she felt herself starting to believe him, wanting to return the exuberance more than she'd ever allowed herself.

For months, she'd marveled at how easy it was to just let go. They'd even talked of marriage when they were both

ready, *absolutely* certain. Karin had been content to wait
for that elusive knowledge, to ride recklessly on those new
exhilarating waves toward unknown horizons.

Then one day Carol had told her as kindly and tactfully
as possible that Eric had started sleeping with a new younger instructor. Karin's sense of betrayal had cut through to
her very core, but when she'd faced Eric, she'd been deadly
calm. He'd said that his feelings for her hadn't changed,
but that he was attracted to the other woman, too. Karin
was also free to pursue additional relationships, if she
wished, because, after all, they weren't married yet....

Karin had felt something shrivel up and die inside her,
and she had refused to speak to Eric again, even though she
saw him daily at the club before her timely transfer to
Kitchener. Now she looked back on her experience with him
as a humiliating failure of good judgment.

Although she'd had a lot of male friends, Eric had been
the only man she'd ever become so intimate with. Before
Eric, there had been an intense intellectual relationship with
Jean Luc, an English-speaking sculptor in Paris, who had
raved about their rare spiritual communion. While she'd
found his company stimulating, she hadn't experienced
anything close to the subliminal heights he'd described. One
day she'd just left Paris, unable to face him and say goodbye.

That was how she was feeling now, suddenly wanting to
flee from all John Martin stirred in her. Perhaps they could
become good friends, despite their different backgrounds,
but she was terrified as to how to handle the strong but un-
fulfilled sexual currents that had developed between them,
not to mention how to treat his own qualms and confusion
because of his strict Mennonite upbringing.

And how had this man who was so far removed from her
image of the ideal, worldly partner managed to affect her

so potently? Because he was real, an inner voice answered—and her safe, unattainable fantasy was not.

But John was at a critical transition point in his own life, and she was always in a stage of transition, so what could they possibly give each other but more confusion and frustration in the present and grief in the future, when they inevitably moved on, following their individual directions?

Suddenly she wished she could chat with Carol, who had two marriages and innumerable romances behind her and considered herself quite an authority on the dos and don'ts of relationships. But it was too late to call. Besides, Karin reminded herself wryly, she already knew what her friend would say. Carol would quote from one of her favorite self-help books and tell her that once again Karin had become entangled with an unsuitable man who offered no hope of any permanence, because deep down Karin was afraid of lasting involvement.

What struck Karin was that this time her friend just might be right. An indisputable pattern *was* starting to emerge. If she was smart, she would make John history, before the pattern once more took on the unwelcome texture of a fiasco.

But an inner chorus of resistance began as she recalled John's seductive eyes, his strong gentleness, the loneliness that so matched her own.

JOHN WAS STARING at the ceiling, his thoughts as drifting and elusive as the play of shadows there. The apartment was too hot, so he had opened his bedroom window a crack. Since he was on the second floor of the apartment building, a block away from the center of town, he was unable to avoid hearing street sounds. But it was not the

unfamiliar city noises that were keeping him awake tonight.

He was thinking of Karin. The memory of her warm lips
under his exploring mouth was tormenting him, refusing to
be suppressed. His response to the woman he'd known so
briefly was a powerful force, its origins running deeper than
simple sexual abstinence. Never had he felt such hunger for
Emma. Never had he felt so threatened by a woman.

He had always believed that the kinds of sensations and
drives he was experiencing must be controlled until marriage. Yet his response to the bewitching Karin had swiftly
managed to make him *want* to defy his upbringing. He had
acted purely on impulse with her and had gloried in the loss
of inhibition. He had shocked himself.

For the first time in his life, he had been feeling in control of his destiny. The church, the community, his family
were not expressing disapproval at his every transgression.
His freedom was like a precious gift to him, his job challenging, rewarding in ways the farm work had never been.
Even his cramped living quarters, functionally furnished,
were a sanctuary, because they were all his own—quiet,
restorative, despite the brevity of the hours he spent here
before returning to Greenbank every day.

But in one night, Karin's presence had invaded his place
and his peace of mind with a tumult he resented as deeply
as he was lured by her temptations.

Once before he had chosen to join the course of his life
with that of a woman, when he had married Emma and
tried to mold himself into the Mennonite ways. That had
been a disastrous mistake, as much as he'd cared for his
gentle wife. His deep dissatisfaction with his choice had
hurt her more than she had ever admitted, even though his
discontent had not been her fault.

He was determined not to repeat that mistake, especially at this time of new beginnings. A relationship with Karin would be filled with risk, leading him in directions he might not be ready for, might not want.

He had known all this and still he had asked to see her, had slipped into an easy companionship with her, had kissed her with restraint, all the while wanting more. In all honesty, though, during their hours together, he had felt more alive than he had in years.

But all his instincts for self-preservation were warning him to bridle his errant desires before *they* controlled him. Never again would he let another human being stand in the way of his personal goals. He knew he was selfish, but he had fought hard for his freedom, and he would not give up all that he'd gained.

But, try as he might, he could not convince himself never to see Karin again. He needed to bask in her golden warmth yet keep his distance from it. He prayed he could do both.

CHAPTER FIVE

KARIN WAS LATE. The plumber had run into complications fixing one of the club's showers, and she'd had to stay until he'd finished. Then she missed the turnoff that led to Greenbank Avenue, because she was worrying about seeing John again, especially in front of so many strangers.

His call at the club a week ago, about two weeks after spaghetti night, had taken her by surprise. The boys would be preparing a special buffet for a handful of guests, he'd told her, and he'd wondered if she would like to come. When he reminded her that he'd followed up on *her* suggestion about letting the teenagers have free rein in the kitchen, she could hardly refuse to attend.

Still, she'd pretended to check her schedule, even though she'd known she was free on the night of the event—she always left early on Fridays, letting Cindy manage the club. She'd used the stall tactic in order to assess the wisdom of a second planned meeting with the ex-Mennonite.

Frankly, he'd been on her mind too much. She kept remembering that dinner, their kiss—one simple kiss, but it blocked out a lot of other considerations, such as the question of why she was wasting time on a frustrating relationship.

Maybe by seeing John face-to-face she would be grounded in reality again, she'd reasoned; she'd find out that he was a different, less appealing person in front of others. Maybe she'd uncover some idiosyncrasy that really bugged her. Somehow she *had* to lose her preoccupation with him. She'd accepted his invitation.

Driving along, she didn't notice a street number, but it wasn't hard to pick out the house by the many parked cars in the driveway and by the well-lighted windows. The two-storied home was one of the largest on the quiet residential street, not far from downtown Waterloo. But since she was an hour late, Karin only gathered fleeting impressions of the place as she rushed up to it—a big and old yet unimposing brick building, a well-treed, fenced lot that stretched a fair distance into the dark backyard, a wide gray porch badly in need of painting.

She rang the bell, and the door immediately swung open. Blinking out at her was a small but solidly built youth with longish, light brown hair and lazy, thick-lashed hazel eyes.

"Is this Greenbank?" The boy just nodded. "Hi, I'm Karin, a . . . friend of John's. I'm sorry I'm late, but—"

"Don't worry. Apparently one of the brilliant chefs got his kilograms and ounces mixed up, so everyone has to wait for the roast to be ready. And Phil's remixing the salad dressing. He thought the jar of garlic powder was Parmesan cheese. What a joke. Glad I stayed out of the whole thing."

"And you're . . ."

"Brad."

"I thought you were all pitching in. I've been looking forward—"

"You thought wrong," he said abruptly, walking down the hall. "John's downstairs in the rec room with everyone else. Down there. Hang your coat in that closet. You're lucky I heard the doorbell. Or maybe not," he added sarcastically, glancing at a closed door to what must be the kitchen, judging by the sudden sound of breaking glass followed by an expletive from a young male voice. With a devil-may-care gait, Brad ambled up the stairs, then disappeared into a room at the top.

Karin decided to meet the young chefs in the kitchen later, fearing their reception might be just as cool as Brad's. After hanging up her coat, she drew a deep breath and made her way down the stairs.

At the bottom she stopped, not spotting John among the small, scattered groups. Furniture had been pushed to the side of the carpeted and paneled L-shaped room to leave space for a series of mismatched tables, with a colorful assortment of coverings and dishes. A fresh bouquet of pink and white carnations graced the center of each table. Suddenly Karin winced.

"Don't tell me you're already regretting coming and you haven't even tried the food yet," said a familiar voice beside her.

She turned to see John emerging from an adjacent storage room with a few bags of potato chips. His white shirt, tucked loosely into dark pants, was unbuttoned carelessly at the neck, and the sleeves were rolled up to reveal his muscular forearms.

"No, I just realized that not only am I late, for which I apologize, but I also forgot to bring the box of after-dinner mints sitting on my desk at the club."

"Don't worry about it. Your day has probably been just as hectic as ours here." His eyes quickly took in her cream-colored silk blouse, the belt sitting jauntily on her slender hips, the simple line of her black wool skirt, her sheer stockings. "You look nice," he said with sincerity.

"Thanks. I thought I'd aim for a conservative look."

Never would he describe her striking, golden-haired elegance as conservative, but he just nodded in agreement. "I'll, ah, introduce you around as soon as I distribute these emergency appetizers. The meal's been delayed."

"I heard . . . from Brad. He let me in."

"The perfect host, I imagine," John said dryly. "Brad's not being very cooperative today. At the last minute he refused to help."

"So he said. Why?"

John shrugged. "Who knows? Maybe the whole thing was starting to seem too much like fun. He's not an easy kid to get close to. As soon as we seem to be making progress, he draws back. Likes to run away, too. We have to keep a close eye on him. Where is he, by the way?"

"Went up to his room, I think."

John whistled. "I wouldn't put it past him to pull something tonight. Hold these. I'll be right back." He rushed up the stairs.

Clutching the foil bags, Karin mustered a healthy dose of bravado and stepped into the crowded room.

"You must be Karin." A thin-haired, lanky man sporting gold wire-rimmed glasses touched her elbow. "I'm Henry, John's cohort in this crazy place we call a home. You must be starving. I'm sorry about the setback, but these things happen. Where's John? He seems to have abandoned you."

"He went to check on Brad," Karin managed to interject, dazed by his fast-talking, energetic personality.

Henry frowned. "If I had my druthers, the boy would be ignored tonight. No excuse for letting us down like he did."

"But we all know you're the tyrant around here and John's the one with some heart," said a slim, gray-haired woman. "Hi, I'm Margaret Sanderson. The one with the unenviable job of putting up with everyone's quirks around here. I'm a child-care worker according to my résumé, although that isn't accurate, either, because I mainly work with teenagers and adults. Are you totally confused?"

"No, I don't think so," replied Karin, immediately warming to the older woman's relaxed manner and friendly face. "Are you here full-time?"

"Heavens, no. I keep trying to retire, but they insisted I work even more hours when John came on board." She leaned toward Karin and whispered conspiratorially, "I'm supposed to be a female influence around here, but mainly I'm a fourth player in euchre tournaments when one of the kids doesn't feel like playing. Henry *loves* euchre."

"Don't let her fool you, Karin. Margaret is great relief help when John or I need a break," said Henry, smiling fondly at his colleague.

"Even so, these two big lugs are doing a marvelous job— in their own way," Margaret told Karin, winking.

"Someday, I'll find out what you mean by that," Henry teased. "Right now, I'll relieve our guest of these hors d'oeuvres. If you'll excuse me, ladies."

"Ever-efficient, that's our Henry," Margaret said amiably as he dashed off. "How long have you known the other half of the dynamic duo?"

"Oh, not long...."

"John's quite the guy, and the boys seem to like him, although they're too 'cool' to show it, of course. Henry's big on rules—and punishments if they're broken—while John likes to talk things out, show he cares. The two balance each other nicely. The boys will have to adjust again when Henry's wife, Melissa, returns. She can be quite strict, too."

"And ambitious," Karin put in. "I understand she's working on her thesis out west—that's a long way from her husband, but I admire her if she's pursuing a dream she's always had."

Margaret nodded. "Actually, she chose Vancouver, not only for access to certain research, but to be close to her mother, who lives there—she's suffering from Alzheimer's disease. Melissa is helping to care for her until space in a suitable nursing home can be found. I think that's why the ministry bent their rules about not having a married couple here. Have you met any of the boys yet?"

"Just Brad."

"Ah, Brad," Margaret said, shaking her head. "At least John gets along with him a little more than Melissa ever could."

"He does seem to have a chip on his shoulder," Karin ventured.

"You guessed it. The Children's Aid Society took him from his mother when he was about four. No father around. She was in rough shape, drank a lot. Brad's been in far too many foster homes since then."

"Has he been here at Greenbank long?"

"Almost two years. I hope he hangs in until he finishes high school. But he's free to leave when he turns sixteen— he's fifteen now. The success rate in this business is not as high as we'd like, unfortunately. It certainly takes special people to work as full-time house parents."

At that moment John appeared in the rec room, his arm resting lightly on the shoulders of a scowling Brad. Around the youth's neck hung a well-worn camera that Karin instantly recognized—with a pang—as John's.

The two women watched as John led the boy to a corner of the room and began instructing him on the use of the camera, aiming it at the set tables.

"I've got to hand it to John—he's innovative," Margaret said quietly. "Come on, I'll introduce you around before the feast arrives—if it ever does, that is."

Karin caught John's querying eye and nodded that she was being well looked after, then followed Margaret. A glass of fruit punch was handed to her by Henry, who was in rapid transit. She met Jessica Gervais, the social worker

who was responsible for seven group homes in the south-
western Ontario region, and Gary Fries, the local supervisor from the Ministry of Community and Social Services.
She was also quickly introduced to a few neighbors and
teachers of the boys, who attended the local high school.

"Your name sounds very familiar," remarked Jessica, a
tall, plain-looking woman wearing a tailored navy skirt and
jacket and a crisp white blouse tied at the neck with a large
bow. Her posture was ramrod-straight.

"Perhaps you've seen my ads or heard me on the local
radio. I've been busy promoting my new women's health
and fitness club in Kitchener."

"Really? Maybe that's it, but I don't usually pay much
attention to that sort of thing. Not that others shouldn't,
mind you, but I'm a firm believer in my own health program—moderation, whether in eating or exercise. I walk
whenever I can, and the only dessert I ever allow myself is
fruit."

"But we don't all have your dogged willpower," Gary
Fries interjected, patting his portly middle good-naturedly.
"I say, you only live once, so why not indulge yourself from
time to time? Chocolates are my big weakness. But let's not
talk about food. I'm starving. So what brings you into our
humble midst, Karin?"

"I'm a . . . friend of John's."

"That so? Pardon my saying, but you two seem so different. Do you see him much?"

There was a shrewdness in the older man's narrowed eyes
that Karin didn't trust. "No, we just met, actually."

"Don't worry, Gary. John isn't shirking his duties here.
You won't find a more dedicated man anywhere." Margaret leaned toward Karin and added, with a daring glint in
her eye directed at the supervisor, "This month Gary is
picking on the latest addition to our staff. He won't be-

lieve me when I tell him that John is beyond reproach. Some people just have a natural talent for helping others, and John is one of them.''

Gary straightened his tie and tried to look dignified as he replied in a lowered voice, ''I hope you're right, Margaret, but I *am* accountable to a lot of folks if we've made a mistake in hiring someone as...backward as John. And we've also had plenty of negative experiences with single fellows whose libidos, shall we say, sometimes interfere with their necessary commitment to the demands of the home.''

Margaret humphed and Karin felt anger boiling inside her, but she put a check on her feelings. Simultaneously they all glanced over at the subject of their discussion, who was gathering one of the groups together for Brad to take his first photograph.

''Don't forget us, Brad,'' Gary called out after the boy had snapped several shots.

''Coming up,'' John said cheerily, ignoring the unforgiving look the boy was giving him. ''Now that you've practiced on your teachers, Brad, let's impress our esteemed visitor from the ministry and these three lovely ladies.''

''How do you want us, Brad?'' Margaret piped in, trying to ease the tension between Brad and John. ''Showing our pearly whites to the camera or pretending to be engrossed in conversation?''

''I don't care,'' he mumbled.

''You've been elected as chief photographer tonight, fella,'' John said, undaunted. ''What's it going to be?''

''Smiling, then,'' the youth said at last, keeping his eyes on the camera. ''It's kind of dark in the corner, though.''

''No problem,'' Margaret said, switching on a lamp. ''Come on, John, if we have to submit to this, so do you.''

"Okay, but just cut me out of the shot," John said over his shoulder to Brad as he joined the group, standing by Karin's side.

"Everybody closer," Brad ordered.

Karin turned sideways and she had a distinct sense of John's presence towering behind her, their bodies brushing.

"Closer...."

John's arm slipped around Karin's waist as he pressed himself against her.

"Okay, smile or something...."

"Something," Margaret repeated in a singsong voice, holding the last syllable. Laughter rippled through the group.

After the camera clicked, everyone broke apart amid a chorus of hoots and hollers. John was the last one to pull away, and he did not look back at Karin as he stepped toward Brad.

Disoriented, she felt as if his body was still imprinted on hers, its strength and warmth penetrating her clothing. She gulped her punch and saw that Gary Fries was watching her thoughtfully.

"Attention, everyone!" bellowed a deep voice that had a tendency to crack.

In the doorway stood a tall young man, dressed completely in black, from his leather jacket and T-shirt to his tight pants and high boots. Even his hair stood in shiny jet-black spikes. "You better get seated. We're almost ready."

"As long as you eat first, Karl," said Brad mockingly. "Didn't you fail home ec?"

"Get off my case, Williamson, or you'll be stuck with all the dishes. Or is that too much for you to handle, too?"

John adroitly stepped in. "On that encouraging note, let's all have a seat. Timing is critical for the true gourmet chef, isn't that right, Karl?"

"Yup... I mean, that is correct, sir." He folded an imitation cloth over his arm as a tuxedoed waiter would. "At theese establishment, ve pride ourselves on our cri...sp vegetables *incroyable* and our juicy roast *au* pot," he added with a hackneyed blend of accents. He kept a straight face, despite the smiles that were spreading around the room, then exited with a flourish.

"He can certainly pour on the charm when he wants to," John muttered as Karin found herself being wedged between him and Gary Fries in the flurry of seating arrangements that followed.

Gary, overhearing John's comment, leaned toward her and said in a low voice, "You wouldn't know it, judging by the satanic look he insists on wearing, but Karl comes from a very wealthy family. His father's one of the Cross brothers—they're into real estate, hotels, you name it. And his stepmother runs a top model agency."

Karin looked surprised. "So why's he here?"

"He's what we call a society ward," John explained. "His folks are preoccupied with their own lives, their careers. He was with nannies a lot and got into drugs pretty heavily and some other trouble with the law, so his parents decided to put him into a group home for a year or so. I guess they figured he could be supervised more carefully."

"And their own guilt could be relieved," Gary added with a snort. "How have the meetings been going with your staff, the Crosses and Karl?"

"The Crosses keep canceling," John answered evenly. "If any of the family members are available, we like to have them involved," John explained to Karin. "In this case,

though, all we can do is keep trying for some cooperation.''

He fell silent as Karl returned. Her interest sparked,
Karin watched the youth field the teasing of the guests and
serve the platters with an air of confidence and refinement
his other two young assistants lacked.

"He does seem to be in his element, doesn't he?'' she
murmured to John, but his attention was back on Brad,
who was about to leave the room.

"Brad,'' he called out. "Let's have one more shot of the
whole motley crew.''

The youth nonchalantly strode back into the room and
stared at the faces looking up at him expectantly. He
glanced toward John, who just shrugged, refusing to in-
tervene anymore.

"Okay, okay,'' Brad mumbled. Going to the far corner,
he adjusted his camera and gave curt instructions as to who
should lean where so that everyone would fit into the picture.

After the camera had finally clicked, he said gruffly,
"Don't move. I might as well get another in case someone
blinked. I think you did last time, Mr. Fries.''

"Just grabbing some shut-eye,'' the supervisor joked,
and Brad gave him a quick half smile, the first glimmer of
lightness Karin had seen in him.

"Is that what you're used to doing back at the office?''
Margaret asked sweetly.

"If you hadn't been around so long, I'd file a complaint
against you for harassment of superiors,'' Gary threw back
at her, clearly enjoying their friendly sparring of long-
standing.

"Someone has to keep you on your toes,'' she returned
just as sweetly.

"Hear, hear," a voice called out from the far end of the table, then everyone chuckled and the camera flashed.

"Grab a seat there," John said before Brad could leave again, reading the boy's intent.

"Nah, it's okay...."

"Here, there's lots of room," one of the teachers said, moving over as an extra chair appeared from a pair of hands behind him.

With a casual swagger that reminded Karin of the macho heroes in old movies, Brad sauntered over and was safely seated. John breathed a small sigh of relief, and she marveled at the ease with which he had drawn the problematic boy into the gathering. In fact, he'd surprised her throughout the evening, mixing congenially with everyone in the room. Margaret was right—he was a natural with people, and he seemed to have an uncanny perception of what was needed of him.

The platter of sliced roast beef was the last dish to join the salads, vegetables, potatoes and rolls already sitting on the table. The cooks took their seats, and Henry stood to propose a toast.

"Thank you all for coming. Here's to the guys who've worked hard at this meal," he said, raising his water glass. "I sneaked a few scraps in the kitchen, and I can assure you they weren't bad...."

"Not bad!" squeaked a red-haired youth with more freckles on his face than patches of pale skin. "Is that all?"

"Coming from Henry, that's high praise, Phil. You better take what you get," John told him dryly as he started passing the food around.

Jessica Gervais scooped a tiny spoonful of potatoes onto her plate, topping them with a drop of gravy. "You lads have an even greater challenge trying to please John here. If *he* praises your meal, that's worth something. He's used to that fabulous Mennonite cooking and baking. Aren't you, John?''

''Hmm,'' he answered vaguely, abruptly changing the subject. ''Dig in before it gets cold, folks.'' Karin looked at him curiously, but he kept his head down as he reached for one of the casserole dishes.

She quickly forgot about his evasiveness as she started to sample the simple but tasty meal. Compliments ran high from the main course to dessert, and before long the three boys who had prepared the meal were beaming. They barely noticed the small portions on everyone else's plates, compared to what was on their own.

''Next time, we'll have to work on quantity, not just quality,'' John muttered to Karin as he politely declined the last slice of pie, which promptly disappeared onto the plate of Jordan, the pale-skinned, fair-haired boy sitting beside him.

Jordan was overweight, with a round, moonlike face. It hadn't taken Karin long to realize that he was also painfully conscious of his stutter—he avoided conversation with everyone but his freckled friend, Phil, who was perched on a stool next to him.

''The average North American eats too much anyway, if that's any consolation,'' Karin replied in low tones to John, when she saw that the two boys were busy with a quiet exchange of their own, and Gary was engrossed in conversation with Jessica.

''Some.'' Their eyes met and in that golden-starred moment it was as if everyone else in the room vanished.

''Are you enjoying yourself? I've hardly had time to chat.'' His voice was hushed.

''That's okay. I'm intrigued to be witnessing another side to the multifaceted John Martin.''

''I hide nothing.''

"I noticed."

"Except how much I battled with myself before I called you," he confessed.

"But you finally called. Why?"

"Maybe I should start keeping secrets. It makes everything easier, doesn't it? When two people are just testing the waters, making sure they don't get in out of their depth."

Before she could reply, Karin felt a tap on her elbow and turned to face Gary Fries. "Is there room for another in your cozy tête-à-tête?"

"Of course," she murmured, hoping he hadn't overheard anything.

"I'm curious about the woman who can capture the attention of our saintly Mennonite."

That was it—he'd pushed her too far. "John, saintly?" she asked, her eyes wide, innocent. "I wouldn't say that."

"Very much the man, eh?" Gary challenged, staring at her as if John was not even present.

"Very much the humanitarian," she replied coolly. "Are you married, Mr. Fries?"

"Yes...."

"Happily?"

"Well, I suppose, but why do you want to know?"

"Too personal a question? I'm sorry. Now, if you'll excuse me, I'd like to freshen up."

She stood, aware that the two men were watching her leave. She glanced back at John, who winked at her, his dark eyes acknowledging her victory.

As she found her way around, Karin was amazed at the size of the fully finished basement, consisting of an office, a huge storage area, a laundry room adjoining a workshop and the party room. The house had to be fifty years old, but it was in good repair.

Thankfully, Gary was gone from the table when she reentered the dining area. John was talking to Phil and Jordan, and they all looked up at her as she rejoined them.

"My compliments to you both," she said sincerely after John had introduced her to his two companions.

"No problem," said Phil, his face flushed, which made his mass of freckles more prominent. His hands were stuck in the pockets of a long barbecue apron with a bold beer logo on it.

"Th-thanks," Jordan mumbled.

"John told me you've been dabbling in the kitchen, but is this the first formal meal you've prepared?" Her glance included both young men, but it was Phil who replied.

"Yeah, 'cept, I used to make a lot of clubhouse sandwiches during the play-offs or World Series, but I guess that don't really count as a full-course meal."

"Not quite. Were they all for your friends?" Karin asked.

His feet shifted. "No, mainly for my...uncle and his buddies. But they didn't care what they ate. They were usually pretty drunk by the end of a game."

"Oh. Well, I'm sure your uncle would be suitably impressed with this meal," Karin said, trying to smooth over Phil's growing discomfort.

"Not that bastard," he snapped, abruptly standing and walking away.

Jordan looked unsure of what to do, murmured something inaudible, then went to help his friend, who was carelessly piling dishes onto a tray, his face hard.

"Guess I stuck my foot into that one," Karin said with a grimace.

"No, he has to learn to deal with what happened," John replied.

"What did happen?"

"His uncle raised him after his parents died, when Phil was ten or so. From what I understand, the uncle worked in construction and got messed up in some dubious investment deals on the side. Some shady characters came after him, and one day he just disappeared. Phil was really upset—he idolized the man."

"Oh, dear...."

"Phil was shuffled around then to various relatives, got into some trouble shoplifting, was given a warning, then got caught starting a fire in a new subdivision. A few homes went down."

"Phew! That's serious stuff."

John nodded. "Since he was over twelve at the time, he was classified as a young offender and subject to charges in youth court. These days the judges are coming down hard on offenders, especially repeat ones, but Phil got off relatively easy. He was put on probation and sent to live here two years ago when Henry first rented the house and started it up as a group home."

"So how's he been doing?" Karin asked, warily watching Phil carry a full load of dishes up the steep stairs.

"Great, considering. Once in a while he lets himself get provoked, like tonight, but usually he has everything under control. He gets along well with Jordan, wants to protect him, which is good for him—he needs someone to be close to. As much as he idolized his uncle, I don't think he was treated very well by him."

Karin shook her head sympathetically. "And what about Jordan? He seems so... frail and frightened."

"A victim of child abuse. He's really started to come out of his shell. Apparently before I came he barely spoke, but he's improving a bit. He's our newest resident, so we can't expect miracles overnight."

Although John didn't admit it, Karin was starting to realize just how stressful his new job could be. The hours he spent with the volatile teenagers were long and the rewards small since progress seemed to be such a slow, erratic process.

"Are there any coed group homes?" she asked.

"Some, but not usually with the older residents. The living quarters are very close, and the, er, dynamics between the sexes can create some unwanted problems. Adolescent hormones, you know."

"Ah, those wild and wacky adolescent hormones...." she said, unable to resist the bit of mischief that caused her to step onto potentially dangerous ground.

"Sometimes they refuse to grow up," he murmured, his eyes flickering with the same mischievous glint he saw in hers.

And suddenly they were both remembering the night when the chemistry between them had ignited suppressed desires, sparking insistent adult hormones....

"Everyone has to learn to control their hormones," Karin said softly.

"True."

And they both knew they were failing miserably at the task at the moment.

"I should leave now. I have an early day tomorrow at the club," she said quickly.

"I'll show you out."

"No! You better stay with your other guests." She glanced uneasily over at Gary Fries, who happened to be watching them.

"I'll walk you out," John insisted, smiling pleasantly at the supervisor.

Karin quickly said her goodbyes while John checked on Brad's whereabouts—he was listening to his Walkman in his room. The other three boys were in the kitchen, trying to restore it to some semblance of order.

When Karin finally stood outside by her car, under the soft glow of a street lamp, she stole a quick look back at the house.

"Checking for spies?" John asked.

"I wouldn't put it past Gary. He's something else. How did he ever get to such a position with his, ah, lack of tact?"

"I asked the same thing of a few people, and apparently, he's better at administration duties than people skills."

"Doesn't his meddling bother you?"

John shrugged. "I don't let him get to me. Actually, I think he's just testing me. There's a high burnout rate in this profession, and he's making sure I have 'the right stuff.'"

"Where'd you hear that expression?"

"I saw the movie—someone donated a VCR to Greenbank. Gary even encouraged me to watch it as often as possible. He says I have a lot of catching up to do."

Karin laughed. "He's right. But you like challenges, don't you?"

"Actually, my hardest task will be to sell him on a long-range plan Henry and I have worked out for the boys. We'd like to get them more involved in the community—volunteer work at a hospital, team sports, part-time jobs, that sort of thing. But Gary prefers that we keep them more cloistered, developing their individual strengths in the controlled environments of home and school. Basically he thinks that guys like Karl or Brad would abuse their freedom. I think that's a risk we have to take if they're ever going to make it on their own."

"And how are you going to convince Gary of that?" Karin asked, intrigued.

"Next week I'm going to Toronto to present my plan to a roomful of skeptics—Gary is surrounding himself with lots of supporters. But I'm not walking out of there until I've convinced them all to give my ideas a chance."

There was such a fierce determination and strength of purpose in his face that Karin knew he would be listened to seriously, but she also knew about the complex interaction of personalities, procedures and policies in any corporation, particularly in the government.

"Well, good luck, but I'm sure you'll do fine, John Martin. I can see you championing a cause, not with fire and brimstone, but with a firm sincerity, like Gregory Peck in *To Kill a Mockingbird*." She looked at him hopefully, but recognition didn't spark in his eyes. "No? Well, put it on your catch-up list of the classics. It was a good movie."

"Okay."

"Actually..." she began, then stopped.

"What?"

She was into it now. "I, ah, just thought I should mention that I'm off to Toronto myself next week to give a status report on my first four months at the club. Plus, I have to come up with a game plan for the next few months. Unless I meet my quota for new members, I'm out on the street."

"That seems cutthroat, considering how hard you've been working."

"Numbers are what count, though. And if I don't live up to Supreme's expectations of me—and my own promises to them—then I don't deserve the job. It's as simple as that."

"It sounds as if you're tougher on yourself than anyone."

"That's how I stay one step ahead of the game," she told him with a resolute set to her lovely face that caused his pulse to quicken.

"When are you going?" he had to ask.

"Thursday or Friday."

"I'm driving down Thursday myself."

"Oh..."

"As a matter of fact, I just got my license. Henry gave me lessons, although I've driven tractors before. And buggies, of course. Locally."

"Expressway traffic *is* different."

"I'm looking forward to the challenge." He looked away, then back at her. "Maybe you'd be safer in my car than on the same road...."

She sputtered, stalling. "That's a tough choice."

"Want to gamble? It might be an experience you'd never forget."

She should think about it, talk herself out of it. But she was going to accept, and he knew it. His face split into a crooked half grin, and she felt as if a steamroller were heading through her stomach. Her opposition was crushed into minute particles, and she smiled back, the radiance of smile meeting smile a powerful force.

As Karin drove away, her spirits were buoyant and her skin was tingling as if he had kissed her again. But he hadn't even touched her.

CHAPTER SIX

"WATCH OUT!"

As if plucked out of danger by an unseen hand, the Honda Civic veered left between two other cars, the space barely large enough to accommodate it. The vehicle skidded to a halt inches from the red brake lights of the car ahead, having narrowly missed the fender to its right. All the other vehicles on the highway were slowing and squeezing together as the construction signs directed.

Slowly Karin exhaled. She tried to gaze nonchalantly at the tall silhouettes of the airport hotels on the outskirts of Metropolitan Toronto.

"I didn't expect that!" John said cheerily.

"No, I guess not."

"One minute we were sailing merrily along, then the next, everything came to a standstill."

"Wait until you get downtown. You'll have to drive even more aggressively to survive."

"No problem."

Karin glanced over at him. "That's what worries me," she mumbled, then added more clearly, "Anyway, I'd forgotten what it's like to get the ol' adrenaline pumping—things are certainly a lot calmer in Kitchener traffic." The cars started moving at a steady but slow pace, and Karin tried to relax. A short time later, she directed him onto the expressway that led to the core of the city.

"Gotcha!" Without signaling, he pulled into the right-hand lane, oblivious to the indignant gesture of the driver whose car he'd just cut off.

"How long did you say you had your license?" Karin murmured, wondering whether fate—in the unwitting hands of John Martin—was going to make her stay on earth short-lived or not.

"Oh, about a month. I've improved a lot since I got my own car, beat-up as it is. Henry's van is a bit harder to handle."

"I can imagine."

Once they were off the highway and driving through the busy city streets, he continued to dart fearlessly around moving objects; he also demonstrated a knack for avoiding parked cars at the last minute and racing through amber lights.

Since neither had had a day off in a long time, they had decided to travel to Toronto a day earlier than their respective meetings. With her Supreme Fitness connection, Karin was able to get them each a corporate rate at the posh Harbour Castle hotel, overlooking Lake Ontario. When she'd warned John about the high yet discounted cost of his room, he hadn't seemed concerned. He considered the jaunt into Toronto not only a business trip, but a holiday of sorts, and he didn't mind dipping into his savings.

At two o'clock they pulled up under the concrete portico that fronted the hotel. A young valet, wearing immaculate gloves and a long-tailed black jacket, helped her out of the car. A quick exchange of keys, and the luggage was unloaded by another smiling penguinlike official, then the first valet drove the car off to the parking area. John watched it disappear down a ramp, suspicion written all over his handsome face.

"You'll learn whom you can and can't trust," Karin said, smiling. "He's one of the good guys. Come on."

"If you say so...." he murmured without conviction. "I can manage those," he said to the bellboy who was loading their two suitcases onto a trolley.

"It's no problem, sir." The youth gently tugged John's worn suitcase away from him.

"I'm no invalid," John retorted with forced politeness, yanking the bag out of the other man's hand and reaching for the second suitcase before it, too, became involved in the battle of wills. His car was one thing, but he would not trust his personal belongings to a complete stranger. "After you," he said to Karin, giving her a wary half smile.

Dazed, she ran up the stairs to the hotel, then marched through the revolving doors that led into the lobby. John followed directly behind her, the corner of one of the suitcases jamming into Karin's leg as they both crammed into the same opening. She tumbled out and he barely had time to exit as the doors continued to revolve.

"Those doors aren't very practical, are they?" he said, looking back with chagrin.

Karin just shook her head and laughed, which felt amazingly therapeutic. Her nerves were stretched taut, not only from the hair-raising car ride, but also from the unsettling effect John Martin had on her. Incongruously, she found him easy to be with, yet at the same time he put all her senses into high gear and left her mind reeling from the unexpected.

"This trip is *not* going to be dull," she said, but he was looking around in wonder and had not heard her.

"What a place!" he marveled, gazing up at the giant sparkling chandeliers and shiny marble posts, then down at the plush carpet and polished hardwood floors.

As they lined up at the registration desk, Karin could not help but compare his ingenuous expression and bright eyes with the blank faces of many of the other travelers for whom hotel life seemed as familiar as going shopping. She, too, had stayed in a lot of hotels, although not many had been as luxurious as this one, but this afternoon, by sharing her companion's enthusiasm, she felt a renewed excitement.

After checking in, they agreed to meet in half an hour in the lobby. Karin wanted to pick up some boxes that she'd stored at her former house—none of her ex-roommates would be home, but she still had a key—and John had gladly volunteered to assist her. Neither was due for business meetings until the morning.

Alone in her room, Karin slowly unpacked. Her mood became strangely mellow, reflective, enhanced by the pastel tones of the room's wallpaper and fabric—a blend of soft peaches, mint greens and butter yellows. Finally distanced from John, she realized that already she had let her guard slip around him. His high spirits about the trip had had a contagious effect on her, which was fine, as long as she remembered to keep their outing on a strictly friendly footing, or more realistically, to control the sexual currents between them. If she hadn't believed that was possible, she wouldn't have agreed to accompany him to Toronto.

Distractedly she wandered over to the window to gaze out at the view. Sunlight shimmered off the dark blue waters of the lake and glinted off the tankers that crawled through the harbor. The stretch of diamond-tipped water was soothing, making her able to see beyond the industrial smokestacks, high-rise condominiums and expressway traffic along the shoreline. Across the bay rose the green horizon-like strip that was Centre Island, the largest and most commercialized of the three islands that were accessible to the city proper by ferryboats and smaller craft.

A flash of a summer picnic she'd shared with Eric on the island zigzagged through her mind, to be quickly erased as she turned from the window.

She decided to wear jeans and a black sweater, because the boxes she needed to pick up would be dusty, and she would have to crawl around in the basement to dig them out. Grabbing her taupe leather jacket, she went to meet John, curious as to how he was faring in the strange new environment.

As planned, he was waiting for her in the lobby. He smiled amiably and followed her out. She stepped through the revolving doors and turned to find John right behind her again.

"Lesson number one," she said, trying not to laugh. "I don't object to sharing, but single occupancy is usually the norm here. For safety reasons."

They both fell out, Karin's purse almost making a second trip.

"Point well-taken," he said, grinning. "Where to next?"

"We have to retrieve your car. Where's the stub they gave you?"

He looked worried. "Up in my room, I think. I'll be right back."

She turned to the valet. "We'll just be a moment. Everything's under control," she added, watching John let another man enter the revolving opening before he stepped into the next available space himself.

A short while later, with Karin navigating, John was driving along Queen Street East in the Beaches area of the city.

As if she were visiting an old friend she hadn't seen in a long time, Karin pointed out favorite spots among the many cafés and boutiques that lined the street: Lick's, renowned for its burgers, cones and long lineups on a summer's night; the wide greenery of Kew Gardens, with its lighted baseball diamond; the popular Balmy pub; the old Fox Cinema, which aroused an instant craving in Karin for its addictive buttered popcorn....

"But where're the beaches?" John asked, puzzled.

"The lake is at the end of those streets to the right, but the water's polluted. Swimming's not advisable. Unless you're crazy or you happen to fall in while sailing or windsurfing. I used to like jogging on the boardwalk that runs along the lake, but dodging pets and cyclists was always a challenge. Oh—turn here," she suddenly directed. As John swiftly obeyed, the car bumped over streetcar rails and a pothole. "Yikes!"

"No problem," he said wryly.

They were driving up a winding, steep road, overlooked by a variety of weathered and renovated houses. Dwarfing many of the homes were tall budding maples, willows and poplars, as well as mature evergreens.

"Everything seems so closed in," John commented, glancing at the lack of space between homes and the tight row of parked cars that narrowed the road.

Karin nodded. "You get used to it, believe it or not. A friend of mine, Carol, used to say that close-knit urban living takes us all back to feelings of security in the womb. Who knows? Hang a right there at the next stop sign, then a left at the first street and keep going a ways," she instructed, wisely giving him more warning of his upcoming moves this time.

"You enjoyed living in such a big city?" John asked after the car had rounded the corners.

"I was comfortable here. I liked the variety of people and places, and Toronto is a very cosmopolitan, safe and clean city. I may decide to return here someday."

"It amazes me that you can be so casual about pulling up roots, leaving friends, familiar territory. The one move I made in my life was very difficult. Do you get more accustomed to it the more you move around?"

Karin was going to be flippant about her answer, but the earnestness in his voice stopped her. "No, each time is just as tough," she admitted quietly. "The secret is not to let yourself get too attached to anything or anyone."

"But how can you control that? Already I can feel myself growing fond of the boys at Greenbank, even though I know I'll have to leave them at some point."

"Pull up there," Karin quickly bid. "Don't worry if you're blocking the driveway. We won't be long."

He followed her instructions, turned off the ignition and looked over at her, waiting for her answer.

"The choice is yours," Karin said slowly. "Farewells are a necessary part of life, so you can either keep your distance at the early stages of making acquaintances or resign yourself to more pain down the road if you *don't* keep your distance. Either way has its drawbacks, but the latter is the hardest, so I just remind myself of that every time I find myself getting too...close."

He studied her for a long moment, and they both knew the conversation had become intensely personal.

"I'll try to remember that," he said with a false brightness, gazing out the window.

The confines of the car became suddenly claustrophobic, and Karin bolted out of her side.

But the claustrophobic feeling didn't leave her. Not when they were carrying box after box of clothes and miscellaneous articles out to the car, John repeatedly wondering whether she collected rocks, judging by the weight of some of the cartons. Not later when they were walking along the boardwalk, lazily eating ice-cream cones and watching waves curl over the sandy shore. Especially not when they were back in the car, returning to the hotel, caught up in their own thoughts.

For Karin had discovered that she had no hope of losing the stifling feeling as long as she was with John Martin. Period. Even when they were outdoors, distracted by strangers and new sights, his sheer presence was a strong overwhelming force. And she'd discovered something else. She actually *liked* the warm, breathless claustrophobic feeling he created in her. She couldn't stop herself from enjoying her time with him. *Enjoy* was too mild a word, though, for the shimmering glow she felt inside.

When they returned to the hotel, John hesitantly suggested they have dinner at the revolving restaurant atop the needle-shaped CN Tower, one of the city's outstanding landmarks, he'd learned from brochures in the hotel lobby. Karin thought quickly. Too romantic? But the place was big, popular. Better than somewhere more intimate. Too expensive? Both of them were in the mood for splurging on this trip. Fact: the view would be worth seeing on a night that promised to be clear....

Which it was. Karin hadn't been able to refuse his invitation, after all. As anticipated, the city and harbor lights were a breathtaking tapestry, a multitude of golden pinnacles on soft black velvet. Karin kept imagining that life was giving her a taste of heaven. Across from her sat a man who seemed perfect in his dark-eyed, strongly masculine beauty, yet human in the way his crookedly knotted tie refused to lie flat, or the sleeves of the worn black lapelless jacket he'd long outgrown kept rising up to reveal at least six inches of white shirt cuff. Unconsciously she memorized every detail of his appearance, particularly the charmingly incongruous blend of old and new that characterized him.

John was clearly awed to be sitting atop the tallest freestanding structure in the world. He absentmindedly ate the stuffed chicken breast on his plate—one of the least expensive entrées on the menu—as he gazed out at the panoramic cityscape and star-sprinkled sky. His face grew softly reflective.

"Lost in space?" Karin asked, forcing herself to eat and not to stare so hard at him.

He gave a small, self-conscious laugh. "No, I was just wondering what Menno Simons would have said if he could have known what future generations would be seeing in their lifetimes."

"Menno Simons?" Karin asked, jarred away from thinking solely of John Martin. The name was vaguely familiar.

"The Mennonites were named after him—he was Dutch, one of the leaders in what was originally called the Anabaptist movement, centuries ago."

"Oh, yes," Karin said, remembering some of the facts she'd learned about the Mennonites since moving to the area. It wasn't surprising that they still opposed violence. The treatment of the Anabaptists by the state-run church had been horrible—public drownings, beheadings, burnings at the stake. All because the Anabaptists did not believe in automatic infancy baptism.

"But what about you? What are your ties to the past?" John suddenly asked, changing the subject, just as he'd done at the Greenbank dinner when the conversation had touched upon his heritage. But this time *he* had brought up the discussion of the Mennonites. Regardless, he no longer seemed entirely comfortable with it.

"Oh, way back there's some Scottish blood, but my relatives have become so North Americanized that I don't feel any great affinity with it." She hesitated, then spoke self-consciously. "Sometimes I kind of missed that, as if I grew up in a vacuum. I remember going through one stage in grade school, when I loved reading about the feudal wars. I imagined brave lords and beautiful ladies, gallant battles, the whole bit, and I pretended that the Sherwoods were right in there, fighting and loving. But I soon grew out of such silly romantic notions."

"I don't think they're silly," he said, the warm lights in his eyes reaching out to her. He liked the fact that she'd shared something private, however small, with him. She didn't do it very often. He wanted to give her something in return.

"You know," he began slowly, "I could never really appreciate the historical aspects of my Mennonite heritage in the same way that my father, grandfather and others did. I was curious about the past, even respected it, but it was all just words, another history lesson that I was supposed to absorb. I felt no... empathy for the hardships my ancestors endured. It was all so removed from my safe little world. I always felt guilty about my detachment. I thought it was just another sign of how different I was inside from the rest of them."

"And now?" Karin asked.

Her question caught him off guard. Setting his silverware upon his empty plate, he leaned back in his chair, focusing for several seconds on the slowly changing view out the window as the restaurant revolved. "A few weeks ago, I remembered something I'd heard as a boy. Apparently my great-great-plus-grandfather actually *walked* the five hundred miles from Pennsylvania, so strong was his desire to settle in Waterloo County. He only had twenty-five cents in his pocket when he arrived. That finally hit home with me."

"How so?"

"I think I'm beginning to understand what it means to strive for something you believe in, something as essential as the air you breathe... whether that's a dream of a life without persecution, some good land to call your own or the freedom to..." He stopped, embarrassed at the sudden outpouring of emotion in his voice, at the way his hand had risen to emphasize his point, hanging in midair, then dropping slowly.

"The freedom to be a daredevil on the highway or dine in the sky," Karin supplied quickly, easing the discomfort of the moment, showing him she understood what he meant.

A faint smile hovered at the corners of his mouth. "Something like that. Mainly the freedom to be yourself, whatever that crazy mix of components turns out to be. But I still can't accept the fact that the Old Order Mennonites cling to the trappings of the past so much, closing their minds to the wealth of experience around them."

"Maybe they feel they've already weeded out the undesirable parts of life and are content with what's left," Karin answered, thinking how she treasured the pride and dignity she'd finally recovered after Eric's betrayal, and how she would never again trade them for the false happiness he'd offered.

"But that's where I'm still different from what my family expects of me," he said fiercely. "I intend to do all I can *not* to sell myself short like that, not to settle for less than the best that life can give."

The force of his unleashed determination was like a physical blow. Simultaneously, Karin felt a stab of fear at

his refusal to compromise and admiration for his undaunted idealism. And something else was bothering her.

"I realize why you chose to move on, but nothing can
change the fact that you grew up surrounded by a large
family and community. Don't you miss all that...
sometimes?" she asked, her eyes pleading for the truth
from him.

"I have many good memories to sustain me through
those...times. That is enough."

"Have you visited your family?"

"No."

"But why? It's been weeks. Surely—"

"My brief chat at the market was awkward enough. I
can't go to the farm yet."

"'Can't' or won't?"

For the first time his eyes flashed angrily at her. "Both."

"But what about for their sakes?" Karin's voice had
risen in a matching anger that surprised her. Maybe she was
just reacting to his obstinacy. Or maybe a part of her sym-
pathized with those faceless strangers who had to accept
that someone they loved had abandoned them.

"They have each other," he said with a note of finality.

But she could not resist adding, "Maybe the boys at
Greenbank have taken the place of your family. What
about when you have to leave them and start all over?"

"What are you saying, Karin?"

She wasn't sure. She could see that he was heading to
where she was by relying on himself and himself alone.
Would he discover, as she had, that it could be an empty
place? Would he learn that the days could feel safe and
comforting but the nights could turn so...hostile?

"I suppose I'm warning you that it's not going to be
easy...being completely on your own," she said at last.

"I've already realized that. But that doesn't change anything."

"So you don't think you'll ever remarry someday, when you've found your niche in the world?" she heard herself ask. She hated when others pressured her about marriage, but something had prompted her to speak. She did not examine why she needed to hear John's feelings on the subject.

He didn't appear to be offended by her directness. Instead, his face took on a look of utter seriousness. "No, I honestly don't think I'll ever marry again. I've already lost one wife to death, and I feel as if I was married to the Mennonite ways, as well, and now I'm divorced from them. I took vows when I was baptized, vows that I've since broken, and inside I've paid dearly for that. I'm afraid of taking more vows, changing, then breaking those vows again. I couldn't live with myself if I repeated that same mistake."

A deep sadness, tinged with acceptance, filled his eyes, and Karin knew anything she could say would be inadequate, so she said nothing....

Moments later, their plates were cleared away by the cheerfully industrious waiter. As they sipped their coffees, they tried to direct their attention to the amiability around them, but they felt vastly removed from it. Karin knew that she did not want the pleasant evening to end on a sour note. When they left the restaurant a few minutes later, she announced her solution.

"We're going dancing," she said firmly, taking John's hand, unprepared for the warm aftershocks of the contact.

"Dancing?" he sputtered. "But I've never—"

"Exactly. You say you want to experience life's riches. Well, here's your chance." She released his hand and pointed to a bright ad for Sparkles, the nightclub that was one floor below them.

His protest was suddenly transformed into a dazzling smile. "You're right." This time *he* took *her* by the hand and led the way to the stairs with renewed enthusiasm.

When they arrived at the nightclub, John stared dubiously at the flashing strobe lights, clouds of smoke and sea of faces that beckoned to them from the other side of the entrance.

"Come on," Karin said with a smile, her body already starting to sway to the thundering beat that was assaulting them.

As they checked their coats, John's eyes were drawn to the way her golden hair flowed down her back and her finely knit rose-colored dress caressed her contours, narrowing to a tiny waist that both his hands could surely encircle, then falling to just above her knee. He didn't know a lot about fashion, but he sensed that the simple lines and flattering shade of her outfit bespoke a natural good taste.

Suddenly he wondered how she saw *him*, whether she was secretly aghast at the clothes he'd pieced together: the new shirt that he'd hurriedly bought on sale, a size too large; the jacket that his mother had carefully mended and remended, which would have to do until he had time to shop for a new one; the tie that he'd spent a frustrating hour trying to knot as Henry had instructed him; the well-worn black pants that at least fit him better than his jacket.

Karin turned around and he looked away, guilty for staring at her so blatantly, conscious of his own haphazard appearance and wishing it was otherwise. These were new feelings for someone who had always been taught that wanting to enhance one's appearance was a mark of vanity.

"Ready?" Karin asked, curious about what was causing his distressed look.

"Lead the way," he said, but it was he who took her by the elbow and propelled her into the flashing red lights of the room, as if he were a charging bull determined to meet his target.

They sat at a table in the far corner, left vacant no doubt because of its distance from the powerful speakers whose music infiltrated every inch of the club at varying decibel levels. The majority of the clientele was squeezed together at a stand-up bar near the small dance floor.

Their drinks were delivered by a long-legged waitress in a short leather skirt, and they sat sipping them without attempting to talk above the music. Because their table was on a platform, they had an unobstructed view of the dancing area. Idly Karin watched the bodies swaying, swiveling and shuffling in an assortment of dance styles as mixed as the partners on the floor. She was reminded of the high-voltage group energy she'd felt so often during an aerobics routine set to music, but there was a more elemental beauty in the rhythm and freedom of these dancers as they responded to the insistent beat.

She glanced over at John, who was sitting stiffly on the edge of his chair, his expression bewildered. His feet were still, whereas hers were tapping with a will of their own. One song merged into the next barely perceptibly, and Karin jumped up.

"Come on," she urged, reaching for John's hand, marveling once more at its roughened warmth.

"I don't think—"

"Don't think—just move!"

A few gentle nudges later, as they made their way past chairs, tables and onlookers, they were standing amid a mass of undulating bodies. Miraculously a few square feet of space cleared for them.

John's only previous dancing experience was a few steps he'd learned while square dancing in a vast barn that allowed ten times the elbowroom of this place. Karin was moving her hips and arms in a seductive way he couldn't possibly emulate, so he stole a glance at some of the men around him and started bobbing, stepping and kicking in what he prayed was a similar fashion.

His heart sank when he dared to look back at Karin. She was trying desperately *not* to laugh, but her eyes were suspiciously watery.

"I'm sorry," she sputtered, leaning toward him, thinking she had never seen such a handsome creature, half chicken, half robot, flapping his wings. "You're doing fine."

He stopped dead in his tracks, not believing her for a moment. "That's it. Let's get out of here."

Her hand lightly touched his arm. "Not yet. Don't copy everyone else. Just listen to the music and do whatever you *feel* like doing. Try it—for me."

Her cornflower-blue eyes were fun loving, inviting, irresistible, and he conceded. His limbs slackened and he tried to concentrate on the pounding beat of the song—it was hard not to hear every inflection, and he wondered if his eardrums would ever be the same. When he started to move again, it was with tentative but controlled steps. He wasn't even aware that his arms and neck had picked up the same rhythm, so deeply was he focusing on his feet.

The tempo of the music increased, and he moved faster. He started to recognize the chorus, and his body remembered what it should do for those bars. Once he even tried a double-step that seemed to fit with the music. But he had to be careful, because he'd already bumped the guy next to him, who'd thrown him an unfriendly look. Out of the corner of his eye, he saw someone else snapping his fingers, so he tried that, too. He found it helped him keep the beat, and his legs seemed to follow more smoothly. He didn't feel as disjointed as he had when he'd first started dancing.

Just when he was relatively comfortable with the changing patterns of this particular song, it merged into a slower-paced one, but his body adjusted easily. He felt very pleased with himself when he finally met Karin's gaze again.

As much as she hadn't wanted to make him even more self-conscious, Karin had been unable not to stare at her partner. Her amusement had soon turned to fascination, though, as she saw how quickly and determinedly he taught himself to fast dance. His steps were rudimentary, lacking the finesse achieved by practice, but he possessed a natural agility. His rangy, well-muscled body was even more gorgeous in controlled motion than at rest. She couldn't tear her eyes away. Her own movements spontaneously synchronized with his.

The next song was a slow one. As the other couples slipped into each other's arms, John hesitated, then moved over to close the short distance between him and Karin. They eased into the traditional dancing pose as if they'd done so a thousand times.

But as Karin felt his sinewy body pressed against hers, one of his hands encircling her waist, the other entwined loosely with her fingers, she experienced a delicious sense of wonder. She was acutely aware of the way her own hand brushed the thick, slightly damp hair at his nape and of his breath fanning her cheek like the first warm breeze of spring.

John's body stilled, then slowly his feet started moving, and hers followed. The dance floor grew more crowded, limiting their shuffling space to a small circle that required little maneuvering skill, which was just as well. Karin simply abandoned herself to the cozy sensuality engulfing her.

Luckily his feet were grounded, because John felt as if he were being swept away to another world—a world where flowery scents, silken hair and feather-soft skin abounded. It was a world in which he could easily become lost, a timeless world inhabited exclusively by him and the woman he held in his arms.

Abruptly the song ended, and harsher sounds once more reverberated around him. John was dimly aware that other couples were breaking apart. Had only a few minutes passed? It had seemed like a breath of eternity. Long enough to create a sweetly intoxicating haze in his head and a fierce fire in his loins.

In jarring sequence Karin felt the bold imprint of John's maleness and a warmly churning response in herself, then the music changed to a discordant tempo, and he was drawing away from her. They were pushed to the side of the dance space. Her startled eyes met his before the knowledge of mutual yearning could be wiped away. Heat radiated through her with lightning speed.

Her heart pounding, blood humming through her limbs, Karin turned and walked back to their table, knowing she could no longer sit there casually with him. She retrieved her handbag, then proceeded to the coat check, aware of John a few steps behind her. While they were waiting for the elevator, neither looked at the other.

"Thank you for dragging...taking me there," he said, feigning lightness. "I enjoyed the dancing, after all."

Karin stared at the descending illuminated numbers above the elevator. "You were great. A fast learner."

He glanced around to check whether they were alone. They were. "Listen, Karin, I'm sorry. I didn't mean to start anything so very—"

"It's okay," she said, briefly meeting his eyes.

He wanted to touch her, to smooth away the creases between her brows, but his arms hung like lead weights by his sides.

She wanted him to touch her, such a crazy, absurd feeling, considering what her better judgment told her....

"Karin, you don't have to fight this...this thing between us on your own. I want you to know that I'm doing my damnedest to fight it, too."

He was saying what she wanted to hear, wasn't he? That he shared her qualms about risking involvement...so why didn't she feel reassured? Why did she still feel as if she were deep in the heart of a problem with a capital *P*?

Not until she was lying alone in her bed, after a short, strained drive back to the hotel, did she let herself think about the reasons she felt so battered inside. She'd only begun to fathom what her willpower was up against—raw, multilayered needs with unexpected cracks in the barriers surrounding them.

JOHN DID NOT GO to his room immediately after he left Karin. He needed to walk—where, he didn't know. Just away. Somewhere with no associations to her.

Many blocks later, he passed the largest church he'd ever seen, the sign calling it a cathedral. Magnificent spires soared into the blackness of the night. Giant floodlights cast a golden sheen on the pale brick, and he briefly wondered why the lights were on when it was clear no one was using the building at the moment.

He kept walking. He came to a park and sat on a bench. A streetcar rumbled along the tracks in front of him. Two old men who huddled together on a nearby bench stared at him dully. Traffic was light on the near-deserted street, a few yards away from the oasis of yellowed grass he'd chosen to stop at.

He sat there a long time and let the starkness of solitude wash over him. He closed his eyes, and unbidden came her image, the strength and softness of her face as real as if she were there in front of him. It was impossible to will her away. So he let himself think about her—precious details that he'd tucked away inside. Karin by the river, wearing earmuffs. Karin showing him that monstrous rocking chair. Karin enchanting him on the dance floor, making him oblivious to everything but the primeval forces between a man and a woman.

He faced himself and knew that he was changing and that it was time to listen to long-hushed voices inside himself. What had once seemed unthinkable to him outside marriage was now crashing beyond the realm of desire toward the realm of possibility... with a tormenting fury.

CHAPTER SEVEN

THE FOLLOWING EVENING, Karin sank chin-high into the bathwater, her hair safely tied up; steaming clouds of tropical heat surrounded her body. Such luxury.... For once she didn't care about energy conservation. Surely the cost of her indulgence was included in the high hotel charges.

Besides, after a long and trying day with the Supreme Fitness hierarchy, she needed to relax, rally her forces, plan her next course of action. But right now she was content to think of nothing but the warm languor enveloping her.

The phone suddenly shrilled at such a close range that she kicked a splattering of foamy bubbles onto the floor. She jolted up to a sitting position. At the second ring she just stared at the offending phone between the tub and toilet. So much for modern technology and the joys of conducting business anytime, anyplace, she thought. Surely Carol hadn't cooked up yet *another* marketing report that she wanted in a hurry....

She reached for a towel, wrapping it loosely around her as she sat on the edge of the tub. "Hello?" she said gruffly, only to meet silence. "Hello?" she repeated, exasperated.

"Karin?"

The deep resonance of his voice seemed to surround her with warm ripples, as the bathwater had done. "Oh, hi...John."

"I'm sorry—I didn't recognize your voice."

She cradled the receiver on her shoulder and watched her legs drip onto the bath mat. "The, ah, phone startled me. I was having a bath."

"Oh. Look, I'll call back."

"No, it's okay. I'm out now. How was your day?"

"Er, full. Quite full."

As ridiculous as the notion was, she kept feeling as if he could see her. She clutched at the slipping towel. "Was your meeting with the ministry officials successful? Did you win your battle with Gary Fries?"

"'Win' is not exactly the right word. He's letting Henry and I try more community work—"

"Great!"

"But he's still keeping a tight hold on the reins. He wants weekly reports from us, and he insists on personally approving every activity. The amount of red tape for the simplest change will be incredible."

"You don't have to tell me about red tape. I know all about it. At least you got what you wanted in a complicated way. I finally swallowed my pride and asked for some extra time to meet my quota, but it was a no-go."

"Why not?"

"Oh, I signed a little contract that they're going to make me stick to. My friend Carol admitted privately that the owners are still mad that they're paying me more than they intended. Anyway, it's all part of the game of business. So how did you find your way around?

"If I said easily, would you believe me?"

"No...."

"Let's just say I'm acquainted with a few corners of the city that I wouldn't be if I'd taken a taxi."

"You didn't walk everywhere!"

"That would have been simpler. No, I ventured onto the subway en route to my meeting."

The Toronto underground system was fairly uncomplicated, but it could be confusing to someone as out of touch as John. "I hope you didn't end up too far out of your way."

"Nowhere that paying closer attention to signs or asking a few questions like 'Where am I?' couldn't remedy. Instead, I chose to follow the masses. I was only half an hour late for my appointment."

Karin grimaced. "Did you find some time to look around afterward?"

"Gary suggested I stroll through the Eaton Centre. He thought I might be impressed by the architecture."

The Eaton Centre, in the downtown core, was a vast shopping complex that was a popular tourist area as well as a main draw for locals.

"And were you?"

"I was more amazed by the number of people there at five o'clock. Gary said something about rush hour, but I had no idea.... All I soon wanted was some fresh air and open fields."

"Well, you won't find either of those in the city."

"No, but I did discover the World's Biggest Bookstore. I couldn't believe the selection!"

"See, there are advantages to the big, bad city."

"Some...except that I bought several bags of books with my new handy piece of plastic. I may have second thoughts when I *really* have to pay."

"Welcome to the marvelous consumer world, John Martin!" She shifted, almost dropping the receiver in the tub before quickly retrieving it. "Whoops! I nearly gave the phone a bath, too."

He cleared his throat. "I'm sorry I kept you so long. You must be getting cold."

"I'm fine," she lied.

"Actually, I called to see whether you'd like to go out for dinner again. It seems silly that we each eat alone. Unless—"

"What time is it?"

"Seven."

"I've been invited to a party tonight—in honor of Carol's engagement."

"Oh, well. Another time...."

Karin had decided it wisest not to phone John herself, but she was glad that he'd taken the initiative. It didn't seem right that he spend his last night in the city alone. "Why don't you come along to the party?"

"No, I couldn't impose."

"You have to know Carol—she's a professional party giver. One never knows who'll show up. Some people can't turn away a stray cat or dog... well, she's like that with people."

"I don't know if I like the comparison, but I certainly felt like a stray today."

"Then you'll have to come. It'll be good for you."

"And you?"

His voice had lowered to a husky probing tone that caused crazy somersaults inside her stomach. "I'd like you to come, too." The answer spun out on the same wave of inner turbulence.

"What time?"

"Eight. In the lobby again."

"Eight then. Karin, is your hair up?"

"Yes...."

"Please keep it that way. For me."

The phone clicked and she was flooded with a host of other special things she would like to do for him. With him....

"ALL RIGHT, give me all the dirt," Carol said at the first opportunity she had alone with Karin. John appeared to be immersed in conversation with a friendly woman who was a Toronto social worker. "I can't believe you held out on me all day about him."

"We did have more official business to discuss," Karin said dryly, not mentioning that Carol had monopolized most of their private moments with details of the *extraordinary* new man in her own life. Carol always talked in superlatives, such as Ken was one of the most prominent criminal lawyers in Toronto; he was the most generous and considerate man she'd ever known, an outstanding squash player, and he was absolutely nuts about her....

After such a buildup, Karin had been disappointed when she'd been introduced to the short, self-effacing man who immediately put her in mind of a Dudley-Moore-like character. But all that mattered was that Carol, who towered over her fiancé, looked extremely radiant. Karin had never met anyone who could be so...resilient despite her two brief failed marriages.

"He's not what I would have expected for you," Carol murmured, not hiding her appraisal of Karin's date, who stood a few feet away. "But I can see what you like about him. Definitely sexy. On the shy side. Those are usually the ones who turn into wild beasts between the sheets. Am I right?"

Karin smiled at Carol's colorful frankness, too familiar to be offensive. "Is nothing sacred to you?"

"Come on, Karin, it gets tedious being respectable and businesslike all day long. We're not at the office or club anymore." She squeezed her friend's arm affectionately.

"Ah, it's good to see you again, Carol. And you look wonderful." She wore a loose-fitting, wide-shouldered black jump suit that minimized the fullness of her figure.

A turquoise sash brought out the striking blue in the large doelike eyes that dominated her face, framed dramatically by short-cropped ebony hair.

"Courtship always brings out the best in me," Carol admitted, waving fondly at Ken, who was giving instructions to the hired bartender in a corner of her posh Harbourfront condominium. "I haven't yet mastered the art of marriage, but I really think Ken's the one to help me do it."

Karin remembered hearing similar sentiments expressed with regard to the hockey player/habitual philanderer—she forgot his name—and husband number two, Robert, the brilliant entrepreneur who turned out to be desperately in debt and up on charges of fraud, involving Carol in bitter legal battles. But maybe Carol had at last found *the one*, however mismatched a couple the two appeared at first glance.

"Enough about me," Carol said impatiently. "Where did *you* meet such a fine specimen of manhood? Surely not at a singles' bar?"

Karin shook her head. "Somewhere less predatory," she answered evasively.

"Regardless, have you checked into John's background? I mean, who he's been with, that sort of thing? These days, one has to be cautious."

Karin choked on the drink she was sipping. "I'm sorry—it's just that no one could be...purer than John. He's a former Old Order Mennonite. I'm just helping him get acquainted with Toronto—we both happened to be coming down at the same time."

Carol's wide eyes rounded even more as she stared from Karin to John, a slow smile spreading across her burgundy-outlined lips. "And you're also educating him to life's forbidden pleasures. Interesting...."

Karin felt herself reddening. "We're just friends, really. Or that's all we *want* to be."

"Sure," said Carol disbelievingly, studying her friend's face. "I know where you're coming from, kiddo, but how could a guy who's just emerged from a world of bonnets and aprons not fall madly in love with a gorgeous, intelligent woman like you?"

Karin just rolled her eyes. "Carol, you're incorrigible. There *are* people around who aren't a slave to their emotions. They make choices. They prefer to stand on their own without... without molding themselves to someone else's life. Not that that can't work for some people, but—"

"'The lady doth protest too much, methinks,'" Carol said softly. "But just pretend I didn't say that."

"Why?"

"Because I'm trying to wean myself from my reliance on all outside sources, from tea leaves to Jane Fonda—my figure will never be like hers...."

"And what brought about this radical transformation?" Karin asked, relieved that the conversation had diverted, however briefly, from her disturbing relationship with John.

"I'm a walking contradiction to every theory I've ever believed in, and besides, every opinion has an opposing view. For example, Ken is a Leo, and we're not supposed to be compatible at all, which we're not in many ways, but I've decided I need that imperfect meshing. Life would be dull without the sparks, wouldn't it?"

"Maybe for you," Karin murmured, her attention caught by John, who was nodding with feigned interest at his companion and looking in her own direction expectantly.

Carol didn't miss the exchange. "You better rescue lover boy." She smiled. "It's been wonderful seeing you again, too, Karin. You're not mad at the world anymore, which is a good sign. And I love your hair up like that. Only you could get away with wearing such an understated outfit," she added warmly, referring to Karin's simple off-white dress and shiny black brooch.

"Thanks...I think." John was coming toward them, the tallest man in the room, with the most captivating eyes.

"One last word of advice, before I totally forget all the wisdom I gleaned from self-help books," Carol said, leaning toward Karin. "I read somewhere that men don't reach their 'bonding zone'—you know, commitment and all that—as quickly as women. So patience and timing are everything if you want a guy for keeps. It worked with Ken. Ta-ta. Catch you later, John."

"You couldn't resist, could you?" Karin threw after her, shaking her head as she watched her friend merge into the conversation of the next group with an amazing finesse.

"Well, did I pass scrutiny?" John asked amiably.

"She's not too subtle, is she?" Karin said, avoiding the question.

"No, but you can't help but like her. Do you know others here?" he asked, looking around at the eclectic mixture of guests.

"A few. That group over there, predominantly wearing white, are the superjocks from the club. Those teenagers—see the one with the Iroquois cut?—are probably friends of Carol's stepson, Tim, from her first marriage. Tim's the one by the window talking to the old guy with the baseball cap. Carol sort of adopted him one day. I gather he combs antique stores to help her furnish the farmhouse she just inherited. But I don't know anyone else...."

"That'll do," John said wryly, his eyes riveted on the long elegant line of her neck. "Why do I always feel as if I'm on a merry-go-round playing catch-up when I'm with you?"

"Because that's the kind of gal I am...." Karin suddenly felt as if he had indeed caught up to her and was spinning her around in giddy circles.

"Do you know how lovely you are with your hair up?" The words seemed to be pulled from him by an outside force. "Thank you," he added simply.

"I take requests from time to time," she returned. The flippancy died in her throat as her world stilled and she was drawn into the warm dark depths of his eyes. She felt herself flushing under his scrutiny and willed herself to look away, straight into another familiar pair of eyes, blue-gray ones that she remembered could swiftly change from lazy to seductive. They were neither right now. Just steellike, appraising.

"Someone else you know?" John murmured, slowly turning to see why her face had suddenly drained of color.

Karin didn't answer. She only looked as if an insect-infested jungle would be preferable to having to stay rooted to the spot as the man walked toward her, his gait self-assured.

"Karin...."

"Hello, Eric." His shaggy blond hair was sun-bleached and his skin browned, but he didn't look as if he were taking very good care of himself, Karin realized. His face was thinner, despite the tan, and his eyelids were heavy. He certainly seemed a far cry from the carefree individual she remembered.

"You never know whom you're going to run into at one of Carol's parties. I'm just back from...a rest in Martinique. I didn't know you were in town." His eyes searched hers, ignoring the presence of the man by her side.

"I'm only here for a meeting. We're leaving tomorrow. This is a friend of mine, John."

He nodded, but said nothing to her companion. "I need to talk to you, Karin. But not here."

"I can't," she said quickly, not sure whether he really was in rough shape, or whether his pleading voice and haggard manner were staged to elicit her sympathy. Eric was capable of that, she admitted with a pang.

"Please. Just for a few minutes...."

"There's no point, Eric." She turned away. He grabbed her arm, and she shrugged him off with less gentleness than had crept into her voice.

"Look, I told you I was sorry," he said impatiently. "I need you back. My life is falling apart. What more do you want me to say?"

He reached for her again, and she pushed him away with a violence that shocked her. "Don't touch me."

Eric smiled, the cajoling smile of a child who knew he'd done wrong but expected to be forgiven. "You know you don't mean that." The backs of his fingers lightly stroked her neck with a familiar practiced ease.

Karin's control snapped in a blaze of fury. She felt her arm rising, then John's arms were around her and she heard him say, "We were just on our way out of here." His voice had taken on an authoritative note, and she made no protest as he led her through the room, ignoring the stares of the other guests.

Eric watched them leave, a stony look on his face as he gulped his drink. No one noticed the slight sway to his walk as he approached the bar again.

THE COOL NIGHT AIR was like a balm to Karin's flushed skin. She was thankful that John respected her need for silence as they walked toward the visitor's parking lot.

Her anger dissipated somewhere between her flight from the party and her arrival inside John's car. She leaned back against the seat, closed her eyes and felt only a great weariness.

"What happened back there?" he finally asked, making no move to start the car.

"You saw what happened."

"I want you to explain it to me." He was staring straight ahead, his hands gripping the steering wheel.

"I want nothing more to do with him. Nothing."

"Why?"

"Because it's all over."

"So why are you so upset? Why did you let him get to you?"

"I don't know…. He caught me off guard. Please, can't we just drive back to the hotel? I want to be alone."

He looked out the window, then over at her, huddled against the door, her face forlorn. "Maybe you should go back and talk to him," he said quickly.

"Are you crazy?"

"You need to get it out of your system."

"Get what?"

"Anger, leftover love, hate, I don't know. I just know it's not good to store it all up inside."

She stared up at the checkerboard of light and darkness created by the windows of the towering building they'd just exited.

"Believe it or not, a big chunk of all those…feelings already came out tonight. I think I can deal with what's left."

"Even the love?"

A sea gull landed on a lamppost next to their car, and Karin's eyes were drawn to the bird—a common sight yet it looked unusually regal in its solitary pose on this particular late-April evening. "I think I learned something tonight," she began haltingly as the bird suddenly flew away. "People don't change. The way we see them does. I saw only what I wanted to see in Eric before."

"And tonight?"

"Tonight I saw a spoiled child with an ego the size of a mountain." Leaning her elbow on the armrest, she kneaded her tight temples with her fingers. "And I can't believe I was so...blind to it all before. I was so stupid!" Tears sprang to her eyes, and she turned away before he could see them. She never let herself cry, especially in front of others.

"Hey...." He reached over, and with a feather-light touch of a single finger on her cheek, he urged her to face him again. He wiped a stray tear away, then another. "It's okay. We all make mistakes. Don't be so hard on yourself."

It would be so easy to let him take care of her, hold her, make her forget.... But easy was not always better. She withdrew from his touch, swiftly wiping away her betraying tears. "I don't know what's the matter with me tonight. I don't usually fall apart."

She rolled down the window and drew deep breaths, as if the fresh air could make her feel like her old self again. In control. It began to work. "The only person who's probably secretly glad I made a scene is Carol," she quipped. "She loves drama at her parties. You'll be a knight in shining armor to her forever for whisking me away."

"I didn't want to have to bail you out of jail for a case of assault," he said, forcing a smile, wanting to relieve her tension.

"I was provoked."

He had to know more. Why, he wasn't sure. Only that he had to know everything. "How did he provoke you, Karin? What exactly did he do to you? Before. Not just tonight."

The tension was back. Around her. From her. Like a million tautly held wires. "Do you have to know every humiliation?" As she looked at him, her eyes were flashing with pride and indignation.

"I want to help."

"I don't need your or anyone's help," she said flatly. "Save your altruism for the poor lost souls at Greenbank."

She'd gone too far, but she didn't care. He revved the engine and the car shot forward, an instrument of the unleashed aggression in him. His face was rigid during the entire drive back to the hotel.

The glare from the bright chandeliers in the lobby hurt Karin's eyes. All she wanted was to escape to her room, and she eagerly stepped onto the elevator. When her floor came, she mumbled a clipped "Good night" and stepped forward. To her chagrin, John followed. She ignored him. At her room, she inserted her key and was prepared to close the door in his face if she had to. But before she could object, he took her firmly by the elbow and propelled her into the dimly lighted room, kicking the door shut.

"What on earth—"

"You may not be able to face . . . him." For some reason he couldn't say the name of the man he'd instantly disliked. "But if you can't face yourself and talk about what happened, then you're going to be stuck in emotional limbo."

"Thank you for the advice, but I know what's best for me. I don't need you as some kind of self-righteous, meddling—"

"You don't know what you need," he snapped.

"And you do?" He was giving her a strange frightening look that made her want to retract the words, but it was too late. Instinctively she stepped back.

They stared at each other, eyes bright, breathing irregular, as if they'd just undergone great physical exertion. The room seemed to ring with a white-hot silence.

Karin saw him move. He was reaching for her with an infinite slowness, or so it appeared to her senses, supersensitive to every nuance. Maybe she flinched when the expected touch arrived, his hand slipping to the back of her neck. Or maybe she let out a little cry. She couldn't be sure. Because she was already anticipating his next move, anticipating the warmth of his lips upon hers, her own lips slightly parted, quivering. She had been anticipating the kiss for a long, long time . . . since he'd last kissed her.

Warmth turned to a potent heat with the speed of fire on dry kindling. His mouth grew bolder, his tongue burning its way into her mouth, demanding a response, which she found herself giving with surprising abandon. His arms pressed her closer with a crushing strength, born of a hunger long denied.

It seemed like one long kiss, because there was no break, no unfrenzied interlude, but really his mouth came to hers again and again, dropping to her neck, then breathing an unhurried trail back. His hands kneaded her back, then his fingers ran restlessly up to her neck, through escaping strands of hair, mindless of the loosening pins until a critical one dropped to the floor, releasing a soft golden weight into his hands.

Karin felt as if tiny erotic fingers were traveling over her whole body, inside and out, maddeningly slow one minute, agonizingly fast the next. She wanted more, then less. Mostly, she just wanted....

John's restraint became like an entity in itself, yearning to be set free on wings, proud and strong and glorious. He was conscious of his body swollen with energy, taut with desire. Yet he was also aware that though Karin's mouth was yielding to his, it was only part of her complex whole. He needed to hear her voice, look into her eyes to understand where they were heading—a territory he sensed to be as vast and overwhelming as heaven and earth combined....

Reluctantly he drew back, his arms slipping to her waist for he could not release her completely, nor could he instantly still the fierce beating of his heart.

"Karin..." he whispered, and the simple utterance of her name became a question, asking what was happening between them, why it was happening, whether it should happen.

If she could look into his eyes forever, she would tell him to forget all questions, but even in her aroused state, she knew that was too simplistic. The outside world and their separate, chosen places in it exerted an even greater influence than the powerful chemistry between them.

She drew a deep breath. "We're not ready, John." And unspoken was the shared knowledge that perhaps they never would be. "You should leave. We both know that."

"In a minute," he said, pulling her to him, burying his face into the thick masses of her hair. He kissed her once more with a deep thirst, a lingering tenderness to carry with him into the long hours of the nights ahead.

At last he gently released her, his hands still resting lightly on her hips. "The past few minutes haven't exactly been conducive to talking, have they? Answering my question might have been easier to handle.''

"That's a tough choice," Karin said half jokingly, half seriously, her breathing shallow.

"Well?"

"Well, what?"

"Are you going to tell me what happened between you and...Eric?" There, he'd said the name. And he felt a surge of anger toward the man who'd managed to wound Karin so badly.

Karin twisted away from him and walked to the window, her arms around herself, as if she was cold. Thankfully, John stayed put. She needed thinking space between them. He was the most direct, persistent man she'd ever known, not to mention overwhelmingly sexy in an earthy, nonpretentious way. She didn't have the ammunition left to dodge him anymore.

Never had she felt so exposed, the rawness of her emotions seeming as evident as the clothing she wore. But she also knew that telling John about Eric could not make her feel any more exposed than she already did.

She searched for the words that would both satisfy him and keep her self-respect. Around her, she was vaguely aware that the complementing pastel-colored shades of the wallpaper, curtains, bedspread and pictures all blended together so perfectly. She wished her life could fit together as neatly and attempted to make it so.

"Eric and I were infatuated with each other for a time. It wore off—as simple as that.''

"Just like that?" John asked skeptically.

Karin turned to face him, schooling her expression to a neutral one. "He was unfaithful to me, which made his feelings ... or lack thereof ... clear to me, even though we weren't married. His actions also opened my eyes to what a fool I'd been. That's when my infatuation died. Instantly." She made herself smile, but her effort was a weak one. "That's it—there ain't no more. No deep dark secrets."

He studied her for long wordless moments. "Do you still believe that love and fidelity are a necessary team?"

Her smile vanished. "I never used the word 'love.'"

"I know." His eyes penetrated hers relentlessly.

"If love exists, then yes, fidelity and love must be one," she heard herself say. "But I've come to think that my version of love is rare, if it exists at all."

"And what is love to you?"

His voice was gentle, undemanding, but somehow it pulled the answer from her as if she were caught up in its spell. "Love is totally selfish and unselfish at the same time. But the two are mutually exclusive—that's the irony of it all. That's why it's impossible to achieve love—in its truest sense—and why I doubt those who think they have."

A bleakness, cold and stark, filled her eyes, and John felt the impact of it like a whiplash. He wanted to go to her, comfort her, fill the jagged edges of her strength with his own. But ultimately all he could offer her was more bleakness, and he cared too much for her to cause her more pain than she'd already known.

"I'm thinking that I'm making your life worse instead of better. And I don't want that," he said.

She expelled a deep breath and turned around. Staring out at the still, night-lit waters of the harbor, she told him, "I have a feeling that when I'm seventy or something, I'll look back on all this and realize you were good for me. Maybe I'll even regret that things hadn't turned out differently. It's not your fault, so don't worry about it."

She was silhouetted in the soft glow of the table lamp that had been on when they entered the room. Once again he stared at the line of her back, at the tall poise that was both delicate and strong. He felt a great wave of tenderness.

"Good night," he said quietly.

"Good night," she echoed.

He continued to stare at her, but his feet wouldn't move. "Karin, I—I just want to tell you..." He stopped.

"Yes?"

"Don't stop believing in love and fidelity. Maybe then you'll find them someday. With the right person. Or they'll find you."

She didn't reply and she heard the door close softly behind him.

She stood there a long time, unaware when the tears started rolling down her face or when they dried. She was grieving for what she would never know, because she could not prove to herself that she was strong enough to risk all for love. She could not trust another person that much. Worse, she was afraid to even try. Pain pierced through her, the pain of a sharp emptiness. She'd never felt such aloneness.

The knock on the door was so soft that at first she thought she'd imagined it. It came again. Louder. More insistent. She walked toward it.

Through the peephole she could see him, larger than life, distorted. But one thing was clear. There was nothing sheepish or apologetic in the way John Martin was leaning against the doorjamb. His stance was purposeful, intense, aggressive.

Slowly she opened the door. Their eyes fused. She felt as though a life force as dazzling as moonlight from a black sky was flowing between them. Neither could stop its passage, and then the force was upon her as his lips covered hers with an anguished need.

CHAPTER EIGHT

"I COULDN'T LEAVE YOU," John finally whispered, the kiss broken, their faces touching. "I stood outside your door for the longest time. All I could think of was how good you felt in my arms, the baffling rightness of it."

He didn't tell her how he had eventually walked away, tormented once more by ghostly voices. They'd whispered that what he'd been contemplating did not belong outside of marriage. But he'd realized that his need for Karin—as natural as sunlight and rain and the changing seasons—came from the very core of his self. Just as he'd faced himself in the park the night before, he'd faced himself in the long unfamiliar hallway of the hotel. His conscience had been at peace when he'd returned to her room.

His voice was filled with emotion as he finally uttered the words that had propelled him to knock on her door. "I want to give you myself, this night. Is that fair to you, Karin? Is that what you want, too?"

Suddenly Karin only knew what she did not want. She did not want to lose the warmth and strength of his arms again. She did not want to confront once more the black abyss he'd just rescued her from. His darkly pleading eyes promised a night to treasure, no matter what happened tomorrow, and at the moment she wanted to convince herself that that was enough for her.

And as he'd said, what felt so incredibly right had to *be* right, or at the very least, could be made right.

Drawing back, she took his hands in hers. "I'm glad you came back," she said softly, trembling.

His eyes flickered with relief. "You've been crying," he said, looking closely at her. "Ah...Karin, I don't ever want to hurt you."

"I won't let you." And she willed it to be true.

Suddenly the strange haunting magic was there between them again, as palatable yet elusive as morning mist, and Karin could not prevent its gentle fingers from reaching deep into her being, pulling her to him.

"I want to make love with you," he said clearly, urgently.

With. Not *to.* She liked that. Her eyes grew bluer than blue, brighter than bright, and the truth spilled from her before she could retract it. "I want that, too." His hand brushed her cheek, and she could feel his barely controlled tremor.

"I'll be sure you won't have a child," he said with the unflinching directness she'd come to admire in him.

"It's not the...right time for that," she returned, thankful that the rhythms of her body had always performed with such clocklike precision. But there was nothing regular in the way her heartbeat was starting to accelerate as she melted into the rich brown of his eyes.

Those eyes imprisoned hers until he lowered his head to kiss her again. It was a different kiss than the others, filled with a new wonder and a growing acceptance that tonight would be special. But the kiss was also more pain than pleasure, because it released a deep yearning in her. She was like a child that has never been held, her need for his touch so profound that the fulfillment stirred an even deeper ache of remembered emptiness.

Then he was cradling her close, and she was content just to nestle against him, her arms tucked around his low hips, her head turned so that she could hear the strong beat of his heart and could feel his warm breath upon her cheek. They stood that way a long time, like two models posing for a sculptor. But there was only the two of them, sharing the sheer joy that they were together, fighting the inevitability of it no longer.

At some indistinguishable point their gentle rocking motion turned to a slow erotic rotation of hip against hip, thigh against thigh, leg against leg. The hand that had been gently massaging Karin's back grew bolder, dropping lower, following the outer curve of her buttocks. Pressed more intimately to him, she was aware of his swiftly hardening maleness. Answering ripples—sweet and warm like melted honey—radiated through her. Her nipples were growing sensitive, straining through her clothing, seeking the play of flesh upon flesh. A small sound escaped her lips.

John's mouth found hers again, and he kissed her with a raw energy that seemed to pick her up and carry her far away—where, she didn't know, only that she was heading to a place that promised to answer the needs being slowly wrenched open inside her....

As if he knew the right moment had come, his hand found the zipper at the back of her dress, hesitated, then slid downward. Their bodies eased apart. Their eyes spoke a wordless sensuous language while John slipped the dress off Karin's shoulders and she stepped out of it. She immediately forgot about the soft pile lying beside her as she saw John catch his breath and smile in a precious crooked way she would always remember....

He could not tear his eyes away from her. Her sweetly rounded breasts peeked over the top of a delicate lacy fabric. She wore the wispiest underwear he'd ever seen and silk stockings that were but a transparent sheath enhancing her

long limbs. Slowly she removed the stockings. The sight
made his throat go dry.

He had never beheld such underthings. His wife had
worn sturdy cotton lingerie and colored opaque hose.
Warmth and practicality had been what mattered most. To
deliberately make the body look more attractive would have
been considered vain. Nevertheless his eyes feasted on the
result of such attention, discovering how alluring the female form could be with a touch of mystery, a brief covering of its charms.

"How I've wished to see you like this," he admitted for
the first time to her, and to himself. "You're so beautiful."

Without breaking eye contact with him, she smiled in a
way that made her even more beautiful, stepped backward
and sat on the bed, waiting for him to join her.

Her openness with physical matters was a quality he had
never encountered in a woman before, but he admired it,
responded to it. His intimacy with Emma had been limited, firstly by their mutual lack of experience and ingrained sense of propriety, then by her illness. But the more
he was with Karin, the more he was finding buried deep inside himself a desire to explore his primitive side, layer by
layer, to shed his inhibitions, one by one.

Yet, for all his inner brazenness, a trace of modesty remained as John undressed in front of her, but he did not
attempt to hide it. He advanced toward her, still wearing his
briefs. Something in her look told him she understood.

The bed coverings had already been pulled back, and he
briefly wondered whether the hotel staff performed such a
simple service for guests. He moved the sheets farther down
as he sat beside Karin. Needing desperately to touch her, his
arm crossed to the inside of her knee, the bare skin there
like cool satin.

Feeling as if he were being reborn, as if he were embarking on a sensuous journey for the first time, he murmured, "We have much to learn . . . together."

Together—both were teacher and pupil at the same time. Again, his simple choice of words pleased Karin, in a deeply intimate way. He was the most protective man she'd ever known, yet he respected her independence, too. And his combination of innocence and intensity was a powerful aphrodisiac to her. She loved to watch that intensity uncoiling. And she knew that she was the first woman to ever truly penetrate its secret depths. She hadn't forgotten that ultimately John would pursue his own goals—without her—and she respected his honesty in telling her so. But what she wanted to remember most was that tonight he would be hers and hers alone in a way that the egotistical Eric Lester had never been. Tonight she had decided to fill her heart with a woman's complete joy so that she would have something to cherish long after she had parted from him.

"Let's begin our lessons," she said huskily, trembling with anticipation. She felt as if she were hovering on an edge before the jump to exhilaration . . . or destruction. . . .

Before she could retreat, he was raining kisses on her face with puppy-dog fervor, her cue finally releasing his tenuous restraint. He kissed her lips, neck, cheeks in a wild random order. But she didn't care. Because she was kissing him back with equal craziness.

Then he was pushing her backward, and she was cushioned between the soft padded firmness of the mattress and the rough tickling hairiness of his chest. In one smooth motion, he lifted her fully onto the bed. Her heels dug into the sheets, pushing them away, easing herself toward the pillow, and then his body dropped alongside hers.

"You must tell me what you like, Karin," he said on a deeply expelled breath. His mouth planted itself just below her ear, nibbling the sensitive skin there, sending a shiver down her spine.

"I like that," she murmured, turning toward him and affectionately running her leg up the soft furlike texture of his. Her shift in position brought his hand just below one of her breasts. His fingers lingered there, gently kneading her rib cage, all the more tantalizing because she wanted him to touch her more intimately, and he seemed to be waiting. Finally, when she could hardly stand the delay any longer, his thumb lightly brushed her nipple through her near-transparent bra, and she let out a tiny sigh of pleasure.

"I like that, too," she whispered. "Very much," she added as his fingers grew more daring and cupped her entire breast, continuing to move ever so delicately, then more insistently as he slipped beneath the fabric. The front fastening released on its own with the pressure, and the material fell away.

He drew back to look at her naked breasts, and a soft smile broke across his face. "So perfect...." he said barely audibly.

"Kiss them, too," she invited, and his lips descended, needing no further prodding.

He tentatively tasted from one nipple to the other, then his tongue began to perform a sensual dance along the pale brown rim surrounding each nipple. Transfixed, Karin watched as his mouth dipped to her again and again, and she thought she would surely burst into flames from the smoldering fever inside her. Her fingers dug into John's scalp, weaving their way through the thickness of his hair. They dropped to his shoulders, journeyed along his arms and rested on his hips before turning toward the dark curling hair on his stomach and playing along the band of his briefs.

He seemed to stop breathing, then exhaled with a low whistling sound. On the last strand of breath, his mouth found hers, as if gasping for more air, her air, and he kissed her deeply, with infinite tenderness, more tenderness than she'd ever known.

"Hello again," she murmured, laughing softly.

"Why, hello," he answered, his eyes brilliant, heavily lidded.

And then their exploring hands, lips, limbs, communicated for them, finding the cool places, the hot ones, the little nooks of euphoria, the wide expanses of burning flesh.

A pair of hands eased away Karin's underthings. Another pair removed John's. She saw how beautifully formed he was in nakedness, how vulnerable yet powerful, his skin vibrant and silken smooth, taut with tension.

His hands lingered on the softness of her hips, suddenly uncertain. "It's okay," she whispered, guiding him to touch her in the most intimate place of all, a place that opened readily for him, warmly greeting his arrival. A multitude of pulses clamored in her throat and chest, where a flush of passion branded her like a sunburn.

She ached to touch him as he was touching her, but she hesitated, as he had done, even though she knew that they had long passed the point of no return. Maybe she moved or maybe he did, but with sudden artistry his warm hard flesh was gliding through her fingers. . . .

They embarked on yet another voyage of discovery with an unhurried pace they would not have known they were capable of moments ago. Time became a fragmented series of one sensation after another, sweetly interconnected—mouths drowning in salty depths, scents mingling with primitive delight, legs tangling and untangling, hands working ancient rituals....

Even when John eased himself on top of her and grew still, Karin's nerve endings continued to tingle with a life of their own. Supporting his weight, he gazed down at her, and she memorized every detail of his face: the stark angular lines, the perspiration-lined forehead, the jubilance of the boy, the seriousness of the man, the deep intensity of the man-boy.

Slowly he slipped inside her, burying his face in her neck. "I want to be lost in you, Karin. I need to be lost in you. I need..." And then he grew incoherent as his body molded itself to hers, finding a rhythm, alternating deep penetrating thrusts with shallow teasing ones.

Lost in a world of pleasure, Karin moved with him until she felt a spiral of excruciating heat start to pulse from within her very center. She opened her eyes in surprise, her body unconsciously stilling. John raised himself to look down at her, and she saw that his face was contorted with a barely controlled passion. His gaze locked with hers as he continued his gentle but relentless onslaught of her body. The elusive feeling returned to Karin with a dazzling, all-consuming force, shortening her breath, making her wonder how much more she could stand.

She arched her back as the explosion broke, and suddenly she was crying out a long, elated gasp of affirmation...and another, as she entered a shattering, star-bright universe of rapture.

Her cry was all John needed to hear. As he drove himself into the heart of her, his fingers digging into her shoulders convulsively, his flesh became hers, his soul hers. Rocking his head back, he called out his release and her name together, and in the mid of those glorious moments, he suddenly shuddered with a nameless fear....

DAWN BROKE SLOWLY, the darkness of the room gradually turning to the dull gray of a drizzling day. John dimly remembered that the lamp had still been on while he'd made love with Karin. She must have been up afterward to turn it off, while he'd been deep in sleep.

Karin appeared to be in that same state now, her breathing soft and regular, her long lashes resting on her lovely face as she curled into the shelter of his arms, her body aligned to his. Her hair spread into a golden veil over the bare slope of her shoulders, resting just above her breasts, and he marveled that skin could be so pearllike smooth, so quiltlike warm.

Bit by bit, details of the previous night came back to him, and he savored each memory with a kind of awe. He had not thought such a powerful mutual intimacy was possible. He had unleashed desires that he had only vaguely suspected existed within himself. He realized how much he had held back from Emma, sweet gentle Emma. But he had held nothing back from the bewitching woman now in his arms. He had given himself fully to her in every sense, and that fact terrified him.

As much as he loved being with Karin, he could not stop the feeling that he wanted himself—his whole self—back. He wasn't ready to lose his independence. Unfortunately nothing had altered that basic, monumental truth.

Karin stirred beneath him, but her eyes remained closed. Sometimes she seemed older than her years, and at others, younger. He saw the youth now, so undefended it ate away at his heart. He stroked her head, wondering what on earth he was to do.

Slowly she came fully awake. "Good morning," she finally murmured. She smiled and burrowed into the dark furriness of his chest.

"Good morning," he repeated, and knew he should try to tell her what he was feeling. He resisted the urge to fold his arms around her more tightly.

"Did you sleep well?"

"Very well...." And he could not hide the betraying strain in his voice. "Karin, as...pleasant as it is here, I—I have to leave soon. I didn't bring my toothbrush...or fresh clothes or..."

She tensed and he knew that she realized he wasn't talking about toothbrushes or clothes. He felt a wave of caring for her, even as he sensed her withdrawal from him. He kissed the top of her forehead, his lips lingering there. "Karin, last night was very, very special," he began haltingly, "but we're still two different people."

"And life goes on," she completed for him, rolling away and sitting on the edge of the bed. "Damn, it's nine o'clock. I'm supposed to be back at the club by noon."

He stared at the beautiful silhouette of her breasts in the morning light. "We'll make it home in time. I don't have any regrets about what happened," he was compelled to explain. "It's just that I can only give you so much and you deserve—"

"Don't spoil it, okay?" She turned to face him. Her eyes were cool blue chips, so different from the blazing brightness of hours ago, but her lips were still red-ripe and swollen from the fervor of their kisses. "Last night was...incredibly nice, and I don't want to have any regrets, either. We both knew what we were walking into, so there's no need for you to make any fancy speeches, okay?"

"Okay," he echoed, hating the inadequacy of it. He knew he'd hurt her, and that was the last thing he'd wanted to do. Unexpectedly, he was even hurting himself, but that was the price of honesty....

She stood and walked swiftly to the bathroom. Instead of following her with his eyes, as he wanted to do, he sat up and bent to retrieve his scattered clothing.

When he was ready to leave, he called to her through the closed door, but she did not emerge. He told her he'd meet her in an hour in the lobby, and she said that was fine. He shouted goodbye and she shouted it back. He asked her to come out, and she said it was better that she didn't. He waited. Finally he left, wishing their parting wasn't so impersonal, but believing that she was right. It *was* better this way, all things considered.

ON THE WAY HOME, Karin was barely conscious of John's erratic driving. They were both quiet, as if the events of the past two days had drained them of words, leaving them with raw mysterious emotions that needed to be slowly assimilated.

Not until they were out of the city, breezing along the rolling farmland that lined the highway, did Karin speak, but she was not ready to talk about their own relationship. "I called Joanna before checking out," she heard herself blurt out.

"Joanna?"

"Oh, one of my father's lady friends of long-standing. She's a well-known politician in Toronto. We met her years ago in the Caribbean."

"Are you friends with her?"

"I don't know her all that well—we just have my father in common."

"So, is that why you called, for news about him?"

"Not really—I just wanted to touch base while I was in town." Never in a million years would she tell him how low she had felt when he'd left her that morning. She'd needed to talk to someone, and Joanna's strong intelligent face had come to mind. Joanna had never married. She was as involved in her political career as her father was in music, which was probably why they had remained friends—and possibly lovers—all these years. She had an air of self-sufficiency that Karin admired, but she was a difficult woman to grow close to.

John glanced at the tense way Karin was holding herself. "You should have called your father directly," he ventured.

Karin glared at him. "Not on your life. *He's* long overdue."

"So what did Joanna have to say?"

Karin was intently playing with the nail on one of her fingers. "Oh, just that my father had been there...in Toronto, about a week ago to see her." She adjusted the vents on the dashboard until cool air rushed against her face. "He could have at least called me, if a visit was too inconvenient. He knows my new number. I just don't understand how he can be so...so selfish or single-minded...or forgetful or..." Rolling down the window a crack, she stared out blankly.

"Maybe he tried..."

"Don't make excuses for him—I've done that often enough," she retorted sharply. Turning, she saw the startled look in John's eyes. "I'm sorry. You didn't deserve that. I just can't believe he wouldn't *want* to see me, talk to me every once in a while. I don't expect him to be around all the time—I'm too used to running my own life. But it would be nice if he thought to say 'hello' or 'how are you?' occasionally...out of duty or guilt, for Pete's sake! Doesn't he have a conscience, at least?"

John was tempted to cajole her, to tell her of course her father cared about her despite his actions to the contrary, but he sensed she needed honesty; he would only irk her more if he offered her empty platitudes. "As hard as it seems to accept," he said gently, "you have to realize that people don't always meet our expectations, and they can't be changed, no matter how much we might wish it." Reaching over, he slipped his hand under her curtain of hair and lightly stroked the back of her neck.

Karin continued to gaze out the window as trees, farmhouses and cars passed in a meaningless blur. Unconsciously she leaned toward the soothing pressure of John's fingers, and her embittered face took on a softer cast. "Just before Mom and Satch split up," she began reflectively, "I sensed something was wrong because he'd been gone longer than usual on one of his trips and Mom had acted so polite—in a stony way—when he came back. One night he took me downstairs to his workbench, the messiest area in the house. He had so many unfinished projects down there—old TVs, broken toys of mine." She smiled at the memory. "One of the things he'd started to work on was a cardboard puppet box for me. It was late, but he told me he wanted us to finish it. It was in the shape of a castle, and he'd been going to build me separate rooms for it...but instead he just painted a lovely garden, open at the front, surrounded by the castle walls, trees, creeping vines and lots of flowers. He was quite a good artist when he put his mind to it...." Her voice wandered off, and she shook herself. "I don't know what made me think of that after all this time."

"Go on," John urged, his hand returning to the wheel to change lanes. "Did he finish it?"

"Oh, yes. And we took it outside, where I could have my first puppet show. I collected my puppets—a princess, a prince, a clown, the old king—and we set up the box in our backyard, by the porch light. I guess we played a long time, because the lights inside the house went out. I thought it strange that my mother didn't join us, like she used to when we sat out and made up stories about the stars. That night the sky seemed very dark, and I looked up for the moon. When I finally found it, it was only a pale sliver. I remember crying out, 'Look, Daddy,'—that's what I called him then—'the moon is broken tonight.' And he'd put his arms around me and made some funny noises, as if he was chuckling, then I felt wetness on my cheek, and I realized he was crying. He told me everything was going to be okay, when that was what I wanted to tell him. He put me to bed, and in the morning he was gone.''

She drew a deep breath before continuing. ''A week or so later, he and Mom had a talk with me, and I learned very quickly that even the things you never expect to change, do. More than you ever dreamed possible. Ever since, I've tried not to be taken by surprise again. I expect change. I expect people to move on, to forget. Now, I do it, too—it's part of life. It can all be very painless and natural. But every once in a while, I let him . . . and others—'' she instantly regretted adding that, but it was too late to take it back ''—do it to me again. When I thought I was immune. When I'm prepared for the worst. I guess we all have our moments of stupidity.''

Suddenly she felt silly, exposed, and she glanced nervously at John. All she could see was a tall stranger crammed into a tiny car, his eyes intent on the road, a deep crease between his brows. It was hard to believe he'd made love to her so exuberantly, so sensitively. A wave of fatigue overcame her and she turned away, rubbing her eyes.

''Are you okay?''

''I'm fine. Just a little tired, I guess.'' She just wanted to be home, alone, away from the vagaries of people, then she remembered she was due at the club.

"We didn't get much sleep last night," he murmured, facing her briefly, but she refused to look his way.

Without the pent-up longing that had brought them together, without the passion their mutual touching created, without the scents, sights and sounds of lovemaking, the words rang out hollowly in the confines of the car, Karin thought. Perhaps each of them was too preoccupied with the recurrence of their own private demons. Her night with John Martin—her last one, she decided with a pang, because she could not cope with the bittersweet aftermath— seemed as distant as the city they had left behind, as fleeting as a dream that can never be totally recaptured upon wakening.

She didn't reply to his comment about their lack of rest, and the words hung in the air, then evaporated. Neither spoke the rest of the journey. When they parted, Karin knew that the only certainty between them was uncertainty.

CHAPTER NINE

"NEVER MIND *WHO* TOLD ME it's been happening. I *know* it has and I want it stopped. Immediately." Karin was gripping the telephone receiver so tightly she was afraid it would crack. Her indignation had risen to a dangerous level, and she drew a deep breath in order to gain control of herself.

When she spoke again, her voice was calm, but firm, brooking no interruption. "I intend to post an announcement at your club for a month, stating that the rumors that Supreme Fitness will be closing are completely false. I will invite anyone who's interested to tour my facilities and compare my services and prices. Also, I have an interview with the life-style reporter for the *Kitchener-Waterloo Record*, in which I will set matters straight. If you don't cooperate, I will make things very difficult for you. Neither you nor the media will have heard the last of me."

Estelle Rogers, the manager of another downtown fitness club, made a few snide comments and ineffectual protests, which prompted Karin's own language to grow more colorful. But by the end of the call, Karin was confident that she would have her way with the announcements, thus squelching the damaging rumors at their source.

"I don't need this," she said into her empty office after she'd hung up. When she'd returned from her trip to Toronto, she'd been informed by Cindy that several members were concerned because they'd heard the distressing news about Supreme's imminent closing from friends who were members of or who had visited Body Beautiful. Naturally, the Supreme Fitness members were concerned about their investments should the Kitchener branch fold, as other clubs had done in the past.

When a local journalist had called Karin the next morning to confirm the rumors, she had practically exploded her denial, realizing how far the false stories had spread. And she'd soon discovered she wasn't just dealing with a few misinformed individuals. She'd followed up on several potential new members, only to learn they had joined Body Beautiful after being told point-blank by Estelle Rogers that Supreme was in financial ruin. Karin's fingers had been shaking with anger when she'd dialed the ruthless manager whose unscrupulous business dealings were well-known. Many of Karin's own club members had signed up after a year of dissatisfaction with Body Beautiful—they'd paid a premium for new equipment and classes that had been promised but had never come to be.

The timing on this mess couldn't be worse. Just when Karin was under pressure to increase membership substantially by her July deadline, she'd encountered a setback and had actually *lost* many she'd counted on.

A knock sounded and she stared blackly at her door, in no mood for further disturbances. Cindy poked her dark head around the corner uncertainly. "Is it safe here yet?"

"Barely."

"The telephone repairman is here. He said he'd never seen wires snap like that—they must have taken a lot of abuse."

Karin could not resist a half smile. Only Cindy could find some humor in the situation. "Okay, so I let her have it, but she deserved it."

"Did you have to tell her you didn't think it was a good idea that she do personal TV ads for Body Beautiful anymore, or ask her whether she was familiar with that wonderful new starvation diet?"

"You heard that?" Karin mumbled guiltily.

Cindy nodded. "You weren't exactly whispering."

"So what do you want, MacLeod?" she asked in her most authoritative voice, her eyes twinkling.

"These just came for you." Cindy held out a paper-wrapped bundle that unmistakably contained flowers.

"Oh, thanks...." Karin said nonchalantly, setting them beside her, then looking up at her assistant with a blank expression.

"Well, aren't you going to open them to find out who they're from? Or maybe you know that already?"

"Thanks, Cindy." Karin's voice held a sweet but dismissive note.

"Of course, it's none of my business...but you're cruel, you know that, boss?" Still grumbling, she closed the door behind her.

Karin stared at the package for several seconds, then slowly unwrapped it. A bunch of daffodils. In full bloom. The brightest yellow she'd ever seen. Just as slowly she opened the card and read the bold scrawl. "Thank you for bringing *Gemütlichkeit* back into my life." *Gemütlichkeit*. The spirit of the local Oktoberfest festivities. Good times. The joy of celebration and fellowship.

On the next line was simply his name. "John." That was all. Nothing as eloquent as the messages Eric used to send, but those words had turned out to be empty, meaningless. John had made her no promises he couldn't keep, and Karin wouldn't trade his honesty for the most romantic lies in the world.

She was grateful that Cindy hadn't stayed. Her assistant would have taken one look at the card and breezily interpreted the note in a typical fashion—something akin to "Thanks for the good time, kiddo. See you around." But Cindy didn't know John Martin. She hadn't met the profoundly idealistic man who had tortured himself about leaving the only life he'd ever known and was now determined not to let anyone stand in the way of his goals. Cindy couldn't fathom the rare genuine quality he possessed. He would always speak the truth, even if the sentiments were imperfect, falling short of expectations.

Nevertheless Karin felt gladness swell inside as she reread the brief uplifting message, accompanied by the cheerful flowers.

She found a tall glass and filled it with water from the adjoining washroom. She arranged the flowers loosely, then cleared a place for the container on one of her cabinets.

But every time later that day that her eyes strayed toward the daffodils, she was bothered. Their beauty was so short-lived. They only served to remind her of the transitory nature of her relationship with the man who had sent them. From the start she had known the terms between them, terms that were compatible with her own desire to keep an emotional distance from him so that their necessary parting would be easier. She was trying to make herself believe that she could handle the unknowns of the future. So why was acceptance of all that so difficult?

Finally she had to put the flowers out of sight, where she wouldn't be distracted by their springlike freshness. She wished that her mixed feelings for John Martin could be set aside so easily.

During the next few weeks, she kept herself so busy that she managed to think about him less and less. She threw herself into her membership drive, working thirteen- or fourteen-hour days, six days a week. By the time she arrived home at night, she only had the energy to fix herself a light dinner—generally one of those reheatable gourmet cuisines for the calorie-conscious.

After her meal she usually soaked in a hot bath, then propped herself up with pillows in her bed to read from one of the bestseller novels that always sat by her bedside. She was lulled to sleep within an hour. Rarely did she remember turning off the light, but every morning the alarm shattered the dark stillness of her room, signaling the start of another long vigorous day.

What kept her going was the fact that her increased efforts were slowly paying off. New members were steadily signing up. She'd decided to lead fewer aerobics classes, so that she would have more time for the marketing and administrative aspects of her job. She religiously followed up on every guest who visited the club, chatting with them about their fitness needs without pushing them to make an immediate decision to join. If a guest was undecided about whether she would indeed make maximum use of the club, Karin invited her back for repeated visits until she was convinced that attending the club could fit into her lifestyle.

Karin knew her promotional budget was wearing thin, so she made inquiries among her members until she found a woman who worked at a printing company and could get her a good discount on flyers. They were ready in time for Supreme to participate in a widespread direct-mail package, not only to Kitchener-Waterloo households, but to homes in the smaller neighboring cities and towns. Karin hoped to reach the growing numbers of individuals who commuted into her area and could visit the club before, during or after their workday.

Also part of her intense spring promotion were introductory letters to major corporations in the twin cities, offering group tours of her facilities and volume discounts to employees who signed up by a certain date. Sometimes she even generated interest in her club by making presentations at the companies themselves. Recently, a large shoe-manufacturing firm had agreed to bring in thirty new members.

Three and a half weeks after she'd received the daffodils, she was busy with the paperwork involved in her latest corporate acquisition, wishing she could see the faces of the Supreme Fitness owners when they received the applications. She was only a hundred names short of her quota with just over a month to go. *Let them chew on that,* she thought elatedly.

She'd told Cindy to hold all her calls until she'd finished filling out all the necessary forms, so when her assistant stepped into her office to inform her she had a call waiting, she looked up in irritation. "But, Cindy, I told you—"

"He said he'd tried before and couldn't get through. It sounded important."

"Who is it?"

"He said he was a friend. I thought he might be the one who sent the flowers."

Karin's eyes narrowed. "Who is it, Cindy?"

"John Martin."

Karin looked down at the flashing red light on her desk, feeling a similar fluttering run through her. "Okay, I'll take it, but no more exceptions," she warned in her most businesslike voice.

"I'm right, aren't I?" Cindy asked slyly. "He's the one, isn't he?"

"Cindy, don't you have an aerobics class to teach or something?"

"He has a great voice," she went on, her eyes daring, dancing. "If anyone with a voice like that called me, I'd drop whatever I was doing, especially if I'd been working nonstop for weeks on end. It's not healthy. Now, a good man can be a very... healthy experience."

"I know all about what a man can and can't be," Karin said dryly. "Thank you anyway, Dr. Ruth."

"Anytime," Cindy tossed back as she ducked behind the closing door.

The probing by her well-meaning assistant unnerved Karin, and her voice was less than steady as she answered the phone in her usual way. "Karin Sherwood here."

"Hello, Karin Sherwood," he said quietly. And the impact of that "great voice" washed over her in full force.

"Oh, hi, John. How have you been?"

"Working a lot, long hours and such, but you're no stranger to that, according to the woman who answered the phone. She sounded concerned about you. Who is she, anyway?"

"Cindy MacLeod. My senior assistant, in terms of responsibility." She'd almost used the description "infuriating," as well.

"Actually, she asked whether I was the one who sent the flowers."

I'll kill her, thought Karin. "Yes, I—thank you. They, ah, brightened my day," she lied.

A long silence stretched between them. "I've just received the prints of you—the ones I took by the river," he finally said in a nervous rush. "Actually, the roll of film went missing, and I only recently found it among my things."

"Oh. Ah, how'd they turn out?"

"They're very beautiful. Among the best I've ever done, I think," he admitted softly.

She swallowed. "That's . . . nice."

"Someday you'll have to see them and judge for yourself."

"Hmm." She was all set to tell him she was too busy to meet with him in the near future, but he didn't pursue anything definite.

"I should be going," he was saying. "I have to pick up the boys from their basketball game. I just called to . . . say hello."

They each feigned a merry "hello" again, then mumbled an equally stilted "goodbye."

As John hung up he uttered a self-directed expletive. "Idiot!" Why had he thought he could make light, chatty conversation with her? The call had turned out incredibly awkward. She was probably laughing right now at his schoolboyish efforts. And he'd talked about the very things he'd warned himself *not* to discuss: the flowers that were linked to their disturbing night together and the lovely photos he'd taken of her in the winter sunlight.

After studying those prints for two nights running, he'd convinced himself there was no harm in calling to find out how she was faring. He had no intention of becoming too involved with her, which was why he'd not called sooner— although he'd been tempted to several times—and fortunately she shared the same feeling with regard to himself. But it had seemed bizarre somehow to have shared what they'd shared and not to keep in touch, no matter how easily he could rationalize the necessity of it.

He hadn't known exactly what he'd expected to achieve from a call to her. Looking at the pictures had triggered an unfamiliar ache inside him. He'd simply needed to hear her voice again. Surely that would help, he'd told himself. But he'd been wrong. He only felt frustrated and foolish after the unsatisfactory exchange.

The phone rang at his elbow in the study at Greenbank, and he was immediately jarred away from his self-directed rebuke. Jed Holmes, the school basketball coach, informed him that Brad had not shown up for the championship game. He knew of Brad's tendency to run away, so thought it best that he let someone at Greenbank know. John thanked him, left a note for Henry, who was at a meeting, then raced out the door.

He drove anxiously to the school, his first instinct to question Jordan, Karl and Phil, who played on the same team. But they could offer him no clues as to Brad's whereabouts. No one had seen him since the last class of the day. Brad loved basketball; it was highly unusual that he miss such an important game.

Brad was a loner, so the boys and basketball coach had no other suggestions as to who might be able to help. While the others finished their game, John combed the school grounds and the popular after-school hangouts—the doughnut shop, the video arcade, the rest of the plaza—but found nothing. It took a supreme effort to control his worry as he drove his charges home.

An anxious Henry was waiting for them at the door. "Any news?"

John just shook his head grimly.

"He's probably just goofing off somewhere. No big hassle," Karl said, slipping out of his black military boots. "We all need our space sometimes."

"Yeah, I can't see him just taking off," Phil offered less confidently. His freckled face was creased with a thinly disguised concern. "Where would he go? He hasn't got any money, especially after he lost that bet with me...." His voice trailed away guiltily.

John didn't want to remind him that Brad had run away twice before from Greenbank. He'd lived on the streets for weeks before he'd been apprehended, once because he'd been kicked out of a bar for drinking while underage, and the second time because he'd been reported loitering in an office building after-hours. Both times he'd managed to avoid having charges laid against him, but John feared that this time Brad might not be so lucky, especially if he grew desperate for money or shelter.

"I'm going out looking for him," John told Henry. "I'll try the bus terminal, the downtown arcades, the highway, in case he's hitchhiking."

Henry glanced swiftly at the others.

"Don't worry. We won't get any ideas. It can get damn cold at night out there," Karl said blandly, then ambled into the den, flicked on the television and flopped into a chair. Phil and Jordan watched him, then looked back at John.

"Go ahead," John said. "There's nothing you two can do." And he was left alone in the hallway with Henry.

"Look, I'll go," the other man said quietly. "He's primarily my responsibility."

"Forget it," John snapped, thinking of the extra time and effort he'd put in with the difficult teenager during the past few months. He'd persuaded Henry to give Brad as much freedom as the other boys had, because only then could the youth prove he was growing more mature and trustworthy. "*I'll* find him," he vowed, turning quickly and slamming the door behind him. He wanted to believe so badly that he had not misplaced his trust in Brad. There had to be some explanation for his disappearance. He would *not* jump to conclusions.

While driving through the city streets and walking into random shops, restaurants and arcades, John tried thinking of clues in Brad's recent behavior that might shed some light on his present whereabouts. The boy had seemed less resistant to companionship lately. He'd been playing chess nightly with John, talking more at mealtimes. Although he was still as serious as ever, he'd seemed more content—not what one would have expected in someone who was plotting his next escape. So, if Brad had indeed bolted, something unexpected had been at the root of it, but what?

After exhausting every concrete possibility he could think of in town, John drove along the expressways that led out of the city, then just aimlessly around in hopes of spotting the familiar small brown-haired figure by chance. He returned to Greenbank several hours later, exhausted and frustrated, hoping desperately that Brad had returned on his own free will.

Henry's somber face instantly told him that he hadn't. "I'm calling the police," he announced bleakly.

John didn't protest, although he knew that the investigation would necessitate informing the ministry of the situation, and that would not bode well for either Henry or himself, especially with regard to the new community programs they had been implementing.

Since it was well past midnight, John sent the remaining three boys off to bed while Henry made his phone call. An officer arrived shortly thereafter to record the particulars. He promised to give out the information to the patrol cars on duty, but he didn't hold out much hope of finding Brad right away. The majority of the missing-person reports that his force received were for Brad's age bracket, he told them, and if runaways wanted to stay hidden, they usually did.

After the policeman had left, John didn't even consider going home to his own apartment, nor did he pull out the sofa bed he used whenever he stayed. Instead, he sat alone in the den, staring at the Insight section of the newspaper, but he didn't absorb a word, let alone gain any insight as to his present dilemma.

He must have finally dozed off, sitting upright in the chair, but the rattling of the outside door jerked him awake, pumping adrenaline through him. He was only a few steps ahead of Henry, who was tearing down the stairs, hastily donning a bathrobe.

The door opened and Brad stepped into the dark hallway.

"Where the hell have you been?" Henry demanded.

"Out," Brad retorted defiantly, blinking hard at the sudden onslaught of lights Henry had flicked on.

"You can do better than that, Williamson." Henry's voice was menacingly low. "It's two o'clock in the morning."

"Are you okay?" John asked, his eyes searching Brad for any signs of injury and finding nothing but mud-caked sneakers and heavy eyes.

"I'm fine. Just tired. I gotta get some sleep." He went to move past Henry, who stopped him, gripping his arm tightly.

"You can't just waltz in here and expect to get off the hook without an explanation. We've been worried sick."

"Next time, spare yourself the worry. I can look after myself." He tried to look tough, but he was so exhausted he swayed on his feet.

"There better not be a next time," John warned, and Brad just shrugged. "You look as if you've walked for miles. Where were you?" he asked insistingly.

"That's nobody's business." His fists were clenched at his sides.

John sensed that the boy was deeply upset and that he was deliberately provoking them into a stronger anger than they already felt, as if he actually expected them to kick him out, back onto the street. So with considerable effort John reined in his own anger—it would not help him understand what was going on with Brad. "I'm really disappointed in you, Brad. I expected more from you, at least a reassuring phone call."

Brad did not reply. He looked away.

"We called the police," Henry told him, his eyes narrowing when he saw Brad's unbending stance.

"Well, call them back. I'm here, aren't I, safe and sound?" He pushed past Henry and ran up to his room, ignoring the other three boys, who had gathered outside their own doors.

"I hope your little burst of freedom was worth it," Henry bellowed after him. "Because your leash is going to be a lot shorter from now on."

Brad's door slammed shut. He and Karl each had their own rooms, while Jordan and Phil shared one in the large five-bedroom house.

"I'll call the police from my room. Tomorrow you better find out what the hell went on," Henry added quietly to John. He rubbed a weary hand through his thinning hair, then shuffled up to his room. "Get back to bed, guys," he murmured gruffly to the silent group.

John doubted if any of them got much sleep that night.

The next day, Saturday, dawned clear and bright, a perfect late-May morning. The house was still when John awoke, sometime after nine o'clock, feeling groggy due to such a fitful rest. He lay on the sofa bed, eyes wide, thinking of the events of the previous evening and rehearsing various tactics to take with Brad in order to draw him out.

The sudden peal of the doorbell annoyed more than startled him. At this early hour the culprit was probably selling tickets for some cause, canvassing for religious purposes or collecting newspaper money.

He pulled on his jeans, ran a hand through his hair and managed only two buttons of his shirt before he peered out the opened door. A policeman and a policewoman stood there, both tall, dark and unsmiling.

"Are you a resident here?" the policeman asked.

"I work here," John replied, puzzled. "What seems to be the problem?"

"One of the neighbors has just reported the theft of his car stereo system last night." He cleared his throat. "We also learned that someone from this address, a group home, as we understand it, filed a missing-person report last night, then called to negate the claim. We have evidence that there's a connection between the two events. We'd like to talk to you."

"Come right in," said Henry behind John, offering his hand. "I'm Henry Gingrich. And this is my assistant, John Martin." He pointed toward the adjoining den, nervously glancing at the outstretched sofa bed. "We'll get things in order here, then I'm sure we can get to the bottom of this."

John deftly maneuvered his bed back into a couch, then they all sat down, each one perched stiffly on the edge of his or her seat.

The female constable, who was at least twenty years younger than her partner, pulled out a notepad and at a nod from him began to speak, occasionally referring to her notes. "Today, at 7:50 a.m., Mr. Moyer of 78 Greenbank Avenue, reported that his car had been broken into last night and that his AM-FM radio, speakers and cassette deck had been stolen."

John glanced swiftly at Henry. He thought he recognized the name Moyer from a previous discussion and, as if reading his mind, his partner was nodding in confirmation.

"There was considerable damage to the dashboard, and one of the windows had been smashed." The woman paused and looked around the room, as if for effect, before continuing. "We questioned some of the surrounding neighbors, and one of them, a bartender who was driving home after working his shift, reported seeing a youth coming from the direction of the Moyer driveway, then fumbling at your door. The porch light was on, so he was able to give us a fairly detailed description of the person. Apparently he slowed his car to get a better look, his suspicions aroused due to the lateness of the hour—approximately 2:00 a.m., he says. He recognized the boy as one of the residents here, and the description matches what we were given by you, Mr. Gingrich, as to the supposed missing person, Brad Williamson. Naturally we'd like to question him. I presume he's still here?"

"He's here," Henry said quietly as John stood and left the room.

Three heads peered out of the upper bedrooms as soon as he reached the landing. "Stay put," he ordered softly, entering Brad's room after a quick rap on the door, then closing it behind him.

Brad was lying in bed, his face to the wall.

"We have some visitors who want to talk to you," John began gravely. "Did you hear what it's all about?"

"Parts."

"Where were you last night?"

"Nowhere near his bloody car."

"That's not good enough and you know it. Look at me."

Slowly Brad turned around. "I didn't do it," he ground out.

"So just tell them where you were, and everything will be okay." John's eyes pleaded with him.

"I have a *right* to my privacy," he said at last. A note of fear had crept into his voice.

John studied him. "You should have called us, at least."

"I didn't think of it," Brad murmured, looking away. "I was...bugged about something. I don't know why it hit me so hard, but it did." His eyes returned to meet John's, and he did not try to hide the worry there. "I'll just tell them that being seen *near* the scene of the crime and being seen *doing* it are two different things, right?"

"True. But you may remember that Mr. Moyer was one of the most vocal and hostile residents on the street when Henry first got approval for his group home. He and some of his supporters have just been waiting for something like this to start things up again. What happened—the theft— is just what he feared would happen. He's not going to give up easily."

Brad slammed his fist into his pillow. "That's *his* problem."

"No, I'm afraid it's yours, too, unless you can answer their questions satisfactorily as to what you were really doing last night."

"Do you believe I didn't do it?" Brad challenged, his voice level.

John looked into the teenager's eyes, and he saw fear and something else—a sort of dignity that he had not noticed there before, and he sensed that Brad was having a difficult time holding on to it himself. "I believe you," he heard himself say.

"Then don't let me get screwed by that narrow-minded bastard. No matter who did the hack job on his car, who is *he* to say who can live here and who can't?"

John stared hard at him for a long still moment. "Get dressed, and help me out down there as much as you can," he finally said. "But if you ever pull something like this again, you're on your own. I don't get angry very often, but when I do, look out. Do you understand?"

Brad threw him an assessing look. "I hear you," he mumbled before flinging aside the covers and reaching for his clothes.

Even after the intense scrutiny and firing of questions by the police, Brad would not offer any explanation as to his whereabouts during the hours in question. He flatly denied any part of the allegations being hurled at him. He refused to meet Henry's furious stare, turning only to John when at one point the senior officer grabbed his collar roughly.

"Let go of him," John bit out, holding the man's gaze until he obeyed. "I think we've hashed this out enough. It's clear you don't have sufficient evidence to charge Brad, despite your curiosity about his activities. You'll have to believe him when he says he wasn't involved. So, good day to both of you, and I wish you luck with your investigation." He stood and led the way toward the front door.

Reluctantly the two officers followed him. "Would you have any objections if we searched the premises before we leave?" the policeman asked.

"But you don't have a warrant," John threw at him, remembering something he'd learned from one of the many TV detective shows the boys liked to watch.

"Go ahead," Henry intervened smoothly, his eyes ordering John to cooperate.

After the two uniformed officials had finally left, having found nothing to help them with the case, Henry asked to speak to Brad alone. But by the futility echoing in his raised voice as he dismissed the teenager, John knew he hadn't gained any new information.

Brad stayed in his room all day, while John and the other boys watched a baseball game on TV. Henry had planned a long-awaited visit to Melissa in Vancouver for four days, and John insisted he go ahead with his plans. He promised he would keep Henry informed of any news, and he assured him he could handle the four boys on his own. Frankly, Henry was the most upset of them all about the incident with Brad, and John knew the tension in the house would be alleviated considerably without him. Besides, Margaret was always on call should he need some help, but he didn't think involving her at this point would accomplish anything.

He tried to speak to Brad again on Saturday night, but was only offered monosyllables in return, so he decided to wait until the teenager was more receptive.

On Sunday afternoon, John drove the boys to their various community activities in the van, which Henry, who had taken John's smaller car to the airport, had left behind. The program had been under way for several weeks now. Brad volunteered as an orderly at a home for senior citizens, while Jordan and Phil worked in the emergency department at St. Mary's Hospital in Waterloo. Brad said little about his post; the other two seemed proud of their new sense of responsibility.

Sixteen-year-old Karl was the only one who had a paying job. He worked as a busboy at the Alpine Inn. Initially he'd balked at having to wear the traditional German costume of lederhosen and feathered fedora, but he had finally given in. The restaurant owners were longtime friends of Henry's who had been persuaded to hire Karl on a trial basis. But everyone had been surprised at how swiftly Karl had mastered the job and endeared himself to the patrons with his jovial charm.

Following his usual route, John dropped Brad off last. He had debated whether to trust someone who had so recently violated that trust, and he knew Henry wouldn't, but somehow he felt that Brad was testing him. John sensed that it was vitally important to give the teenager a second chance. If Brad really wanted to run, he could certainly sneak away at any time. He had to *want* to stay at the home, not because he was forced to, but because of the love he knew was always there for him. The only way that John could teach Brad to accept that he belonged at Greenbank was to persistently show he cared about him.

"You like working here, Brad?" he asked as he pulled up to the quiet shady grounds of Maple Haven.

"You want the truth or something positive for your reports to show how well adjusted I'm becoming and what a great job you're doing?"

Brad's resentment of the progress reports John and Henry had to furnish to the Children's Aid agency that had placed each resident was shared by the rest of the boys, too. The regular treatment plans that went to various supervisors at the ministry were also met with scorn. But this data was a necessary tool for the support network associated with the running of the home, including psychologists, social workers and probation officers.

"I want the *truth*, Brad," John answered evenly. "Whether you believe it or not, the reports are written with your best interests at heart, not mine or anyone else's."

"Then I don't like working here. It's depressing."

"Do you want to try somewhere else?" John asked. Brad stared straight ahead. "Look, you don't have to stay if it's that bad for you."

"I'll stick it out as long as I can."

"I'm sure we can find something more suitable. It's up to you."

Brad shoved his way out of the van, his fingers lingering on the door handle. "That's a switch." His voice was edged in a deep bitterness, and suddenly John was reminded of the pain and rejection Brad had suffered since childhood, first by losing his mother, then by being placed in one foster home after another.

"I'll see you in a few hours," he said matter-of-factly, deliberately keeping the doubt out of his voice.

"Yeah," was all Brad replied before he sauntered off, the back of his denim jacket flashing a decal of jagged silver lightning.

To John's relief, Brad was there waiting for him when he returned sometime later on his pick-up rounds, but he refused to speak to anyone. After a quick dinner in which everyone tried to ignore Brad's foul humor, John was once more trying to load the group into the van for the youth gathering they attended each Sunday evening at the local church hall.

Brad had been dawdling, and finally he told John he didn't want to go.

Time was running short, as was John's patience. "Why?" he'd demanded, glancing at his watch.

"I've got some studying to do."

Karl, who'd overheard the exchange, slyly piped in, "What for?"

"The history test," Brad answered quickly, glaring at him.

Karl called his bluff. "You've still got a week for that."

Brad turned pleading eyes on John. "I just don't want to go. I'm . . . bagged."

He did look tired, but John had no choice, nor was he willing to give in to the boy's every whim. "I can't leave you here unsupervised, Brad. You know the rules. Come on."

"No."

"We haven't got time for this. Get a move on." From outside, either Jordan or Phil honked the van's horn.

Defiance and frustration crossed Brad's face as he stared at the two of them. Then slowly, silently, as if in pantomime, he raised his fist and struck the mailbox built into the entryway. The force of his pent-up anger was strong enough to splinter the small wooden door. Another quick jab created a gaping hole and made the metal slot at the back of the box clang noisily.

"Hey, man—" Karl sputtered, stepping forward, but John's arm restrained him.

"Get in the car," John snapped, barely able to control the white-hot fury that was growing inside him. He towered over Brad, his height and blazing eyes making him a formidable opponent.

Without a word Brad pushed his way out the door and sat sullenly in the back row of the vehicle. No one spoke on the way to the meeting. John's knuckles were white as he clutched the steering wheel and tried to regain his professional calm.

At the church, the other three teenagers piled out. "I'll be back at nine," John told them quietly, and no one questioned his decision not to stay for the gathering as he usually did, nor to force Brad to join them.

The ride home was just as wordless as the trip to the church. John did not try to deal with what had happened until he had fully regained control over the rage building inside him. At Greenbank he let Brad escape to his room. For a long interval that could only be measured by the number of conflicting thoughts tumbling around inside his head, John stared at the large hole beside the front door.

Finally he went down to the basement work area. The sound of hammering echoed through the house. He returned with a rudimentary wooden frame, which he set over the hole in the mailbox and nailed into place.

Rather than repair the damage or force Brad to, he'd decided to let it stand indefinitely. Brad would be reminded of his destructive behavior every time he walked by.

Satisfied with his work, his anger cooled, John sat in the kitchen with a cup of coffee. For the first time, he wondered if he had the mettle to handle this stressful, often discouraging job over an extended period of time....

When it was finally time to pick up the guys, he climbed the stairs to Brad's room and saw that he was fast asleep, fully clothed on his bed, his face softly boyish in sleep. John made up his mind not to disturb him, gambling that the youth would still be dead to the world by the time he returned.

During the short ride home, Karl occupied the front passenger seat while Jordan and Phil sat in the back.

"Everything okay back at the ranch?" Phil asked immediately.

"I think so," John answered. "He was sleeping. I decided not to bother him."

"Someone was asking about him tonight," Karl offered hesitantly.

"Who?" John was instantly alerted by something in Karl's tone.

"A chick. Amanda Hampstead. She seemed upset—wanted to know where Brad was. In more than a casual way. Promise you won't say anything to him, guys?" He glanced back at the other two, who nodded, their faces solemn.

"Why do you think she was so interested?" John pressed.

"Said she had a big fight with Brad...on Friday. The same day he ran...or tried to...or whatever happened."

"Did she say what it was about? Are she and Brad serious?"

"Are you kidding?" Karl scoffed. "She's...not bad looking, but she's one of those snotty types. Only wears things that *look* expensive, if she can't flaunt the label. Reminds me of my stepmother. Drives her mom's BMW to school. I doubt if she'd give someone like Brad the time of day. She wouldn't even *talk* to me the one time I ever tried. Who needs a bi—someone like that?"

"Hmm, thanks for telling me," John said pensively, pulling into Greenbank's driveway. "But you're right, Karl. I don't think it would be a good idea to say anything to Brad. It could be a touchy subject."

"I don't want my face to look like that mailbox," Phil said as they approached the house.

"M-me neither," Jordan echoed.

They entered and both wore puzzled expressions as they stared at the homemade wooden frame around the broken chute.

Karl gave a low whistle. He turned to John and murmured with admiration in his voice, "I like that. It'll drive Brad crazy."

And for the first time that long weekend, John exchanged a smile with someone, but the smile was short-lived, because he knew the deep-rooted problems with Brad were far from being solved.

To John's relief the next few days passed without additional visits from the police, but he was on tenterhooks the whole time, fearing that more incriminating evidence against Brad might turn up. Yet all his instincts were telling him to believe the youth was not involved in the car theft....

On the night before Henry's return, he was sitting on the porch and gazing up at the slate-paved sky. Neither stars nor moon was in sight. From the blackness suddenly rose a vivid memory of Karin. It wasn't her face or form that he saw, but a shining blue-gold essence that he felt. He remembered how often he had tried to make himself numb to that feeling, yet it kept coming back to haunt him at the strangest times....

CHAPTER TEN

HENRY ARRIVED HOME late Wednesday evening, and John filled him in on the events of the past few days. Both men agreed that the disappearance and mailbox incident must be discussed with Brad in further detail. They hoped that confronting the issues after some time had elapsed and emotions had had a chance to calm down would help Brad put his negative feelings in perspective. John wanted to be the one to counsel Brad, but Henry was skeptical about that.

"Whenever I've encountered any crisis situations like this one, I've always found it worked best to refer the boy to one of our professional therapists. They are better equipped to deal with the specific behavior and to figure out what problem is being consciously or unconsciously 'acted out,' as they like to put it."

John shook his head. "I just have a feeling that in this case, we'd only alienate Brad more. Involving others would make him distrust us even more, as if we were setting him free to the wolves. He's had enough of that in his life already."

Henry smiled wryly. "I don't think our therapists would appreciate being compared to a pack of wolves, but I see your point. You're saying that's how Brad would *perceive* it. You may be right." His long fingers kneaded the stubble on his chin as he studied John. "But if we decide to try counseling Brad ourselves, I think I should be the one to do it.''

"Why?"

"Because I don't know how objective you can be.''

"I *am* closely involved with what's happening to Brad, and I *do* care about him a lot. I want to help him, not that you don't, Henry, but...I *have* to see this through. Please. I think I'm learning how to read him—especially his defenses, and heaven knows he's got a lot of those. I don't expect any instant breakthroughs, but I do know that, given time, I *can* get through to him. Please, give me the chance.''

Henry had not moved a muscle during his friend's impassioned speech, nor did his expression indicate what he was thinking. Finally he said simply, "Okay. But if he's still clammed up after say, a week, we will have to refer him to our more qualified staff. Okay?''

John smiled wearily. "Thank you.''

"Come on, you look as if you could use a rest as much as I.''

For the first time, John noticed just how tired and preoccupied Henry was. "You must have had a draining trip. How's Melissa's mother?''

"Oh, she has her good and bad days. It's hard on Melissa, too, watching someone she loves getting progressively worse. But one of the best nursing homes out there is expanding, and Melissa hopes to be able to place her mother there sometime in the fall. She'll visit her as much as she can....''

"That'll be more difficult once she returns to Greenbank, but at least she'll know her mother is in good hands, as you say,'' John said gently.

"Hmm.'' Henry looked distracted.

"Is everything okay with you and Melissa?''

"Oh, fine," he answered after a moment. "We miss each other, of course, but she's quite involved with her studies and determined to finish her thesis."

"I imagine she's looking forward to coming home when it's all done, though. If all goes well for her mother's placement, is she still aiming for October?"

"October? Yes, I suppose that's about the time. We had so much else to discuss, I—I..." Again, the strange vagueness was back in his eyes. "Let's hit the sack. I'm beat. 'Night." Abruptly he left the room.

John was too tired himself to dwell on the reasons for Henry's troubled behavior. Maybe he was reading more into it than was there. The circumstances of his trip—his enforced marital separation, his mother-in-law's debilitating disease, the rigors of traveling such a long distance in such a short time—would be both mentally and physically exhausting for anyone.

Since the hour was so late, John slept at Greenbank once more. The next day while the boys were at school, he returned to his apartment for a change of clothes, then ran a few errands. But the upcoming confrontation with Brad, which he'd planned to initiate after dinner, was foremost on his mind.

Brad made no mention of the framed mailbox hole, but he avoided looking at it whenever he passed through the hallway. After dinner he did his share of the dishes, declined Karl's offer for a game of Ping-Pong, then bolted to his room.

John knew there was no perfect time for the talk, so a few minutes later he knocked on Brad's door. He was glad that Brad wasn't sharing a room, although another resident would certainly put Greenbank in better financial shape. Henry was currently discussing a new placement with the agency, in fact, but the two boys available were only ten and nine years old, respectively. The agency was stalling, because they felt that either child would be better suited in a home with residents closer to his own age.

Brad did not answer the first knock. John rapped again and finally heard an acknowledgment. "Yeah?"

He opened the door. "Just checking to see how you're doing, Brad."

"Great. Just great." The boy was sprawled on his bed, staring at the ceiling, his hands behind his head.

Without waiting for an invitation, John entered the room and sat on an unsteady wicker chair shared by a pile of Brad's dirty clothes. "How's the studying going for that history test?" he began.

"It's going."

"About that hole in the mailbox—"

"I'll pay for it...from my allowance. It may take a while...."

"We're not planning to fix it, not right away, anyway."

For the first time, Brad looked at him, his eyes narrowed, calculating. "That's fine by me," he said evenly.

"What's more important is getting some answers to a few questions. Such as why, Brad? What's bothering you?"

"The way you keep meddling in my life, for one thing," the youth retorted hotly. "Why don't you try your—your do-gooding on Phil or Jordan? They're much more gullible. They need the attention. I don't."

"I'm here with you because I want to be, and I'm not leaving until I get a few answers." John leaned back and waited.

Five minutes passed and the only sound in the room came from a clock by Brad's bedside.

Finally he spoke again. "The police called yesterday."

As John expected, Brad's interest was pricked. "So what'd they want? I suppose they're still itching to nail me."

"As a matter of fact, they have charged someone else with the theft. One of the mothers on the street found parts of the stolen stereo hidden in her son's room. She knew of the incident with Mr. Moyer and called the police. If it's any consolation to you, the officer on the phone was most apologetic about the inconvenience he caused us here."

"'Inconvenience'!" Brad fairly spat the word out. "It was a pile of sh—all of it."

"The police were just doing their job," John said quietly, "but I know how you must feel, being the one who was wrongly accused. That's not the main issue here, though, Brad. I know something *else* was going on with you that night, and I think you need to talk about it."

Brad's mouth clamped into a tight line, and he stared rigidly ahead. "Come on, Brad," John urged, his voice strong without sounding impatient. "There's someone inside you that none of us know. You've got a lot of different feelings bouncing around inside, getting in each other's way. You've got to deal with them, or they'll eat at you. Let some of them out. Show us who you really are."

Brad snorted, suddenly unable to contain his anger any longer. "You know, I used to think I was a nobody. My mother has probably forgotten I even exist, and my father probably never even knew I existed. And I can't even remember how many foster homes I've been in, but you can bet they were all as happy to get rid of me as I was to get away from them."

"But you've been here at Greenbank almost two years. It's your home now. That's what counts."

"Yeah, I'm finally a somebody. Somebody to put down. Feel sorry for. Mistrust. Fear. You know what some of the kids at school call Greenbank? Slumville or Scumville, depending on who you're talking to.''

"You know that's ridiculous. This is a home. You're part of a family. . . .''

"That's garbage. We're different. People can't forget where we come from, that some of us are on probation, that we're troublemakers. They expect us to fly off the handle. And most of the time they're right.''

"Brad, you can prove them all wrong. You can be whatever you want—now. In the present. Put the past behind you.''

"What's the use? Not when people see you in a certain way only. I know they're right. I *am* born to be a loser. Sure, I can bluff my way and pretend I'm not, but deep down..." His color was rising and his voice growing higher in pitch as he went on, "What's the point when . . . even parents of so-called friends, people who don't even know you, don't want their little darlings contaminated—'' He shut his mouth suddenly, realizing that he'd said more than he'd intended.

"Is that what happened with Amanda?''

Brad blinked, then stared coldly at him. "Who's Amanda?''

"I'm asking you.''

"Well, you're asking the wrong guy the wrong question.''

"Brad, talk to me. I'm here because I care about you.''

"Is that what they taught you to say in your training . . . in Group Home Psychology I? Well, it won't work with me. I know you're just doing your job. You'd like me to 'open up,' 'mix well with my peers,' '' he said the words with a sneer, "so it'll look good on those fancy reports you send to all the other little gods out there. You don't want me to run away again because it'll make *you* look bad. All you and Henry really care about is covering your own asses."

"That's not true," John said evenly, wishing there was some way he could convince Brad how genuinely concerned he was about his welfare. He tried one last stab in the dark.

"Did Amanda have anything to do with why you tried to take off?"

Brad's face seemed to tighten.

"If she did," John went on, "you're only showing her the Brad Williamson she expects to see. Not the person who's tougher, more of a survivor than any of us can even imagine. Don't base your life on the narrow-mindedness of other people, like the Mr. Moyers of the world, for example. You have to build your own strengths."

Brad turned to face the wall. "Is the lecture finished?" he drawled. "You're really an amateur, you know. And, believe me, I oughta know. I've heard all this same garbage over the years."

John knew he'd lost him. It was futile to continue probing when Brad was only trying to lash out, to hurt. Wearily he stood and walked to the door, turning to look back at the rigid form of the youth on the bed. His hand clung to the doorknob, as if for support. "If you ever want to talk, you know where I am. Talking *does* help. I learned that myself, the hard way, when—"

But Brad wasn't listening. "What do you *really* know about life, anyway? You took off your black hat and your suspenders and—and you drive a car instead of a buggy, but that doesn't mean anything. You should have stayed with your own kind. You're way off base here, man."

John felt as if he weren't getting enough oxygen to his lungs. "There's a lot of us out there, Brad. On or off the base, who knows? All we've got is each other," he said with all the air he had left in his chest. Then he turned and walked out.

He was driving home, his mind and body overstimulated, not only from the strain of the past few days, but from the extra cups of coffee he'd sipped while discussing his progress—or lack thereof—with Henry. Suddenly an idea started growing within him, competing with his frustration, refusing to be ignored. He found himself heading for Karin's apartment, unsure of the wisdom of going there, but knowing he deeply needed to talk to her.

KARIN STRETCHED OUT on the couch, feeling gloriously decadent. She'd just finished soaking in a hot, hot bath that had been heaven to joints and limbs that had endured extra aerobics classes all week because Kim had been off with laryngitis.

The source of her pleasure sat beside her—not the tall tumbler of juice but the huge bowl of popcorn, soaked in butter and well-sprinkled with salt. She'd had a nutritious quiche and salad for lunch, so she had decided she could afford to satisfy her craving for one of her favorite snack foods, substituting it for a late dinner. It was nearly ten o'clock.

Her hand dug into the bowl again and again, but she had to tell herself to slow down so that she could fully savor the golden-topped, freshly popped kernels. At such times she was grateful she lived alone. No one could lecture her about her indulgence. No one would be bothered by the old Joni Mitchell album she was playing none too softly. No one could see her in her favorite tattered terry robe, thick socks and ponytailed hair. And lastly, no one would tease her about reading the tabloids that she and Cindy secretly traded back and forth when one or the other hadn't been able to resist an appalling headline while waiting in the supermarket lineup.

When the knock on her door sounded, she bolted up, spilling popcorn all over, feeling as if she'd been caught at some illicit activity. She didn't worry about the popcorn, but she made sure she stuffed her reading material under the couch before she went to the door, pulling her robe tightly around herself.

She expected to see either her landlord or the one neighbor she'd befriended—a lonely widow who'd invited her over for tea a few times and who'd often dropped by with fresh-baked muffins. Karin was not in the mood to visit with anyone at this hour, especially dressed as she was. She peered through the peephole and felt the shock of recognition run through her.

John Martin stood there, looking as gorgeous as he had so long ago in the hotel corridor. It was too late to do anything about her attire, but she tried to appear dignified as she greeted him, half hiding behind the open door. "Hi. I, ah, wasn't expecting company."

His eyes seemed to feast on her face, her eyes, barely conscious of the rest of her. "I'm sorry it's so late. I was just passing by and thought I'd stop in. But if it's a bad time..."

"No, no. Come in," she said a little breathlessly, and then his tall striking presence seemed to fill her room.

Although she'd tried to block out all thoughts of him during the past few busy weeks, she was glad to see him; in fact, she was more than glad—her heart was soaring recklessly.

"Do you like popcorn? I happen to have plenty," she said, gesturing toward the huge, half-filled bowl abandoned on the couch.

"I see that," he said, smiling, then he turned to look at her fully for the first time. His eyes were drawn to the deep V of skin that the loose-fitting robe did not cover, even more apparent because her hair was pulled back, bobbing sprightly from the crown of her head.

"You look..." He stopped.

"If you say 'cute,' I'll have to work hard to forgive you."

No, even if "cute" had been a common word in his vocabulary, he would not have chosen it to describe her. He was barely conscious of what she was wearing; he saw only the summer blue of her eyes, the autumn gold of her hair, the classic beauty of her face, an intriguing blend of girl and woman. She radiated a comfortable warmth, and he had the unmistakable feeling that he'd come home.

"No—you look wonderful," he said soberly. "And I haven't realized how much I've missed you until now."

She didn't know what to say. His directness unnerved her, pleased her. "Let me take your coat, have a seat," she said quietly at last. The jacket's fresh, outdoorsy scent was hauntingly familiar to her, carrying intimate memories of the man who'd worn it. Walking over to the stereo, she lowered the volume, then turned to see him watching her intently from the couch. "Help yourself to the popcorn." Her arms wrapped themselves tightly around her middle as she leaned against the wall, strangely reluctant to move closer to him.

"Thanks, but I'm not hungry."

For the first time, she noticed how tired he looked. "Is something wrong?"

He shrugged. "Oh, I had a run-in with Brad tonight."

"What about?" When he didn't reply, she added, "I'm interested, really."

Pausing often to measure his words, he briefly recited the events of the past few days—from Brad's mysterious disappearance to his stubborn refusal to let anyone get close.

"Maybe he has to work out some of his problems on his own," Karin murmured.

John stared ahead reflectively, then over at Karin, his eyes opaquelike, their spirit dulled. "When I first joined Greenbank, everyone told me not to expect miracles with the kids. They warned me about the high burnout rate in this profession, not only from the stressful parts of the job, but from the inevitable failure rate in the work itself—some kids make it on their own and others simply don't. Many end up giving something to society, while others will always take from it by committing crimes, relying on the welfare system and so forth. But I didn't want to believe in failure. I believed that I could make a difference in *every* case. I thought that effort and caring would pay off. I was naive," he said with a pained smile.

"It sounds as if you've done your best, though. That's what really matters."

He shook his head. "Tonight I felt as if I was merely interfering in Brad's life, not helping him, not making a difference. And I tried so hard, but it wasn't enough. He discounted everything I said by telling me I was just doing my job, and not very well, either."

Karin felt his frustration. She wanted to go to him, but she held herself back. "Hey, I don't know a lot about other kids, but 'difficult' was the favorite tag I got from people who could never understand me. Brad would definitely fit that description, too. Often, it's not *what* we say, but what we *can't* say that means the most. Don't take things at such face value, John. And don't be so impatient. Making a difference is going to take time, no matter how good you are or how hard you try."

"Ah...patience—another virtue that keeps evading me."

Karin didn't want to get into a discussion with him about virtues and their counterparts, vices, fearing where such a discussion might lead. Instead, she said softly, "Don't blame yourself or Brad if he needs time to get his act together. Some of us are *still* trying to figure ourselves out...which may take a lifetime."

He was looking at her across the room and thinking how he'd done the right thing in coming to see her. "It's good to talk to you again, Karin," he admitted, and her smile seemed to light him deep within. "But you're too far away. Come here." The words were low, husky, not the way he'd intended them to come out.

Her eyes fell and she seemed flustered as she returned the record to its jacket, then played with the dials of the radio until she found some mellow classical music that he couldn't identify. She went over to the couch and crumpled into the corner opposite him.

"Come here," he bid again. "Please, just for a while. I need to hold you." And slowly she slid over until she was curled into his outstretched arm, her legs folded beneath her, the bowl of popcorn propped between them. The analytical parts of his mind on hold, he experienced a deep feeling of contentment. Karin, too, seemed to relax.

She reached for a small handful of popcorn, which she slowly fed to herself, one by one. She offered the bowl to him, but he just shook his head, more interested in the nonchalant way she was nibbling her food, her lips moist, her chin endearingly grease stained.

Seemingly oblivious to his scrutiny, Karin paused in midair, a fluffy white kernel poised in her fingers. "You know, I think Brad counts on you more than he realizes."

"And how do you figure that?"

The kernel disappeared into her mouth. "I don't know—
I watched him at that dinner...at Greenbank. Maybe it was
the way he watched you teaching him about the camera, as
if he looked up to you but hated to admit it."

"Hmm...how'd you get to be so smart?"

"A heavy diet of popcorn," she said just as airily. "Try
it." She popped a kernel into his mouth, then another, her
eyes merry as he licked his lips in satisfaction. Soon he was
helping himself greedily.

"As I fill myself with wisdom, why don't you tell me how
things are going at Supreme. I didn't mean to monopolize
the conversation."

"Just the popcorn," Karin teased, glancing down at the
bowl he was rapidly emptying.

"Well, you had a head start...."

Their mood stayed light, comfortable, as she proceeded
to tell him about the setback she'd encountered at the club,
her retaliation, the success she'd finally met due to her increased canvassing efforts, the recent lull in new members
just when she was short by a hundred names, her deadline
fast approaching....

He told her she was doing a marvelous job and she
shouldn't worry, and the way his hand was idly stroking her
neck and his arm was protectively encircling her took her
cares away. She didn't want to think beyond the tranquillity of the moment, enhanced by the pastoral Brahms sym-
phony that filled the room from her stereo.

"Ah, Karin, if only I could hold you like this forever,"
John murmured after a time, pulling her even closer.

She felt herself stiffen, an involuntary response. "And if
only I could cash in on all the 'if onlys' in my life," she returned, drawing back, surprised at the sharp edge that had
entered her voice without warning. Her defenses swiftly
rose up, as if they had been hovering nearby, waiting for her

to call upon them when the time of respite had to end. Suddenly she desperately needed to move away from him. She leaned forward to set the empty bowl on the floor and went to stand. The tail of her robe caught under her, the two sides splitting open as she pulled impatiently at the material.

John reached for her hand before she could adjust the loosening belt. "Karin, I didn't mean to upset you. I—"

"I—I just need to stretch." She tried to free her hand, but his grip had tightened, and she felt his gaze trail along the naked curves of her flesh like a flaming feather.

"I thought you were enjoying our...affection." His voice was barely above a whisper. "It seemed that we both needed some tonight."

"Affection is one thing. This is another," she said unsteadily, glancing down in embarrassment at her exposed body.

As soon as he released her hand, she wrapped her robe firmly around herself once more. But his eyes, dark with desire, continued to bore into hers, electrifying every corner of her mind. It didn't matter that she was fully covered again. She felt herself swiftly being stripped down to essentials, defense by defense, to the stark need that he so readily evoked in her.

Then his face was level with hers and his strong hands were upon her and his mouth was hungrily molded to hers. Her lips wanted to betray her, wanted to meet his with an equal hunger, but she turned away.

"I swore that I wouldn't let this happen again with you," she whispered hoarsely.

"I'm not sure we have a choice anymore," he said, unable to still his hands from their fevered journey downward, seeking the soft golden skin that his eyes had so unsatisfactorily caressed before.

"But aren't you afraid of this?"

"Of what? Of this?"

She felt the hard warmth of his palm as it cupped the curve of her breast and it was as if through him her womanhood was defined. With a gentle flick of his thumb over her nipple, a deep sensuousness engulfed her. Karin both loved and hated his control over her body, the way her mind was wavering.

"Yes!" she hissed, tearing herself away, her eyes wide with a nameless dread. "Of everything. This . . . this thing between us. Sex, attraction, kismet, whatever you want to call it. It controls us. It's powerful, addictive. And someday we'll want to be free from it . . . only it'll have its hold over us. And I'm afraid I won't be able to bear that." She felt tears behind her eyes, but she fought letting them fall.

"When that day comes, I promise you we will be strong . . . together. I'll never deliberately hurt you, Karin. We'll be friends, always, wherever we are. . . ." His arms hung motionlessly at his sides; his eyes, genuine and caring, were windows to the promise of his words. "I'm just learning myself that we shouldn't be afraid to live, Karin. We can give each other so much—and not just with our bodies. It's more than that, much more."

She remembered how deflated she'd felt after the last time they'd made love, then drifted apart. But he was here again, and it was as if he were pleading for a fresh start. There was something different about him, something she couldn't pinpoint, but she found herself responding to it, putting her fears aside. He was telling her she could trust in today because he would help her through whatever tomorrow would bring. But would that be enough? Was the fulfillment he offered worth the pain of a parting he wouldn't deny?

She was one step away from finding out. One step away
from the joy she had no doubt he could release in her, body
and soul, if she was truly brave enough to face an unknown future. It was a huge gamble...but she took the step.
Perhaps the choice had already been made from the moment he walked through her door....

He let out a deep breath as he took her in his arms and
held her with a fierce possessive need. Trembling, she lifted
her mouth for his kiss.

"Karin," he murmured against her lips, "you will always be a part of me. Do you believe it?"

"Yes..." she cried softly.

Their mouths locked. He slipped her robe from her
shoulders, then fell to his knees and began a deep worship
of her breasts, raining kisses on them with the reverence of
sprinkling holy water. Her fingers dug into his shoulders as
he drew hot shafts of sensation from her seemingly endless
reservoir.

With a boldness that came from her profound need to
share her pleasure with him, she pulled him back up to full
height, then began unbuttoning his shirt, only stopping
long enough to fan her shaking fingers over the firm,
heated expanse of his chest and stomach.

Her exploring hand encountered the cold metal of his
belt buckle and the crisp denim of his jeans. And then his
hands were there, too, helping her, tugging, and within
seconds of their combined efforts, he was as naked as she.

His eyes willed her to touch him, swollen hard with need.
And when her hand closed over him, he let out a soft groan
that sent a tremor running through her and gave her the
confidence to continue her caress. She felt a deep satisfaction that she could affect him so strongly. With erotic
abandon, she slowly sank to her knees on the soft carpet,

tasted of him with her tongue, then her mouth in a warm wondrous rhythm.

His face tilted in surprise. Achingly sweet moments later, a vulnerable look crossed his features, his breathing quickened, and his hand gently stilled her.

"Enough," he whispered, dropping to his knees, too. He drew her close to his sheltering warmth, and hands and lips that had been briefly idle grew familiar with her soft flesh once more. His fingers sought out her heated womanly core, enhancing the magic transformation that had already begun.

Karin's breathing was as irregular as his had been, her sense of urgency mounting as swiftly as his had. They fell to the floor. When he eased himself down into her, the intense pleasure was almost torment. His pace quickened and the welcome friction caused ancient fires to spread through her, licking at her, dancing within her, consuming her, until she knew nothing but the powerful surge of his essence deep within her....

MORNING SUNLIGHT POURED into the bedroom like molten gold, brazenly reminding the lovers of the new day.

John's arm was securely around her and his leg sprawled over hers when Karin awoke. Blinking in the bright light, she remembered everything, her body still tingling from its sensual onslaught. After they'd finally untangled themselves on the carpeted floor that neither had paid mind to during their lovemaking, John had asked to stay the night, and Karin had been unable to think of a sane reason for refusal. She'd put the future on hold, so intoxicating had been the lure of the present. Mainly she'd wanted the luxury of waking up with him by her side in her own bed. But nothing she'd imagined was close to the pleasure she felt as she turned and met his lazy smile.

"You're awake," she said, staring at the rich darkness of his hair against the peach-colored pillow and at the glossy penetrating quality of his eyes.

"Hmm . . . have been for a while."

"Why didn't you wake me?" She stretched, her limbs rubbing against the masculine crispness of his legs.

"I've been thinking, and your warm body helped my thinking process." His hands stroked the sensitive dip of her waist.

"What were you thinking about?" she asked casually, bracing herself for something that could shatter her fragile happiness, suddenly recalling how swiftly he'd made her withdraw from him in the hotel room.

"Two things. First, I'd like you to visit the farm with me."

Of all the possibilities she expected to hear, that was the most remote. "Why?" she sputtered.

"That's what I've been wondering about. I just want you there. Kind of like a bridge between the old and new."

She studied his face and saw the troubled look he was fighting to hide. "But . . . I'm an outsider. I'd only put more of a strain on the situation."

"Please. . . ."

At least he was facing his heritage again, and she sensed that was a critically important step for him. Besides, she was curious about his background. She wanted to learn more about him. "Okay, if you want me to go with you, I will."

His lips found the hollow of her throat, and the arm spanning her waist pulled her even closer. "Thank you. . . ." He paused, then began hesitantly, "Ah, there's something else I've been thinking about."

"What's that?" Her suspicions were fully alert once more, despite the persuasive distraction of his flesh against hers. Maybe he was worrying, belatedly, that they'd risked pregnancy, but once more their timing made that an unlikely possibility.

"I've been thinking how you've opened up a whole new world for me and made me lose so many inhibitions I didn't even know I possessed."

Moved by his admission, she murmured, "I hate to see wasted potential." Goose bumps erupted on her skin as he nibbled close to her ear and blew lightly there. "Hey, that tickles."

"In that case I'll have to resort to a few of the other things I know for a fact you won't object to...." His hand lightly played with her breast until the tip became a concentrated peak of sensation. "I didn't know that a woman could respond the way you do, Karin," he said in a quieter voice. "I'm amazed that I...that you and I...I'm afraid it all has a very potent effect on me."

"Yes, I can see that," she said with a smile, then they were expressing themselves again in a myriad of wordless ways....

CHAPTER ELEVEN

ONLY A FEW CLOUDS RODE the sky, none of which obscured the sun on the warm Sunday in June that Karin accompanied John to his family farm.

He'd arrived an hour early to pick her up, suggesting that the weather was perfect for a short drive around the countryside. But Karin sensed that he also needed the diversion to ease his nervousness about his long-postponed return to his former home.

John had not said anything about their last passionate encounter, and Karin shied away from mentioning it herself. She was content to enjoy the new familiarity that existed between them, knowing that the delicate harmony they'd achieved could end as easily as a balanced scale could be tipped by shifting weights. She asked about Brad, but all John would say was that the boy had remained aloof and was seeing a therapist. Since John was not inclined to be more expansive, she did not pursue the subject, preferring to share his enjoyment of the pleasant ride.

They were driving north, beyond the outskirts of Waterloo. The two-lane highway was sandwiched between gently rolling hills, a patchwork of yellow, green and brown cultivated fields, which made up some of the most fertile farmland in Ontario.

The car slowed at a traffic light in downtown Elmira, only one of the many picturesque villages in the vicinity. Just ahead of them, a Mennonite buggy pulled up at a

McDonald's restaurant. Taken aback, unable to resist a smile, Karin glanced toward John.

"As I told you, some orders are less resistant to progress than others," he said with a wry grimace, then instantly changed the subject that was too close to the unpredictable event awaiting him. "Did you make it out to the Maple Syrup Festival here in March?" he asked as the light changed and he pulled away, more at ease behind the wheel than he had been on the unfamiliar Toronto streets.

"No. I think I was catching up on my sleep that day or something equally exciting. Did you?"

He nodded. "The boys seemed to like it, especially the free pancakes and syrup, and the hundred or so booths selling other homemade goodies. If you don't mind the crowds, you'll have to visit the festival next year."

"Sure—if I'm still here," she answered without thinking, but in the silence that fell between them, she had time to consider the implications of leaving Kitchener... and him.

At the next interchange the car turned. As brightly as she could manage, Karin asked, "Where are we going?" She knew they were miles away from the farm.

"You'll see."

So she leaned back and occupied herself by looking for signs of life in the verdant fields and aging farm buildings. Minutes later, they approached a pretty hamlet called West Montrose. The car veered onto another roadway, and Karin exclaimed in delight at the unexpected sight. The sparkling waters of a river were spanned by a long covered bridge, its roof moss covered and wavy, its wooden frame russet colored. The single lane of the tunnellike interior was dimly lighted as the Honda ventured inward, but a lovely stone house could be seen on the other side.

Midway through the bridge, John put the car in neutral and leaned toward his companion. "Welcome to the only covered bridge left in Ontario."

"Is it safe?" Karin asked, staring ahead at the dipping floor, then back at him, but in truth she was more concerned about the topsy-turvy effect his eyes had on her when they gave her a full measure of their warmth and light.

"It's been here for over a hundred years so far. In fact, it's been preserved as a historical site. We're lucky there are no tour buses here now."

"Are we?" she asked softly, feeling the familiar intensity building between them again.

"Yes, because I'm about to demonstrate why it's known as 'the kissing bridge.'"

His mouth approached hers and caught the smile waiting there in a sweet unhurried kiss... until a horn sounded behind them.

John waved friendly at the other driver as he pulled away. "I've always wanted to try that out," he said, grinning impishly.

"I was happy to oblige," Karin answered, feeling as if she'd been transported back to an innocence that had nothing to do with time.

John looked very pleased with himself as he pulled the car over to the side of the road. Karin marveled at the subtly growing change in him—she'd always been attracted to his unpretentious masculinity, but his newfound male confidence was additionally appealing to her.

"Can we stroll around a bit?" she asked, wistfully eyeing what looked to be an abandoned blacksmith's shop and the winding riverbank, dotted by sprawling willow trees.

John sighed. "Not today. We should be at the farm for a visit before the midday meal. In case we're not invited to stay."

She looked at him in surprise. "Didn't you tell them we were coming?"

"No."

"Oh." Tension rose inside her to match the faint creases that suddenly appeared on his face.

Soon the car was speeding along the highway again. They came to St. Jacob's, nestled valleylike at the bottom of a hill, home of a charming mix of craft and antique shops, country restaurants and guest houses. Many occupied the village's original buildings, including the mill, blacksmith's shop and general store. Hanging baskets of colorful flowers added a festive, summery flavor. Suddenly Karin remembered that the town was located near the Waterloo Farmers' Market, where she'd met, for the second time, the intriguing man beside her. That encounter seemed so long ago, but in reality only a couple of tempestuous months had passed, she realized with a pang.

Two quick turns later brought them out of the village and back onto rural expanses and near-deserted roads. Karin soon guessed that they had arrived at the Martin farmstead, because John unconsciously slowed the car well in advance of the distant buildings that were holding his attention. She gazed curiously ahead at the neat rows of budding apple trees, the wide grassed yard and the thriving garden. A large brick house, surrounded by an avocado-green fence and porch, seemed to sit harmoniously between earth and sky.

The car turned by a weathered sign that read, No Sunday Sale. As they drove down the long gravel driveway that led to the home and its outbuildings, Karin felt a strange peace and a vague familiarity, as if she'd been here before, which, of course, was ridiculous. Nevertheless, her apprehension eased.

They stepped out of the parked car and slowly looked around. "Nothing has changed," John murmured after a time. "I always loved the land, the old house. I just wanted something they could never give me."

"It *is* a lovely place...."

Then both their eyes jerked toward the sound of a screen door slamming. A young dark-haired woman, wearing a simple blue dress that hung just above her plain black shoes, took one look at them and let out a cry of disbelief. "John!" She ran forward and flung her arms around his neck.

His eyes closed briefly as he hugged her, then he drew back to study her beaming face. "Mary, you look wonderful. Don't tell me you're faring that much better without our daily spats?"

She grinned wickedly, turning so that her arm was still linked with his. "That's only part of the reason. The other part is that I'm to be married."

"But...to whom?" He looked as if the earth had fallen from his feet.

"Joshua Brubacher."

"But you hardly know him."

"Enough," she said willfully.

"He's only eighteen, younger than you...."

"Hush." She glanced back at the open window of the house. "He's here today. You'll see for yourself, John. Marriage will suit both Joshua and I just fine. And I'm not a child anymore." Suddenly she remembered the stranger standing next to John and looked shyly over at her.

It took John a moment or two to shift his mental gears. "This is Karin," he finally said.

With a detached awe, Mary's eyes took in the guest's pale yellow skirt, crisp short-sleeved blouse with its delicate lacing around the collar and the fine straps of her matching white sandals. "H'llo," she said uncertainly.

"Hello. I'm pleased to meet you, Mary." Karin smiled warmly, but did not force her welcome with an extended hand.

The screen door creaked open again, and three more people hesitantly emerged: a tall youth whose limbs had long outgrown the pants and shirt he wore; a thin elderly man who seemed lost within his baggy black clothes; and a rounded middle-aged woman who was hurriedly untying a soiled apron, beneath which she wore a fresh white one.

"Company's here," Mary said softly.

It was John who finally stepped forward. He nodded at Joshua, patted his grandfather on the shoulder, then took his mother's hands and kissed her on the cheek.

"How are you, Mother?" His voice was tight, his eyes searching hers.

"As well as can be," she replied, trying to be formal, dignified, but her eyes gave her away. They were shining with pure joy.

"Jacob, come out here," she called, inclining her head toward the closed door, releasing John's hands. "Your son has come to visit."

No one moved, and then what seemed like an eternity later, a chair scraped hard on the floor inside the house and footsteps approached.

An austere-faced Jacob Martin slowly exited and went to stand behind his wife, his hands buried in the pockets of his dark trousers.

"John," he acknowledged with cool civility.

"Hello."

"So you have not forgotten about us," his father said reproachfully, glancing with narrowed eyes at the parked car.

"No, of course not."

"Already, you look . . . different." Jacob's eyes squinted against the sun, eyeing John's longish hair, his unfamiliar new jeans and camel-colored shirt, his unmistakably thinner body.

"I *am* different, yet the same."

"Will you stay for the Sunday meal?" his mother suddenly asked, refusing to look at her husband, her face bright with expectancy.

John broke contact with his father's rigid, unsmiling gaze and grinned down at her. "I'd like that. Very much."

"And your guest?"

"Oh—I'm sorry." He brought Karin forward, looking at her apologetically for his unintentional neglect. "This is one of my new friends . . . Karin Sherwood."

"Hello," she murmured, feeling as if she were under a microscope as five pairs of eyes scrutinized her, nodding and mumbling greetings in varying degrees of loudness.

"Well, you both certainly look as if you could use a good meal," Erwin Martin bellowed with the forthrightness of age, his dark eyes twinkling in welcome.

Both Karin and John smiled at him.

"Now, at least Joshua won't be the only one under pressure to fatten up," Mary said, joining the group on the porch and standing beside her young fiancé.

"Isn't that what you try to do with the cattle?" John teased in the way he used to.

His mother shook her head, pretending to be distressed, her face creasing with affection. "The same old *boose boo*. Bad boy," she added for Karin's benefit, and everyone but

Jacob Martin chuckled as they were ushered into the big house.

Chairs were pulled up and places set at the long kitchen table for the unexpected guests. Whatever tension lingered seemed to be eased by the business of passing the staggering number of bowls and platters that suddenly appeared. Karin was glad that she'd come hungry. Just by trying a little of everything, her plate was soon heaped. There was schnitzel and spiced sausage, accompanied by pickled beets, sauerkraut, fresh bread and apple rings that had been schnitzed—dried and sliced then plumped with hot water, all to be washed down with homemade cider.

She was pleasantly surprised to see how much John was enjoying himself, despite his previous self-imposed estrangement and nervousness. But it would have been hard for anyone not to respond in kind to the heart-swelling, quiet feeling of togetherness that seemed to exist among the family members. It didn't matter that few questions were directed at her. She had been welcomed into the home as John's guest, and she was content to sit back, sample the delicious food and partake of the unfamiliar, almost foreign, aura of a real home.

Something about the kitchen itself added to the cozy atmosphere. She was fascinated by its cleanliness and simplicity, but there was nothing stark about its functionalism. The room radiated life, humanity, comfort. The warmth that came from the old stove was moderated by the fresh spring breeze from the open window; two tawny cats huddled together on the bare floor in a strip of sunlight; hats, aprons, jackets and capes hung on wall pegs, and boots sat on the floor, ready for use in the many facets of daily rural existence. Once, she caught John's eye as she stole looks around, and he seemed to be watching her with as much interest as she had in her surroundings.

When everyone had been served and started to eat, John asked to be filled in on all the news.

In lilting Pennsylvania Dutch accents, Mary and Anna Martin each tried to outdo the other with a firing of information.

"Samuel Snyder is recovering at home from the boar attack."

"Ten calves were born this spring—all healthy, already grazing in the pasture."

"Grandfather's skin rash reappeared, but cleared up after a week of treatment with Mrs. Reesor's herbal plaster...the same remedy that has been in their family for generations."

"The fields have all been harrowed and seeded, the garden planted..."

They seemed to be running out, when Mary exclaimed, "Oh, Elizabeth Snyder is engaged to one of Joshua's brothers."

John blinked twice as comprehension settled, then said, "I'm happy for her." He looked at Mary, then Joshua. "And I understand you two have also...added to the local gossip. When is the big event?"

Mary glanced shyly at Joshua, who suddenly flushed. "We'd like to wait until after harvesttime, the same as you did—" She stopped, and her eyes flew from John to Karin. "I'm sorry."

"Don't be," John said quickly.

"But we may have it sooner—in October," Mary continued, "so Joshua can be on hand during our own harvest."

John turned to the young man beside her. "You must be about eighteen now, Joshua?"

"That's r-right, sir." And the youth's method of addressing him, his formality and lack of confidence, made him seem even younger.

"Since Joshua is the third of five brothers, he won't inherit a farm of his own," Anna Martin cut in, "so we are very pleased that he will move in here and help your father."

Her voice had been void of any accusation toward John, but still the implication that his departure had caused a need for more assistance hung heavily in the suddenly quiet room.

"I don't need help," Jacob insisted, keeping his head low as he dug into a dripping mound of sauerkraut.

"But you do," Mary said. "You've been working so hard you've had trouble breathing sometimes, and you won't rest or see a doctor."

"No point in wasting the money—it's just a little congestion in the chest, left over from that hard winter."

"But surely it wouldn't hurt to check with a doctor," John interjected, concern etched on his face. "If you're worried about the cost, I'll—"

"I said there's no point," Jacob returned forcefully, the set of his jaw brooking no further discussion.

"And how do you like your...new job?" John's mother asked gently, slipping into her well-honed role as peacemaker between the two men.

John gave himself a shake before he could answer. "Fine." He glanced around the table. "We will never have the same ties as a family related by blood, but sometimes a special feeling is there among us, and I know I'm doing something . . . right in giving the boys the chance to experience it. One night comes to mind—the one they prepared their first dinner for some guests. I was so proud of them. Actually, it started out as Karin's idea."

All eyes turned toward her, taking her off guard. "Ideas are easy," she said swiftly. "The hardest part is to put them into action. John and his crew did a fine job of that, except for a slight delay at the beginning and somewhat of a miscalculation of quantities...."

"Minor technical difficulties," John elaborated, smiling with her.

The others all wore faintly curious expressions. Perhaps they were trying to fathom the world that John now lived in. Or maybe they were wondering what he had in common with this flaxen-haired woman who wore such modern clothes and surely knew secret ways to make her complexion, eyes and body so flawlessly beautiful.

"Not a day goes by that I don't face some seemingly insurmountable challenge, whether it's faulty plumbing or a runaway teenager," John felt compelled to try to explain to them. "Many times I've wondered what I'm doing there. But there have been many more times when it's been worth every aggravation."

Although his enthusiasm was tempered, something in his face prompted his mother to say softly, "It is good to see you happy, John. That's all I want for my children." Her eyes shifted to meet Mary's across the table in silent question, but her daughter looked away.

"We are all blessed with more than we realize," murmured Erwin Martin.

Already Karin knew that the stooped and shrunken-eyed figure at the head of the table spoke rarely but wisely, with a detached air of authority. Neither John nor his father, who were both restless, intense men, had achieved the calm acceptance with life that the elder Martin possessed.

She also saw that John was watching Mary closely as she pushed food around her plate, eating little. She acknowledged just how close he was to his younger sister, and more.

She also realized just how hard it had been for him to walk away from this family who loved each other with a quiet indomitable strength that was not without its painful edges.

Conscious of John's eyes on her, Mary stood abruptly and began to gather empty bowls and plates. "Do you also work at the same place as John, Karin?" she asked, unable to disguise her fascination with the attractive guest, her eyes lingering on the tricolor braided gold bracelet that Karin wore.

"No, I manage a woman's health and fitness center in downtown Kitchener."

"Oh.... Can anyone go?" She ignored her mother's anxious glance.

"On a trial visit or two, but after that you must pay a membership fee of several hundred dollars a year, if you decide to join."

"Don't you be getting any fancy ideas, Mary," Jacob Martin told her sternly.

"I was just curious." Haughtily, she walked toward the counter, her arms piled high with teetering dishes, and her mother joined her.

"Can I help?" Karin asked during the women's second trip.

"No, no," Anna Martin said brusquely before returning to the table with another stack of smaller, clay-glazed plates and an apple schnitz in which a creamy fruit filling was surrounded by a scalloplike arrangement of apple segments.

Karin soon learned that the most expected of her at this gathering was to keep eating. She obliged. "That was wonderful," she raved when she didn't have room for a single bite more. "Tell me, do you use recipes?"

Anna Martin looked appalled. "No, no. We just know from many times making."

Never in a million years would Karin admit that she hadn't even mastered a recipe for a supposedly no-fail pastry crust, or that she'd once caught her former roommates playing catch with the cookies they'd called raisin rocks....

While coffee was served, Anna went on to explain to her that she was always prepared for company—sometimes up to dozens of hungry mouths at harvesttime—with a well-stocked pantry and a cellar that stored hundreds of jars of preserves as well as pickled vegetables and meats. Karin, whose kitchen was torn apart on the rare occasions when she entertained—never more than a few people at one time—listened with heartfelt interest as Anna Martin reminisced about some of the other crowds she'd fed following barn raisings, funerals, weddings or Sunday service.

It was John who finally had to interrupt to tell Karin he wanted to show her around the farm before leaving. He insisted that Mary be allowed to temporarily abandon her kitchen duties so that she could join them. He even whisked his sister out of the room before she could include Joshua, who was clearly uncomfortable being left at the table with Jacob and Erwin Martin.

Once outside, John immediately headed past the driving shed toward the giant old barn. Karin followed closely behind with Mary by her side. All that she had time to notice in the yard was the seemingly never-ending neat piles of firewood, and she thought it was no wonder that John had developed such muscles in his chest and forearms, even if he'd helped chop only a fraction of that wood.

The powerful scent of livestock, manure and straw accosted Karin as soon as she entered the barn. Her nose automatically twitched in distaste.

Mary noticed and laughed. "Believe it or not, you get used to it."

"Really?" Karin countered skeptically.

John was well ahead of them, already inside a horse stall, patting and greeting the animal like a long-lost friend. "Hi, pal. How have you been? Ah, you are such a magnificent old boy, and I've missed you terribly." The horse nuzzled his hand, reciprocating John's affection.

"And who's this?" Karin asked, dubiously approaching the huge glossy creature.

"Meet Wicked," John said with unmistakable pride.

"Your alter ego?"

"Something like that," he admitted, grinning crookedly, and her heart turned over.

Mary reached out to stroke the animal's long neck. "I think he missed you, too. We all have...."

"And I've thought of you a lot." He wrapped his arm around her shoulders. "But what's all this about Joshua? Six months ago you wouldn't have looked twice at him. You even told me he was immature for his age."

Mary stiffened and went to pull away, but he held her firmly against him. "Well, things change, and that was before I knew him. He's very sweet, really. He's just shy, but he's getting better with me, and he'll improve with others, in time, once he knows them...."

"But Mary, *you* have to be one hundred percent sure about your own feelings. You have to love someone for the way they are." His eyes searched hers relentlessly.

"Joshua is a good farmer, and we need him around here. He will work hard and will make a good husband. I am sure of that."

"Marriage is an enormous step. It's... it's more than a manual convenience. It's for *life*, Mary. Father can hire the help he needs...."

"I know what I'm doing," she retorted stubbornly.

"Do you love him?"

She hesitated, glancing over at Karin, but out of a need for diversion or out of discomfort, Karin could not be sure. "Perhaps I should leave," Karin said quickly.

"It doesn't matter," Mary returned. "Nothing will change my decision. I know Joshua is fond of me, and he will take care of me and our children as the years go by. Our feelings will grow with time. That is enough...." She eased herself free from John and smiled reassuringly at him. "Don't worry."

Guilt was clearly written on John's face as he contemplated his role in his sister's premature engagement. "Promise me one thing."

"What?"

"Promise that you'll think about this marriage, and if you realize it's not what you want, you'll have the courage not to go through with it." His voice was tinged with emotion, his eyes boring into hers. "Promise?"

"Thanks for the blessing."

John said nothing, continuing to stare hard at her.

"Okay, I promise," she finally said hotly, then stepped back. "I should go rescue poor Joshua now. You know how hard it is to talk to Father and Grandfather." She picked up her skirt and brushed past them, flattening and crackling the straw that bedded the barn's floor as she hurried out.

"Well, that's that," John said wearily, idly stroking Wicked's smooth brown coat.

"She's a very determined young woman. A lot like her brother...."

"That obvious, is it? Come on, I want to show you the rest of the place, in some fresher air."

"I thought you'd never ask," Karin said with exaggerated relief, and they stepped outside.

With the same nostalgia and pride that he'd displayed
with Wicked, John led her around the various outbuildings—the silo, the chicken coop, the storage sheds—patiently answering all her questions. He pointed out the
many pieces of equipment that carried out the farm work
from spring cultivation to fall harvesting. He told her that
the Martins' only tractor was essential for certain heavy
tasks, such as plowing the soil, then discing the newly
worked ground in preparation for seeding, but an old
horse-drawn wagon was still used for sowing small grains.
Jacob Martin also owned his own rudimentary thrasher and
binder.

John explained that the farm only maintained one cash
crop—wheat, which was sold to a local mill for flour. The
rest of the land was used as forage. This year those fields
would yield corn, oats and barley to be planted together,
and a hay crop consisting of two kinds of grass—red clo-
ver and timothy—mixed with alfalfa.

If the land was kept sufficiently fertile by constant re-
seeding and crop rotation, the forage would feed the farm's
beef and dairy cattle and pigs, ideally with some of the crop
left over for resale. The amount of winter feed needed was
approximately two tons per cow, so proper management of
the land was essential just to stay self-sufficient in any one
year. Other weather and economic factors could also make
or break a farm's productivity, John added grimly.

Karin was fascinated by the glimpse into the inner work-
ings of a farm. Clearly it was not an easy life. They finished the tour by wandering toward the large vegetable and
herb garden that jutted into the front yard, protected on
one side by the house and on the other by a row of spruce
trees.

"This is my mother's beloved domain," John said, stooping to break off a tiny dark green leaf from one of the plants, sniffing it, then handing it to Karin.

The potent fragrance of mint assailed her as the warm breeze suddenly whipped her hair back from her face. Slowly she turned for a kaleidoscope view of the green-gold patches of field, the weathered gray barn and the sandy-colored brick home protected by tall emerald evergreens. Her eyes finally settled on John's darkly striking figure, even more imposing because of the elongated shadow that stretched from where he stood, feet slightly apart, hands on hips. "You seem such a part of all this—" her arm swept around "—this land, a home, those good people. Don't you ever think of what you left behind?"

"Of course I do. But I also think of what I've gained... and why I had to leave." He stooped to scoop up a handful of dirt, letting it fall from his fingers. "I love the earth, I marvel at the cycles of the seasons, but I don't want to be a farmer for the rest of my life. The earth doesn't live, breathe, cry, love, die, as people do. It's people I want to spend my days with. Not cattle or tractors or..." He stopped, began again. "Farming is a life of painstaking routine."

"But there's always people to work with. Your family—"

"I can't work with them permanently if we don't share the same goals... although I do regret how my choice has affected them." He reached for her hand, smiling sadly. "Come, we have been gone long enough." Their fingers touched, as warm as rocks heated by a steady sun. "Thank you for coming, Karin."

"I'm glad you asked me." She was blinking against the bright glare and thought she caught a strange look on his face before he turned abruptly and started walking back toward the house, still holding her by the hand.

He stopped by the green-painted front porch, rather than by the side kitchen door from which they'd exited before.

"Why don't you spend some time alone with them?" Karin suggested. "I'll wait here."

He looked toward the house, then back at her. "Are you sure you don't mind?"

"Not at all. It's so nice outside today." She sat down on the steps, stretching her legs out to the inviting sunshine.

"I won't be long," he said, his fingers brushing the top of her head as he passed.

Karin leaned back, closed her eyes and let time slip by as the sun's heat lulled her into a state of delicious drowsiness. *Why don't I do this more often?* she asked herself, her last coherent thought before a voice behind her brought her fully awake.

"I hate to disturb you," Anna Martin was saying, "but I want to give you this before you leave."

She was holding out a plate of raspberry pie, set in an open box. "Why, thank you," Karin said, surprised. She stood to accept it, gazing into the woman's keen dark eyes, John's eyes....

Anna Martin smoothed the folds of the apron she seemed to wear permanently over her printed dress, looked toward the empty yard, then back at Karin. "Is John as happy as he appears to be?" she asked softly.

"He's as happy as he lets himself be," Karin answered honestly.

Anna nodded, with a trace of sorrow in her eyes. "He is not easy on himself. We tried so hard to help him, but he would not let us. Perhaps it is better that he start over, but his father still will not see it...."

The door opened behind them and John appeared, taken aback to find them both there together.

"Look what your mother kindly brought for me," Karin hastened to say, holding out the pie.

"I was just about to tell her to save a few pieces for herself before you get at it," Anna Martin added.

John chuckled. "I wouldn't think of robbing Karin of her gift, unless of course, she *chooses* to share it with me, for which I will forever admire her."

"I'll think about it," Karin teased.

His eyes lingered on her, then he turned to his mother. "Thank you for a wonderful meal, but we must be going now." He took her arm as they all walked toward the driveway.

"You must come again soon—both of you."

"To return the plate...to be filled again, of course," John suggested, and they all smiled at his audacity.

Karin stepped forward. "Thank you for a lovely meal and visit," she said, her eyes meeting the other woman's as their hands clasped. Impulsively she bent to kiss Anna Martin on the cheek, the affection she so often suppressed rising to the surface.

John was watching the two of them until his eyes were drawn solely to Karin's face. The sun caught her golden-colored hair, her eyes sparkled like precious gems, and the vision etched itself on his consciousness, becoming part of everything that was Karin Sherwood to him.

In the startling clarity of the moment, he realized a fundamental truth—he loved her. His chest constricted with a strange heaviness. He'd been heading toward this moment since he'd met her. Yes, he loved her. And the knowledge was both simple and complex at the same time, as invisible and elusive as the wind, yet capable of a power he could barely fathom.

Seconds passed in slow, vivid motion, and then a low cry sounded from behind. Turning, John saw his father leaning against the barn door, his face ashen, his body half crumpled over.

John bolted forward, knowing something was terribly wrong.

CHAPTER TWELVE

JOHN SLOWLY AWOKE after the deepest sleep he'd had in many weeks. In no hurry to lose the languor of a good rest, he burrowed into the pillow he'd curled up around his head.

Then suddenly his eyes jerked open and he rolled over onto his back. He was remembering everything: the hospital; his father hooked up to all those wires and machines; the doctor's grave but reassuring words.... Jacob Martin had had a mild heart attack; his prognosis for recovery was good, provided he rested for the next few months and restrained from any strenuous physical activity.

John had visited the farm several times while his father recuperated in the hospital. Fellow Mennonite neighbors and relatives were pitching in to do the necessary chores, but their own summer workload was demanding, too—weeding and spraying fields, caring for livestock, preparing for the harvest of the early crops....

John helped out whenever he had a few hours to spare, but he could not shake the feeling that his contribution was inadequate. Both Mary and his mother were exhausted, trying to keep up their share of the daily tasks as well as spend time at the hospital. But, worst of all, his father was worrying about the maintenance of his beloved farm, and worrying was the last thing he should be doing.

John was torn. He couldn't just ignore his own job and the other people relying on him. His reports were long overdue, and he was poorly prepared for the regular in-service meeting that he had to attend tomorrow. Plus, he felt guilty that Henry had taken on more than his share of the burden at Greenbank, so he'd promised to do some shopping and banking today. Somehow he also had to fit in spraying the apple orchard at the farm, which had to be done every two weeks.

At the back of his mind was the realization that he had spoken to Karin only a few times on the phone since their day in the country, and they'd mainly talked about his father's condition. Between his demanding schedule and hers, they just could not seem to make room for each other. Or maybe there were more complex reasons keeping them apart that neither was ready to face. For his part, John knew that his love for Karin was like a seed of truth to be cherished inside, to be turned over and examined again and again. He needed time to absorb the knowledge, to trust in it before acting on it. The time was not right now, and sometimes he wondered if it would ever be....

He swung his legs out of bed and hastily performed his morning rituals, trying to figure out how on earth he was going to accomplish everything that was expected of him today.

"YOU'RE WEARING YOURSELF OUT, John," Henry said the next day. They were reviewing their notes before the group meeting that kept their support personnel updated on the happenings at the home and gave themselves a chance to raise any problems for discussion.

"Don't worry, it's only temporary. I can manage."

Henry did not look convinced. "But your father is going to be laid up most of the summer and fall, isn't he? In the meantime, you are going to be run ragged trying to be everything to everybody."

"You've been very supportive, Henry, and I can't tell you how much I appreciate that."

"In many ways you're lucky your family has accepted your new life. I wish mine had been so accommodating...." Henry rarely spoke of his estrangement from his own Mennonite family, an even more conservative group than John's was, but when he did it was with a trace of lingering pain.

"Perhaps in time..." But Henry just shrugged disbelievingly. John's gaze was sympathetic as he went on, "I want you to know that my work here won't suffer, if that's what you're concerned about. The boys are still my top priority."

"Look, I understand how difficult it can be juggling priorities. That's why I'm going to suggest a possible remedy."

John immediately rallied his defenses in case Henry was going to relieve him of his duties at Greenbank.

"School's out in a week. Why don't you take Brad and Karl with you to the farm to help out? They might get a kick out of it. I can manage Jordan and Phil on my own. In fact, I've been invited to a friend's cottage, and there's only enough room for three of us, at the most..."

"Karl and Brad will be delighted they have to work, instead," John said dryly, trying to be fair, but hope flared at his colleague's unexpected proposal.

Henry shrugged. "Why don't you ask them? They might surprise you. Karl's always game for a lark, and I know he's disappointed since his father decided not to take him for the summer. And Brad, well, unfortunately I don't think he'll really care one way or another."

Shadows crossed both their faces as they contemplated how Brad had changed after his runaway crisis, hiding behind barriers that no one could penetrate. His self-image had never been lower, his depression never more apparent.

"We could certainly use more help at the farm, and I know my father hates to overburden his neighbors...." The idea was slowly growing more feasible to John.

"So we'll present our case at the meeting today," Henry said, smiling with confidence. "I think the arrangement could work out just fine for everybody."

TWO WEEKS LATER, his prophecy was already becoming self-fulfilling. Approval had come from all Greenbank superiors and colleagues; Jacob Martin, home from the hospital, had begrudgingly agreed to accept help from strangers; Karl had jumped at the chance to "get back to nature"; and, as expected, Brad had complied indifferently.

On a typical day, John and his two charges arrived at the farm just after an early breakfast. One of their first duties was to hook up each of the five dairy cows to the electrical milking devices, clean out their stalls, then proceed with whatever field or garden work was most pressing.

Jacob Martin, who was forbidden to do even light manual labor, hovered around the barn and yard, saying little. He did not even try to hide his resentment at his uncustomary inactivity.

On a hot and humid July morning, John stopped at the barn door to tell the boys the horse-drawn wagons were ready to pick up the bundles of wheat that had dried out in the field during the past weeks. Since the wheat crop had been sown the previous fall, it was able to be harvested during the summer months. What he saw inside the barn made him stop in his tracks.

Jacob Martin was showing the two boys how to milk manually. The black-and-white holstein, tied safely to a post, seemed to be patiently enduring the demonstration. "If those machines ever break down, every pair of hands on a farm has to know how to take over," Jacob was saying. "There's a knack to it, but once you learn it, you'll never forget it."

"Like riding a bicycle," Karl murmured, and Jacob just shrugged.

"You can't do it halfheartedly, as if you're afraid of her. You've got to show her you mean business. Nip at the top here and squeeze downward, as firmly as you can. There she goes."

Under Jacob's able hands a steady stream of milk squirted from the animal's teats into the waiting pail. "Here, you take over," he said to Brad, who was watching the procedure with a mixed look of distaste and fascination.

The older man knelt beside him as Brad squatted on the stool and gingerly touched the animal's udder.

"Look, she's got more reason to be afraid of you than the other way around. Start squeezing hard before she realizes how green you are."

Brad bit his lip in concentration and proceeded to vigorously move his hands up and down as he'd been shown.

"That's it," Jacob said with more animation than he'd displayed in a long time.

"Hey, this isn't so bad," Brad muttered, his eyes gleaming as he watched the pail slowly filling.

Jacob glanced over at Karl. "You start cleaning the next one, then you can have your turn."

Not wanting to be outdone by Brad's instant success, Karl quickly applied the disinfectant onto the cow and immediately began to pump away with determined gusto. The animal shifted on her feet and kicked to the side, but no milk dropped into the empty pail. Karl cursed.

"Hey, hey—have a little more patience. And be firm, but not too firm," Jacob added, clucking.

Karl grinned. "Gotcha. Come on, baby." He tried again, and this time the animal cooperated, except that the milk was missing the bucket by an inch or so. Karl maneuvered the pail closer with his foot, but knocked it over and spilled the first results of his efforts. "No problem," he bit out, starting over.

"You've got no class, Cross," Brad told him gloatingly, his face shining as he finished filling his bucket without a hitch.

"I'm working on it ... I'm working on it.... " Karl did not dare to look up, but he, too, was clearly enjoying himself.

"Performed like two old pros," John said, finally joining the group.

"Not bad," Jacob agreed, "considering that they didn't have the advantage you had, John. You could milk a cow before you could tie your own shoes."

John met his father's eyes and thought of all the times the two had worked side by side in the barn. But then he noticed his father's unsoiled white shirt, and he remembered how much had changed....

"I could really get into this," Karl was saying.

"Well, you better hurry up," John said, "because we've got a lot more work ahead of us. This is kid's stuff compared to tilling the rows of corn and loading the bales of wheat."

"Slave driver," Brad accused, but he was smiling, and John could not recall the last time he'd seen that young face so carefree.

"Think of the muscles we'll have by the end of the summer. We'll have to hang out at the beaches to drive the chicks crazy and—'' Karl stopped, glancing over at Jacob Martin.

"You better watch what you're doing, lad," Jacob said dryly as Karl's pant leg slowly whitened with splattered milk.

Brad laughed heartily. "Like I said, no class."

"Everything's under control," Karl countered good-naturedly.

And on this bright and clear summer's morning, John thought, he was indeed right.

As the days passed the boys seemed to thrive in the farm environment. Wearing old baseball caps and T-shirts, they developed distinctive farmers' tans on the V of their necks, the tips of their ears and their lower arms. They devoured every last morsel of the delicious meals Anna and Mary prepared for them. At first, Karl had tried flirting with the quiet, rosy-cheeked Mary, but he had swiftly interpreted the warning looks shot at him by the Martin men. Brad watched Mary a lot, with a kind of awe, but he never spoke to her.

Rarely did the boys complain about the hard physical labor. Instead, they were filled with questions about the maintenance of the farm. Caught up in the novelty of the experience, Karl was mildly interested—the simplest answers satisfied his curiosity. But it was Brad who wanted to know everything, from the basics of agriculture to the technological advances in the industry. Whenever the men relaxed under the shade of the big maple tree by the house, he fired question after question, not only at John, but at Jacob and Erwin Martin, who usually joined them outdoors for the noon meal. He wanted to know which crop had the highest yield per acre. He asked the men to explain how some of the equipment he'd spotted on more modern, neighboring farms worked. He queried how different weather conditions affected the results of the plowing, sowing and harvesting, and on and on. His memory was excellent, his mind highly analytical, and soon *he* was telling *them* about facts he'd learned from his nightly reading of the library books he'd been determined to borrow.

He became opinionated enough to challenge Jacob Martin's insistence on keeping only one tractor, supplemented by a plodding horse-drawn wagon. "You need an extra tractor, Mr. Martin," he suddenly stated one day. "Both could be running in hay-making season—there's going to be a heck of a lot of work in cutting, conditioning, raking and baling the hay. Plus, in the spring, it would be so much easier to have two tractors, one for harrowing, one for discing. You could drive one . . . and that neighbor boy you said was going to help you next year could drive the other."

Buying an additional tractor was a subject that John had tackled numerous times himself, but he had never made any headway with his unbending father. To John's surprise, though, Jacob did not take offense to Brad's know-it-all, pushy approach. He was calmly chewing an apple and studying the teenager pensively. Maybe he didn't want to dampen Brad's budding enthusiasm, John reasoned.

But true to form, Jacob repeated the worn arguments he'd used many times before. "My way has worked fine since I can remember. Why change for change's sake?"

The question seemed absurd to Brad. "'Cause it'll make everything so much easier!"

"Besides, new equipment costs money. I already had to use a good portion of my savings for medical bills."

"Banks give loans and you could probably get a good deal on a used tractor. And think how much your time and health is worth."

"God didn't intend us to sit around and do nothing," Jacob retorted, bitterness lacing his voice. "Next year I'll be able to work ... really work again."

Brad and John exchanged worried looks. "You should take things easier, Mr. Martin. An extra tractor would help," the youth said quietly.

Jacob set down his apple core and gazed out at the tall rows of golden corn in the adjacent field, his eyes narrowed. "'Should' and 'can't' are two different matters."

"Would your church object? Is that it?" Brad persisted. "The Brubachers have two tractors, plus a seed hopper and a spinner, and they're Old Order, too, aren't they?"

Jacob nodded, giving the boy a shrewd look. "Their farm is much larger than mine.... The Brubacher sons are taking over."

"Wouldn't hurt to think about it, at least ... for next year."

"Are you this bossy with your own father, young man?" Jacob asked with a trace of tolerant amusement.

John glanced at him sharply, not only because he'd rarely heard his father use such a mellow tone during similar discussions, but because he suddenly wished he'd told his parent more about the boys' backgrounds. All he'd said was that the family situations varied, and Jacob had asked no further questions.

"I've never met my father. And I don't think my mother even knew who he was. At least that's what the agency tells me, and I haven't seen my mom since I was a kid, so I can't check with her."

He spoke matter-of-factly, without anger, and the moment seemed to pass as naturally as a cloud crossed the path of the sun, then moved on.

"Well, maybe I won't let all that bossiness go to waste," Jacob said slowly. "I'll mull over your advice."

"Good," Brad murmured, biting into his own apple with a self-satisfied smile on his face.

AS KARIN DROVE down the long driveway, her stomach suddenly knotted tightly. When she'd made the impulsive decision to visit the Martin farm to return Anna's pie plate and to check on Jacob's progress, she had expected to feel slightly awkward, but not this nervous.

Was her trepidation so strong because she hadn't seen John in more than a month and she might run into him today? Weeks ago, she'd bumped into Henry at the Waterloo market. He'd been stocking up on supplies for a cottage vacation, and he'd told her that John was still spending most of his time helping out at the farm with Brad and Karl. At first she hadn't minded that they couldn't be together—she'd been as busy as John—but more importantly, she needed to take things slowly with him. Yet she'd felt as if she'd been suspended in midair since she'd last been with him. The need to see him again had grown into a gnawing obsession.

Several male bodies were gathered around the maple tree in various reclining positions as she pulled up, feeling like an invader into their cozy circle. But it was too late to turn around. All eyes were on her as she stepped out of the car, cool looking in a simple blue sundress. Bravely she called out, "H'llo."

John stood and came toward her, his face sun browned, his hair tousled, his clothes earth stained and damp with perspiration, lending him an aura of rugged virility. "Why...hello, Karin."

Never had the familiar greeting carried with it such a host of turbulent messages to her senses and emotions. "I just stopped by for a moment to, ah, return your mother's plate, for one thing. I don't want to keep you from your work."

"Work! We don't work much around here, do we, guys?" John said mockingly, looking back at his father, Brad and Karl. "We just lounge around all day, following the shade, don't we?"

"Sure," drawled Karl. "These calluses are just figments of my imagination."

"Spoken like a true city slicker," Brad said lightly, and Karin thought she'd never seen him so relaxed looking.

John took her by the elbow and led her toward the group. "How are you feeling, Mr. Martin?" she asked politely.

"Can't complain."

"He's a tough supervisor," John said on a teasing note.

"Someone has to keep an eye on you fellas," Jacob answered, resisting the smile that tugged at the corners of his lips.

Karin could hardly believe the different vibrations between the two men, compared to the tension that had been present at her first visit.

"You're not working today?" John asked. Although the question was casual, there was nothing casual in the way his eyes held hers.

"I took the afternoon off. I decided I haven't been getting enough natural vitamin C." She stretched one arm out to the sun and did not notice John's sharp intake of breath.

The door off the kitchen opened then and Mary emerged, wearing a wide-brimmed bonnet and carrying a few baskets. "Hi," she said to Karin, smiling a warm welcome.

Karin smiled back. "Hi. How are you, Mary?"

"Fine."

"And Joshua? Is he here?" she added, looking around.

"No, he's back working at his own place, since we have plenty of help around here."

"His own father is likely getting the most from him before October—isn't that when the big day is?"

Mary nodded, suddenly self-conscious.

"What happens in October?" Brad asked.

"Mary intends to marry Joshua Brubacher," John said quietly.

Brad failed to hide his surprise. "The kid next door?"

"Yes."

"Oh. No one told us." He couldn't stop staring at Mary in amazement.

Karl, too, looked taken aback. "How old are you, Mary?"

"Nineteen," she replied, glancing down, her cheeks pink. Clearly she was uncomfortable being the center of attention.

"Nineteen, eh?" he repeated. "Wow, these days that's kinda—"

"It's *our* way," Mary said shakily before he could finish his sentence, raising her eyes to meet his. "Excuse me, I've got to . . . pick some lettuce and peas for dinner."

"If she has time, maybe Karin would like to stay and help you," John blurted out.

The two women looked at each other. Karin spoke first. "Sure, that is, if you could use the help."

"Yes—I'd like that."

Karin handed the plate to John. "Is your mother around? I should thank her for the pie first."

"She's at a friend's for the afternoon. I'll tell her."

But his eyes were windows to another more intimate message. Something powerful passed between them, wordless but unmistakable. She saw something there that she did not understand, a private dilemma he did not want her to comprehend. Its intensity frightened her, because she sensed it was deeply connected to her.

"Okay. See you later." She turned quickly and felt his gaze pinpointed on her as she walked with Mary toward the garden.

They hadn't been working long together when the heat of the sun's rays bearing down on her became too much for Karin. Mary disappeared and returned with an old straw hat and shirt to cover Karin's exposed face and shoulders.

As they continued picking vegetables, side by side, the two chatted pleasantly. Mary never seemed to tire of hearing about the world Karin inhabited—particularly the club and the faraway places she'd traveled to, but she seemed to accept that she would never be a part of such a world. In turn, the young Mennonite woman answered all of Karin's questions about her own life. Karin also subtly managed to gain an accurate picture of just how busy John had been during the past few weeks.

She didn't say goodbye to him, because he was working in the fields when she left, but Mary invited her back to help in the garden anytime she wanted. So Karin took to dropping by for the occasional visit during the course of the next few weeks....

Sometimes she saw John, but they were never alone. Most often she just sat with Mary and Anna Martin, surprised that they all found enough in common to talk about. But they did somehow. Karin was keen to learn how to cook some of the delicious food she'd sampled at the farm. Although the two Mennonite women kept no written recipes, they gladly estimated measurements for Karin, who took careful notes.

Anna Martin loved to reminisce about her children's early years: their home births attended by a Mennonite midwife; the time John sprained his ankle skiing from the back of a friend's buggy on a snowy winter day; the lively baseball games played by many families together after their big Sunday meals; John's frequent truancy on sunny days from the Mennonite School he'd attended until he was fourteen.

Karin was a willing audience, fascinated by the simple joys and close ties within the Mennonite community. She knew she would always be an outsider to this family, but she grew to feel more comfortable with them while respecting the many differences between her life and theirs.

And lately she'd needed some diversion to ward off a nagging feeling of depression. Strangely the ''low'' had hit her just after she'd reached her July quota, a few days before her deadline. She'd put on a good show in front of Cindy and the rest of the staff. They'd all celebrated heartily with a bottle of champagne. But when Karin had sat alone in her apartment later that night, she had finally admitted to herself how anticlimactic the news was. She'd convinced herself that the feeling was only a temporary one; it was the calm after the storm of hard work she'd put herself through in order to attain her goal. And being at the farm did seem to help. She always left in better spirits than when she'd arrived, as if some of the Martin women's tenacity and serenity rubbed off on her.

She told herself she kept returning because of the uplifting female companionship and the fresh air, a pleasant break from the air-conditioned club. But every time she caught a glimpse of John or exchanged a few words with him, she knew she was only fooling herself if she didn't admit he was part of the reason, too. Never would she be indifferent to this man. Yet, strangely, she deliberately avoided being alone with him—and he seemed to be doing the same with her, as if they both needed this unpressured interlude.

JOHN AND BRAD had spent all morning working the field of mixed grasses and legumes. The process of haymaking was a familiar one to John. Riding the tractor, he ran through row after row of the forage crop with the binder, which scooped the cut sheaves off the ground and tied them in bundles. Brad followed and arranged groups of ten bundles—stooks, as they were called—to dry out. After about a week, depending on the weather, the stooks would be hauled to the barn to be fed into the threshing machine that separated the grain from the straw.

At midmorning the two stopped to quench their thirst from the water jugs they carried. Thankfully, the humidity of mid-July had passed, but the temperatures had risen even higher during the past week. Their soaked shirts clung to them like a second skin as they sat cross-legged in the lone patch of shade offered by the tractor.

"Phew! I'm beat. Karl's dad couldn't have picked a better day to take him to Ontario Place—it's always cooler by the lake." Brad drank greedily straight from the jug, then splashed his flushed face.

"It would be a lot easier on all of us if this heat spell would break."

"What I wouldn't give for a cold beer right now...."

John wasn't naive enough to think that Brad or any of the boys had not tried beer, but alcoholic beverages were not permitted at Greenbank. It was the first time, though, that Brad had ever mentioned drinking in front of him. He merely smiled at the youth's harmless wish.

"Your old man ever let you have a beer while you were working on days like this—or aren't Mennonites allowed to drink?"

"Sure, in moderation...usually at social occasions. But I never acquired a taste for my father's homemade brew."

"He really makes his own?"

John nodded, cringing in memory of the bitter flavor. "And whiskey. He keeps the kegs down in the cellar. I remember he especially likes a shot to warm the bones, or so he claimed, before going to bed on winter nights."

"You really think he's going to be okay...physically?"

John took a swig of water from his own container. "As long as he paces himself, not only now, but down the road, too. He's not a man who likes to be idle."

"I noticed...."

"He's worked hard all his life, so I know it's difficult for him to suddenly change. Farming is ingrained in him, too. He misses it."

"I can see how it can grow on you, get into your blood." Brad hesitated, then added, "Actually, I never thought I'd like it here as much as I do, not when I could have been lazing around the lake with Henry."

"You really don't mind being here, instead?"

"No..."

"You've been a great help to all of us. And you never know, what you've learned here might come in handy with future jobs, even a career direction," John suggested.

"Career? I'm lucky if I can get by one day at a time. It's mind-boggling to think in terms of something so...lifelong, so permanent."

"We all need goals, Brad, and you're no different than everyone else."

"Why set a goal if you doubt whether you'll ever reach it?"

John stared off at the field they'd been working on, at the sun-bleached stalks that were standing upright in neat bundles. "Sometimes you look at everything that's ahead of you, and you think you'll never get through it, but if you stick with it, step-by-step, somehow it all gets done. You can even get over something that's disturbing you the same way. That's how I grew to accept my wife's death two years ago.''

"You were married?"

John nodded, crackling a long blade of grass between his fingers.

"What did she die of?"

"Cancer."

"Oh." Brad swallowed. "You miss having a wife?"

"Sometimes," he answered truthfully.

"You ever wish you had any kids?"

"Sometimes," John admitted, and felt a return of a sadness he had not acknowledged in a long time. He still longed to be a father, but he knew that was not likely to come about. It was yet another of the sacrifices he was prepared to make in order to protect his new course of freedom.

"You can always marry again."

He shook his head in automatic denial. "For the first time in my life, I'm on my own, and I like it, I really do. Besides, I don't think a woman could fit into all my plans, or that it would be right to expect anyone to try. At least not for a long, long time."

"Not even Karin?"

John threw him a wary, assessing glance. "Especially not Karin."

"She's a nice lady."

"Hmm...." His voice trailed off, and the only sound came intermittently from some well-hidden crickets.

Brad cleared his throat. "There was a girl I liked...at school. Amanda. You asked me about her once."

"I remember," John said as casually as he could.

"I was really hung up on her...in a physical way, I guess you'd call it. I *thought* she kind of felt the same way about me. Anyway, I even got up the nerve to ask her out." He let out a low, scornful sound. "She shot me down pretty quickly. Told me she liked me, but she would never be seen with someone like me. And her parents would freak out if they ever found out. She didn't have to say what she meant about me, 'cause I knew. Someone from Greenbank. Someone who's all screwed up, who's been kicked out of lots of different homes, a loser...."

"And you believed her?"

"Yeah, that night I did. That was the night I tried to run. I just went crazy. I made it out to the highway, but no one would pick me up. I knew I'd have to spend the night somewhere, so I started walking, toward the city. I just kept walking until I was back at Greenbank. By that point it didn't matter where I was."

"We're all glad you came back."

Brad looked away self-consciously, a faraway expression in his eyes. "For a long time, I hated Amanda, hated myself, the person she saw, the person I was, everyone who tried to interfere. I couldn't make myself even talk about it." He shot a glance at John, who was listening with a steady gaze and no intention of interrupting. Brad did not speak for several minutes, staring off at field and sky.

"Something weird has been happening lately," he finally admitted quietly. "I just feel...stronger. Some days, when I've been working like crazy or just lying around after lunch, watching a bird or something, I get this feeling that maybe, just maybe, *anything* is possible... that I can be better than everyone expects, even better than I expect from myself. You tried telling me that once, and I think I finally clued in to what you meant."

"I still think you're going to do just fine, Brad. I really do. If you believe in yourself."

A haunted look returned to the youth's face, and he struggled to find the right words. "And then there're times—scary times—when I can't help thinking…I mean, what if something happens to shake me up again, to make me go crazy, like before?''

John drew a deep breath. ''You have to meet those kinds of things head-on, not run from them anymore. Then *you* will be in control. I guarantee it.''

''Yeah?'' Brad looked down, bit his lip and said nothing more.

The silence that fell became an unstrained one. After a while they stood to resume their work, and John was aware of something different between them, a new feeling of undemanding companionship.

CHAPTER THIRTEEN

KARIN STOOD ON THE BRIDGE that spanned the Conestogo as she watched the changing hues of the sunset—soft streaks in deepening pinks, peaches and mauves that stretched over the horizon, as if freshly spilled from an artist's palette.

Her mind traveled back to the first time she'd stood on this same bridge, although in this stifling July heat it was hard to imagine that cold wintry afternoon. She thought of the optimism she'd felt then about her new life in Kitchener—the challenge of opening her own club, the adventure of exploring a new city and the excitement of meeting new people. She remembered how determined she had been to cure the emptiness buried deep within her. Finally she faced why she was here again.

She wanted to recapture that sense of anticipation, wonder, hope—desperately. As much as she'd tried to convince herself otherwise, the anticlimactic feeling she'd experienced after she'd met her quota had not disappeared. Her condition had not proven to be temporary. Not only had it persisted, but it was starting to grow to frightful proportions.

Although she was still responsible for maintaining the club and adding to the membership, the pressure was off her, and she'd lost the sense of challenge that had been driving her. And she couldn't help but wonder if more than that was at the root of her bleakness—some kind of inner deficiency that made it impossible for her to ever be happy.

Her visits to the farm had made it easier for her to avoid facing what was eating at her, but her time there also aggravated another set of problems—all the unresolved emotions that John Martin released in her. By seeing him often, she had grown more and more obsessed with him. Slowly the knowledge had crept through her that if she was to release the tenuous hold she'd been enforcing on the relationship for the past several weeks, she'd be completely enslaved by her obsession. She could not let that happen—something had to change. She deliberately hadn't been to the farm in a week.

She suddenly decided to walk along the riverbank, as she had done once before so long ago. Tall dry grass scratched her bare legs until she came to the path, now trampled to a sandy-brown base instead of a snow-white one. A mosquito landed on her arm, and she slapped it away. In her cotton T-shirt and shorts, she was easy prey. She figured she had about twenty minutes before twilight arrived—and an onslaught of hungry mosquitoes really struck.

She came to the place where she'd met John, near the black walnut tree. Her steps slowed. She remembered what John had told her about the tree signifying fertility to the Mennonites, and in its leafy greenness that was easier to believe than when it had been bare and snow covered.

Karin climbed the bank toward the tree, drawn to it. From her new vantage point, she watched the sky's fading lights play optical tricks on the river waters, and she tried to become her own best friend again.

THE SUNSET WAS SPECTACULAR that evening—a pastel-colored panorama, and John felt a strong desire to watch it by the river. But after a day spent threshing in the barn,

his body was too bone tired to walk there. He heard a peal
of laughter from the direction of the garden. Karl was over
helping the women, who preferred to work outdoors during the cooler evening hours. And Brad was fast asleep in
the new hammock that swung below the maple tree. John
had purchased it for his father, who took his afternoon nap
there, hating to be confined indoors.

Slowly John wandered through the barnyard and sat on
the fence of the empty corral. Unbidden came a yearning
to have Karin by his side, sharing the peace and soft fieri-
ness of the setting sun.

Maybe he felt her absence more because she hadn't been
to the farm for a while. He'd grown accustomed to seeing
her around, even though they hadn't had much chance to
be alone. Whenever an opportunity loomed near, Karin
had been like a skittish colt—unapproachable. He supposed he could have tried harder himself, but he'd needed
the time apart from her, too, for reasons he finally forced
himself to examine.

Since he'd been working at the farm, his old and new
lives seemed to be meshing. He felt more harmony than he
had in a long time. But he was working there out of loyalty
to his family in a time of crisis, not for his own sake, and
he would have to leave again soon. As far as he knew,
Henry's wife was still returning in October, although Henry
had only given him vague answers when he had tried to get
an exact date from him. Halfheartedly, John had sent out
a few applications for other jobs. Eventually he would have
to investigate them all further and arrange interviews, but
he simply had not had the time yet.

Most likely he would find a group home in another city,
and how was Karin going to fit into his life then? he suddenly wondered. If they both *wanted* to be together, it
wasn't an impossible situation. He could not deny that he

wanted to continue seeing her. He loved her. Strangely he knew that would never change, even though her feelings for him were a mystery. She was unpredictable, giving herself to him physically but always holding back a deeper part of herself—yet he couldn't fault her for that emotional caution, given his own.

All love needed a foundation on which to grow, he had always believed, so how could they build on a base that had a habit of shifting? He valued his freedom above anything else, and that would undoubtedly stand in the way of a permanent relationship with her. For her part, Karin had admitted that she'd led a nomadic life, that she *needed* frequent change, that her stint at the club in Kitchener was probably only temporary. So even if he tried to hold her back, to keep her close to wherever he lived, she would likely resent him for it.

And how long would she be content with what he could offer her—a periodic relationship that would likely be a long-distance one? His schedule would always be erratic. He knew he wanted to continue working in group homes. The hours were long and demanding, whether he had live-in privileges or joined a staff-operated-type home that involved shift work.

Sighing, he wondered where she was tonight...he knew so little about her existence apart from him. Two people's lives were certainly more complex than the simple beat of love or the peculiar chemistry that drew two lonely spirits together, he thought....

"You look as dog tired as the boy over there." His father was suddenly standing below him, one arm against the weathered fence rail.

"Oh...I didn't hear you coming up. I was...just watching the sunset."

"Looked as if you were doing more than that—trying to figure out what exactly *made* it set, maybe?"

"Just thinking about a few things...."

"You ever think of staying on here?" Jacob asked in a casual tone that was clearly forced.

John answered gently. "No.... I hope to be moving to a new group home once Henry's wife returns." He could see his father's fingers tighten on the rail ever so slightly.

"Thought I'd ask, anyway."

"That's okay."

Jacob drew a deep breath, then said gruffly, "I want to thank you for coming back when we needed you. I—" His voice thickened and he cleared his throat. "I don't know how we would have managed."

"You don't have to thank me. I ... wanted to help out. I'll always do what I can for you, Father. Sometimes that won't be easy, depending on my job, where I'm located...."

"No matter. By the fall, we'll be in better shape. Joshua will be around and I'll be my old self."

John slid off the fence and stood next to his father, who looked as robust as ever, but he could not forget that he tired more quickly. "You *are* going to take things a little easier, aren't you?"

"Sure...." But there was a familiar stubborn defiance in his voice and something else on his mind. "You know," Jacob began slowly, "you do have a way with those two boys. Maybe it's not such a bad idea that you're doing what you're doing with them ... and the others." He glanced sideways at John. "You can bring any of the lads around here anytime, down the road ... we can always use extra help, and it doesn't hurt them to know a little about God's earth."

"Thank you," John said gravely, deeply moved by his father's words, sensing how difficult it had been for him to utter them. He found himself stepping forward to embrace him.

They slapped each other on the back, then drew back to survey the other. Their half smiles carried no trace of awkwardness, despite the rare show of demonstrativeness between them.

Together they turned to watch the twilight sky.

"SIX TICKETS! How on earth did you get six seats behind home plate to a Blue Jays/Yankees game?"

"Corporate connections," Henry replied gloatingly.

John called his bluff. "How did you really get them?" He didn't know much about professional baseball, but he had learned enough to realize that tickets like those to a game between the two popular teams were at a premium.

Henry threw up his hands. "Okay, steal my big moment of glory. Karl's father coughed them up somehow—after he'd informed the agency he couldn't possibly take Karl back this year. Seems he's going to be spending a lot of time developing international markets and traveling to them. Doesn't want a kid tagging along. There's nothing we or the agency can do."

"Hmm. . . . How's Karl taking it?"

"Fine, considering. Actually, I think he prefers living here than with his dad. Told me he'd be back into drugs for sure if he had to cope with that 'basket case' every day, as he put it. And I gather the stepmother is out of the picture now. Anyway, it's good to see you, John. We have a lot more catching up to do."

"Yes. . . ." John had been surprised to find Henry at Greenbank when he'd arrived there with the boys earlier that evening. During one of his brief and infrequent phone calls to his colleague, Henry might have mentioned his date of return, but the days had started to blur together for John, and he had not remembered it. "First, tell me how you all enjoyed the cottage."

"Great, although we did have a few guilty moments by the lake during that heat spell when we thought about you three slugging it out at the farm. But so far Brad and Karl have only had good things to say about it."

"They're real troopers . . . a big help."

"And Brad?"

Briefly John filled him in on how much the youth had opened up. "I think he's getting a grip on himself, finding some direction. . . ."

"Good, good. We'll talk more later. For now, I need to know whether you can make the ball game in T.O. Thursday night. Thought we'd also take the guys out to the Spaghetti Factory for dinner beforehand."

John didn't have the heart to tell his colleague, who had been incredibly resilient about his stint at the farm, that he was in the middle of threshing and that he should be using every available nonsleeping hour. He also knew that both of them would be needed to supervise the boys on an out-of-town excursion. "Of course, I can make it. Sure."

Henry was not fooled. "But it's a bad time?" he asked quietly.

"One night won't make a big difference. Count on me to be there."

"In case you were tied up, I came up with a contingency plan. Maybe Karin would like to come along. The fellows tell me she's been out to the farm a fair bit. They seem to like her."

"Yes," John murmured, thrown off balance by Henry's unexpected suggestion, "but I hate to bother her, especially with only two days' notice. She's a busy woman...."

"But you wouldn't mind if I gave her a call, anyway?" Henry was peering at him intently, trying to gauge his reaction to mention of the fitness instructor.

"No, of course not. But why don't I call her first thing tomorrow? It's...it's been a while since I chatted with her."

"Fine...."

KARIN WAS ON THE GYM FLOOR teaching herself a new aerobics routine when Cindy paged her. By now her assistant knew better than to push for details, but her eyes were alive with interest as she delivered the innocuous message to call John Martin immediately at his apartment.

Karin thanked her with feigned nonchalance as she walked to her office and closed the door for privacy. Her legs felt weak and she knew the reason wasn't solely her practice workout. John answered after the first ring. He seemed apologetic as he explained his reason for contacting her, giving her every chance to refuse.

But Karin was a longtime baseball fan. "I'd love to go. The summer is slow around here, anyway. I don't work as many nights as I used to."

"I feel terrible—I've been so absorbed in my own duties that I haven't even asked you about your job. Did you meet your quota? Wasn't July 1 your deadline? I'm sorry. That has come and gone and I never thought—"

"Don't worry about it. I made it, just under the wire."

"That's great. You should be proud of yourself."

"Yeah...the funny thing is, though, that I miss the edge of striving for it," she admitted without intending to. "I'm trying to keep busy working up a whole new program for the fall, but it's not quite the same."

"So you're staying here in Kitchener?" he asked casually.

She rolled the phone cord around her finger and didn't answer right away. "I haven't decided. I'm starting to get antsy again. I'll see...."

John cursed the impersonality of the phone. He longed to see her face, her eyes, to read the expression there. "After this week, I should have some free time. Let's get together, Karin. It's been too long since we...talked. I'll call you again. Soon."

"Whatever," she said with a noncommittal tone to her voice.

"No, I *will* call. I promise."

"Whatever," she repeated flatly, amazed at the strength of her resistance to him, at her refusal to let him stir up a whirlwind inside her again. "Look, I have to go. Tell Henry I can meet him tomorrow any time after four, okay?"

Her dismissal became like a roaring in John's ears. He was losing her, and that knowledge filled him with a great need, a great urgency....

"Karin?"

"Yes?"

"I...love you." She said nothing, and he was filled with both regret at his rashness and relief at finally releasing the words. But nothing could take them back. "I didn't want to love you," he went on, desperate to make her understand. "But I do, Karin. I do. And I don't know what to do about it. I—I have so little to offer you. But suddenly it just seemed that I had to *do* something...."

Karin felt the struggle in him. *I didn't want to love you.* A part of him would always fight his love. And then she heard another voice, as if the phone were connected to another time, another place....

"What about Karin?" her mother was saying, her voice muffled on the other side of the closed bedroom door. "You can't just leave her, us, Satch. You can't."

"I never wanted Karin," her father replied sadly. "I love her, but I never wanted her. You did. I can't stay with you because of her.... I'm sorry for not being a better person, Marie. I'm so sorry...."

"Karin? Are you still there?" John's voice jolted her back to the present. "I know my timing is all wrong. I'll make it up to you someday.... Please say something."

She knew he waited for her to say loving words, too. But she couldn't, wouldn't. "It's not going to work, John."

"How do you know that, before we even try? I'm applying for new jobs, all here in Ontario.... Likely the one I pick won't be too far away. We'll see each other when we can, wherever we are. Let's at least talk about it."

A part-time love. A conditional love versus her growing, frightening obsession with him. "No, John. I'm sorry, but . . . I don't want that anymore."

"Karin...." His voice was growing frantic. He drew a deep breath to control it. "I thought you gave me your trust, the last time we . . . made love."

"I—I expected too much from myself. I can't—" She needed to escape. She needed to scream. She needed peace. "I have to go now. Bye."

"Karin!" he cried as she hung up, and the answering drone matched the heavy frustrated beating in his chest.

THE CROWD ROARED as George Bell crossed the plate, making everyone witness to yet another of his illustrious home runs. His feat put the Blue Jays ahead by one run and sparked another series of mass waves to ripple around Exhibition Stadium.

When her section's turn came, Karin rose and swung her arms wildly from side to side, glad for a release of the infectious exhilaration that gripped her. It had been a long time since she'd attended a game, and she was truly enjoying herself. The flashing neon lights of the scoreboard, the announcer's deep wizardly voice, the warmth of the summer's night and the controlled hysteria of the fans around her, all gave the game an otherworldly, magical aura. It helped her forget everything she did not want to think about.

Henry sat between Jordan and Phil, who had a bet going as to the victor. Right now, Phil was impatiently scowling on the edge of his seat, while Jordan was grinning like a Cheshire cat. On either side of Karin were Karl and Brad. They were watching the game with keen interest, but eyeing her boisterous participation in the wave with a detached amusement. Clearly *they* would not stoop to such a juvenile display of excitement.

The next batter struck out, and a mass groan erupted as the field cleared.

Standing, Brad announced, "I'm going to grab a hot dog."

"How can you even *think* of food after all that pasta, half a loaf of garlic bread and two servings of spumoni ice cream?" Karin sputtered.

"Can't come to a game without eating a dog," Brad told her, shaking his head as if an explanation were completely unnecessary. "Anybody else want anything?"

To his surprise the others declined the offer. Shrugging, he went to make his way out along the long row of knees to his left.

"Why don't you go with him, Karin, and grab a few Cokes while you're at it?" Henry handed her a five-dollar bill.

"I'll get them," Brad said, turning around.

"Karin will help you carry them," Henry insisted.

Brad's eyes darkened. "Afraid I'll skip town with your money?"

Henry did not reply and Karin jumped up. "I need to stretch, anyway. Come on, Brad."

"He doesn't trust me," Brad murmured a few minutes later as they were waiting in line.

"Should he?"

"A few months ago, no. Now, yes."

"He'll catch on. Give him time."

"John would have let me go alone."

"Well, he probably knows you better."

"Guess so...." While Karin placed her order for the drinks, Brad smothered his foot-long hot dog in mustard and relish, then bit into it, raising his eyes heavenward. "Hey, can I have a beer?" he asked, wistfully eyeing the next stand.

"I don't think that's such a good idea."

"It's no big deal...one beer. I bet you cheated before you were the legal age." And he bestowed her with a rare flash of roguish charm.

"Okay, we'll split one," she relented, making her way to the other booth.

"Thanks," he mumbled when she returned. "You're all right, Karin."

"Just keep this between us."

"Sure." He attacked his well-packed bun with an expertise that allowed none of the gooey filling to escape, then took a big gulp of the beer, smacking his lips afterward in an unpracticed imitation of experienced beer drinkers he'd probably observed enviously.

They backed up to the wall, out of the path of the jostling crowd. "It must feel good to have a night off from the farm," Karin said. "You've been working there quite steadily."

"I haven't minded," Brad replied, wiping some mustard from his lips, then tossing his empty napkin into a waste receptacle nearby.

"That has to qualify you for Guiness-book material," Karin marveled. "You finished that hot dog in record time."

"A talent I've been perfecting. Don't know if it'll get me rich, though."

"Probably not," Karin said, grinning, then impulsively adding on a more serious note, "Any idea what you'd like to do after you graduate?" She half expected him to brush her off with a flippant answer, but to her surprise he paused to consider her question.

"I can always get a job in a games arcade, I figure. But I might get tired of looking at Pac-Man all day. Lately, I've been thinking about studying agriculture at college. It ... kind of interests me. When I go back to school in September, I may talk to the guidance counselor about it. Just to get a rough idea of courses I'd need and stuff...."

"Wouldn't hurt. You know, I think you'd be really good in the agricultural field. You've learned so quickly out at the farm—everybody thinks so. And, if you *like* doing something and want the goal badly enough, you'll get it, Brad."

"That sounds familiar. Has John been talking to you about me?" he asked suspiciously.

She didn't want to lie to him. "A little. I know he was quite upset when you disappeared. He wanted to help you."

Brad looked down. "We cleared that up. I guess I freaked out when a chick I liked wouldn't go out with me ... because of who I was. Dumb, eh?"

"No, we all have to come to terms with who we are." She hesitated, then decided to elaborate. "My parents were divorced when I was quite young. I started to lie about it to my friends at school, concocting all kinds of stories about where my father was. I guess I was ashamed of my folks' problems, as if they were a reflection on me. Ever since, I've wanted to be judged on my own merits, and I've worked damn hard to develop those merits. I wasn't proud of that girl who had to lie. It's much better to build your own truth about yourself."

His eyes met hers. "But what if the way you are keeps changing? Some days I like myself and other times, forget it. Who's going to want a guy like that?"

"Someday, you'll meet a girl who'll accept you for the whole package, the good and the not-so-good. The most important thing is to be yourself. Because then, no matter what happens—and I won't pretend you'll never get hurt— at least then you'll have yourself and whatever dignity you manage to salvage." Her voice caught as she thought of the loss of her mother, her father's neglect, Eric's betrayal and John's conditional love. She looked away, but it was too late.

"Hey, I didn't mean to upset you," Brad said, gingerly touching her arm.

"I'm okay," she said, forcing herself to smile. Cheers echoed from the stands. "We're missing the game. Let's go. Any of that beer left?"

Brad glanced at the empty cup and shook his head sheepishly. "Sorry. We could always get another."

The look of boyish charm was back on his face again, but this time Karin managed to resist it, shaking her head in mock sternness. "I'll have one of these Cokes, instead." She stepped forward, but Brad stopped her.

"So, if I meet another girl, I should try to forget what happened last time. Start over, like?"

"That's right," she said slowly. "Just go for it, next time around."

"And if I get turned down again?"

"Anything that's worth having is worth fighting for," she heard herself saying. "And if that doesn't work, she probably doesn't deserve such a prize as you anyway, so don't worry about it."

Brad grinned. "You're good for a guy's ego. Wanna date?"

"You can go after anyone *but* me," she replied, grinning back at him.

"You taken?"

"No, but I'm not so good at heeding my own wisdom. Come on, Henry will think we *both* skipped town with his money."

As they made their way back to their seats, Karin couldn't help but think that she was the last person who should be giving Brad advice about the opposite sex. She was caught in an emotional paralysis of her own with a man whose power over her she was terrified to face.

LATER THAT NIGHT, alone in her apartment, Karin was curled up in front of the television set. She should be exhausted after the long day, but her body was overcharged. She'd screamed herself hoarse as the Jays had fallen behind, then won the game in the last inning.

A pair of koala bears was crawling over the desk of the talk-show host, but she wasn't really paying attention....

She was thinking how much she'd enjoyed not only the game, but her time with the teenagers. Her talk with Brad had left her feeling warmly satisfied. He'd *listened* to her somehow. She understood what drove both John and

Henry to stick with such a job, despite the many frustrations.

She thought of her own job. She liked the upbeat atmosphere of the club, and she'd met hundreds of people. But her conversations with most of them were about calories, target heart zones, muscle building.... What did she expect? She was working at a health and fitness club, for heaven's sake. Yet the simple truth was that she was no longer *committed* to what she was doing, not in the way she knew John and Henry were with the boys under their care or with their chosen profession. She envied them.

She flipped through the channels for a late-night movie that might hold her interest. Nothing....

She knew she'd only been postponing the inevitable for weeks. It was time to recharge her batteries and to plan her future with the utmost care. She needed a change. A big change. She especially needed to be free again, free from the dangers of depending on John Martin for her happiness—only heartache could come from giving herself to a man who loved her unwillingly. She needed to be free from their strangling, limbolike relationship and her hopeless obsession with him.

And then it came to her. She'd go on a trip. A long trip—that had been a sure remedy for her in the past. She'd saved some money. Maybe she could get a leave of absence.

She reached for last Saturday's newspaper, lying in a clutter on her rug. She found the Travel section.

Her mind waded through various possibilities that had always intrigued her: the beaches along Australia's Great Barrier Reef, an African safari, a mountain trek in Nepal. She waited for the familiar excitement to fill the aching void within....

CHAPTER FOURTEEN

"CINDY, CAN I TALK TO YOU?" Karin asked during a slow afternoon at the club one week later.

"It's about time." Cindy stepped into the office, watching suspiciously as the door was closed. She'd observed Karin's mysterious behavior during the past several days, but she'd known instinctively that her boss was not open to discussing whatever was going on. Her imagination had therefore run rampant.

What's more, Karin had refused to answer her own phone. Fighting her near-unbearable curiosity, Cindy had relayed many of Karin's calls from Supreme Fitness personnel in Toronto—not just from Carol Levine, but from the owners, too. As instructed, she'd also told John Martin countless times that her employer was unavailable. One day, though, she had let him know that Karin had gone to Toronto for a few days—he had sounded so concerned. He'd been to her apartment, and since Karin hadn't answered her door, he'd thought she might be ill or he'd feared she'd moved away permanently.

Cindy, too, wondered if Karin was unwell. Her sweat suit seemed even more loose fitting than usual, as if she'd lost weight, and her cheeks had a new hollowness. Her eyes were tired, but strangely her body gave off a tightly coiled energy.

"I don't see any pink slips on your desk," Cindy began nervously. "That's a good sign."

"I'm sorry I've been so evasive, Cindy, but I really couldn't talk until everything was in place."

"Until what was in place?"

"How would you like to take over as manager of the club?"

Cindy's mouth dropped. "I was geared up to hear that we were folding or that the fees were doubling, but that's the last thing I expected.... Where will you be?"

Karin's smile was quick, strained. "I've been granted a leave of absence, which wasn't easy, believe me."

"But why? What will you do?"

"I'm going on a trip. To Australia. I just need to get away."

"From what or whom?" Cindy asked quietly, remembering all John Martin's aborted calls.

"Nothing," Karin said smoothly. "I'm heading *toward* something. Toward new adventures, new experiences. Who knows what awaits me? I just know that I was starting to stagnate here. I exceeded my quota, though, and that's what counted with the Toronto gang . . . luckily."

"So why not quit? You say you're just taking a leave of absence. Why?" Cindy was studying her with troubled eyes.

Karin avoided looking at her. "I don't want to burn *all* my bridges. I'm going to need a job when I return, broke."

"And they accepted that?"

Karin shrugged. "They're big on mobility—they intended to transfer me again in six months time anyway, or so they said. To a new club that's opening in the northeast end of Toronto. I've proven myself as a manager, and I guess they don't want to lose me. And I convinced them that you'd be perfect as a manager here. You know everyone, so there would be a sense of continuity."

Cindy leaned back in her chair and rubbed her hands down her black-leotard-clad legs. "Slow down. You're hitting me with a lot at once. When is all this supposed to happen?"

"Don't worry. I'll stay on until you've been given the proper training. You have a few interviews in Toronto first, but I'm sure you'll be able to sell yourself to the top brass. And at the moment they don't have anyone else who's as qualified as you. Aren't you excited?"

"Sure... I know I could do it, but—"

"The raise won't hurt, either."

"Look, are you positive you want to go ahead with this, Karin? I mean, just leave everything? I'll miss you around here... we all will."

"I'll miss you, too, Cindy, but I have to do it. I just have to...."

KARIN WAS WORKING LATE, trying to sort out all her paperwork before handing it over to her new manager. Cindy was currently in Toronto to sign the final promotion papers, having sailed through her initial interviews with flying colors.

Since the club had closed an hour ago, the only interruption Karin expected was a call from her travel agent. When the phone rang, she immediately picked it up. "Oh, hi, Mrs. Sawyer. Here, let me find a blank sheet of paper. Okay. Fire away." She proceeded to jot down the preliminary details of costs, flights, hostels and hotels that the agent had drawn up for the Australia trip.

"A stopover in Tahiti sounds wonderful. New Zealand? I don't know. Maybe I should concentrate on Australia. It's going to be hard enough fitting in Ayers Rock, Sydney, Cairns, Melbourne and all the rest, even though I have several months. How about a brief stopover on the way back via Europe—say, Paris? I have some friends there...."

The door to her office was ajar, and she sensed another presence in the room before she heard anything. She looked up into the dark angry eyes of John Martin, and she remembered she'd forgotten to lock up....

Folding his arms, he stood boldly listening to the rest of her call. But her concentration was blown. She thanked Mrs. Sawyer for all her work and told her she'd get back to her as soon as possible. She hung up, but her fingers clung to the phone as though it were a lifesaver.

"You were just going to leave without saying goodbye, weren't you?" he accused with incredulity.

"I don't know," she murmured weakly, but she couldn't deny the charge.

"How could you, Karin? How could you, after all we shared?"

"Because it would be easier," she said defiantly, starting to regain her equilibrium after his unexpected appearance, starting to feel angry at him for his intrusion.

"Easier!" He spat out the word as if it were repugnant to him.

"Okay! Goodbye, John. It was nice knowing you. Good luck with your life. There, does that make you feel any better?" With shaking hands she began to gather the papers spread out in front of her and stuffed them into her briefcase. She grabbed her purse and stood. "Now, if you'll excuse me. I was just on my way out."

He was blocking her path, but she pushed past him, through the reception area. He hadn't moved.

"I have to lock up. Please, John, let's be civil about this."

His lips were tight and his face was set in a rigid expression that was anything but civil. Staring hard at her, he

walked to the other side of the entranceway and watched
stonily as she turned the key.

She ran up the stairs that led to the street and stepped out
into the night air, breathing deeply of it. A steady rain fell,
but she was damned well not going to go back for her umbrella. Anyway, the last thing she cared about right now
was whether she got wet walking the short distance home.

"Good night," she called back to him, striking out on
the slick sidewalk.

He caught up to her and grabbed her by the elbow.
"Karin, we have to talk."

"What's the point?" She shook him loose and stepped
away as quickly as her feet would carry her.

He followed, a single stride behind, and she was growing exasperated, but she was compelled to keep walking.
Finally, he grasped her firmly and cornered her in the empty
sheltered doorway of a darkened storefront. Her purse and
briefcase dropped to her feet.

As they stared at each other, their breathing was la-
bored. Droplets of rain slid down their cheeks. Slowly John
reached out to push back a wet strand of hair from her face.
His hand lingered there. She saw the fierce determination
in his eyes and knew that he was going to kiss her.

"No," she whispered, knowing that physical release was
no longer the solution she sought.

His hand dropped. "Tell me what you plan to do," he
commanded softly.

Karin drew a deep breath and stepped away from him,
shivering with the dampness, wrapping her arms around
herself. "I'm taking a leave of absence from Supreme. I'm
traveling to Australia, for about five months—it's just what
I need. Then, when I return, I'll consider managing another new club in Toronto. I've been told it's mine if I want

it. The arrangement is perfect, really," she added, feigning more excitement than she felt.

"What are you running from, Karin?" he asked, his eyes narrowed.

She was prepared to answer the familiar question as she'd done with Cindy, but he didn't wait for a reply. "I think you're running from us. From love . . . now that you've realized it's there. Demanding something from you. Something that terrifies you."

She started to protest, but his dark eyes were penetrating hers, radiating contempt for further evasiveness. In a thin, scratched voice, she said, "Love is more than . . . a feeling, a desire between two people."

"You can't just ignore that feeling when it's there, strong and real—"

"But the feeling has to coexist with living," she said fiercely. "Two people have to share the same direction and dreams. It's time I find my niche elsewhere. We always knew that time would come, John." She looked out at the gray slashes of rain that transformed the passing people and cars into a surrealistic blur.

He stared at her for a long, pained moment. "I can understand why you might need to get away, for a time. But I can't understand why you are closing off all possibilities with me. With what we had, have—"

"There is nothing to hold me here," she cut in, her eyes searching his. She saw a deep caring there, but she also saw the anguish that had been in his voice when he'd told her he loved her on the phone. He was not ready to make a final leap of faith with her—and never would be.

"Do you love me, Karin?" he asked quietly.

His eyes were intense, alive, and they were working their powerful magic over her. But she had to anesthetize herself against them, against him. The words were torn from her. "I don't know. But love wouldn't make a difference. I want to move on, John," she said with passionate resolve. "It's the way I am, the way I've always been. But this time it's harder for me to leave than you'll ever know."

Her eyes had filled with tears, and she didn't see his face as she picked up her bags and ran off, oblivious to the slanting summer rain.

As vulnerable and helpless as when he'd lost his wife to an illness he could not fight, John let her go, knowing love could not be forced. He also knew that he had failed her. He had not been able to conquer her fears, because he had not yet conquered his own. . . .

HERE'S TO ANOTHER *big Saturday night,* Karin toasted silently, raising her tumbler of lemonade to the air. A fresh bowl of popcorn sat beside her. She settled back to watch *Crocodile Dundee,* the movie she'd rented upon the recommendation of several women at the club. Supposedly the comedy would give her a feel for bush country in the "land down under"—not that she intended to stray *too* far from the civilized track, but she certainly could use help in building enthusiasm for her trip. Of course, she was looking forward to it, but she hadn't yet felt that bubbling, overwhelming excitement that she'd expected to experience. She wasn't too worried, though. She knew that the reality of her adventure would finally hit her once she was sitting on the plane.

As she watched the film, she smiled often at the rugged charm of the Australian film star, Paul Hogan, who was playing the part of an Outback native. But when, like a fish out of water, he was trying to adjust to a new life in Manhattan, all Karin could think of was John Martin in Toronto—crowding her in the revolving door, dancing like a cross between a robot and a chicken, sharing his fascination with the city, the hotel . . . making love to her. . . .

She jumped as the phone shrilled. For a brief second she thought the caller might be the subject of her fantasies, but she swiftly refuted that possibility. He had too much pride to pursue such an unwilling lover anymore.

She put the movie on hold and reached for the receiver. "Hello."

"Kary? It's Satch."

Her heart jumped. "Satch?"

"One and the same. How have you been?"

"Fine. I've been fine." And she could not prevent coolness from entering her voice as she tried to remember how long it had been since he'd last been in touch. A long time. She'd tried to thank him for the Christmas gift, but he'd moved and left no forwarding address.

"I know it's been a while since we've touched base," he was saying. "Joanna gave me hell when she found out how remiss I've been with you lately, kiddo, so you might as well let me have it, too, then we can have a decent chat. Go ahead."

The same old Satch. Roguish. Infuriating. Irresistible. He made it hard to stay angry, but Karin wasn't ready to let him off the hook, either. "Okay, you're selfish and unforgivable."

"Guilty as charged," he said, sighing loudly.

"You drive me crazy, Satch. You really do. You back out at Christmas and send me a consolation prize, instead. You move and don't even give me a clue as to where. I thought at least you might want a recent picture of me, that maybe that's what the camera was intended for, but—"

"I did *try* to call you once," he cut in, "after you wrote with your news of moving to Kitchener."

"Once? Well, all is forgiven then. . . ."

"I *am* sorry, but I just get caught up in what I'm doing. I've been traveling all over the map, it seems. I have the best intentions to call, but I'm the world's worst procrastinator. You should know me by now."

"I should...." She was starting to soften, but didn't want him to know yet.

"The best thing I do is play the sax, so that's what I do. I'm just not cut out to be a family man. Not even a good part-time one, but I do think of you a lot, Karin." She was silent. "So, Joanna tells me you like working at that sweatshop."

"Health club, Satch," she said dryly. "But actually I'm taking some time off. I'm going to Australia in a few weeks."

"Australia? That's great, I suppose. Why Australia?"

"Lots of reasons."

"You don't seem too thrilled about it."

He'd always been able to see right through her. "Sometimes you just have to *act* on your intuition, follow your gut feelings, and everything will work out for the best, right?"

"Any handsome traveling companion in the plans?"

"I'm going alone," she said abruptly. "But I'm bound to meet a lot of interesting people."

"Hmm..."

"Surely you're not worried about me. You know I can take care of myself."

"And I'm proud of your self-reliance, Karin. I think it's the most important quality a person can have, but I'm less than a model human being, so what do I know?"

"Probably more than we all give you credit for." She smiled, feeling their old rapport returning despite the time and distance between them. "It's good to talk to you, Satch. I've missed you, blunders and all."

"You know something, kiddo? For the first time in my life, I've even been getting a little lonely on the road myself. Maybe I'm getting old or soft or something. But don't get me wrong—I'm too much of a music fanatic to ever change. And I don't think anyone would have me...."

"Even Joanna?"

"Joanna, least of anyone. She's one of the best friends I have, and heaven knows I should see her more, too, but she's too smart to try to make me into something I'm not. At least she's been there for me when I needed her, even though I probably don't deserve her."

Satch had always played the buffoon. He'd never spoken so freely to Karin of his personal life with the woman he'd known for more than twenty years. She listened carefully as he went on haltingly, "Sometimes I wonder what I've missed.... I've lost a lot of people I've loved by my own thoughtlessness. I haven't given you much over the years, Kary, but if I could give you one bit of advice— please don't make the same mistakes I have. You've got a lot of love stored up in you. Don't ration it out too stingily."

"I know what's best for me."

"I've been told I'm one of those rare breeds who's reasonably content in his own crazy little world, as long as I have my music. You're different, Kary. You're more like your mother was. You need people. People you can be close to. People you can love. Not just a bunch of strangers or acquaintances."

"But it's the ones closest to you who can do the most damage, if you let them," Karin admitted softly, trying to keep her voice level.

"That doesn't mean that you don't need them. Don't blame everyone for the weaknesses of a few. Give the right ones—or one, if you're lucky—a fair chance."

She was hearing a new side to Satch, a reflectiveness that was reaching out to her in a more honest way than he had ever tried before. Karin could not speak past the choking sensation in her throat.

"I may not show it very well—in fact, I've been a miserable failure in that department—but I do love you, Kary." The phone crackled faintly, matching the catch in his voice. "Never doubt how special you are to me. There was a time when I didn't appreciate all that I had, but those times are behind me."

"I love you too, Satch," she said, not caring that her own voice wavered or that she'd just sniffed loudly. "Hey, why don't we try to see each other before I leave? I'll be stopping over in Vancouver in a few weeks. Is that where you're still stationed?"

"Off and on. I'm with a new band now. We're off to a jazz festival in San Francisco next week, then we're touring the West Coast steadily for at least six months." He had swiftly reverted to his usual aloof, absorbed self. "Maybe you and I can coordinate our schedules, but I can't be specific about dates until my agent finalizes the band's agenda. I'll let you know...."

"Sure, Satch," Karin said, shaking her head as the typical scenario was once more being played out.

"Here, I'll give you this new mailing address I have in Vancouver. I even remember to check it from time to time."

She copied down the information, then they chatted pleasantly for a few more minutes. He wished her well on her trip and made her promise to write him all about it. A Christmas reunion would be impossible this year since they'd be on different continents, they agreed, but as soon as Karin returned he wanted her to get in touch with him, and they would try to arrange a meeting, especially if the upcoming one fell through....

After the call Karin was in a pensive mood, and she never did see the end of the movie. She thought over everything her father had said, and she was filled with renewed fondness for him, and something else—a new acceptance for the way he was. She no longer condemned him so harshly for his treatment of her—he gave her all that he could. And that was okay. Somehow she felt more *objective* about him, and that was a good thing.

John Martin was another self-professed loner, a man with a large capacity for emotion, but it was a capacity he controlled. He was a man with strong family ties, but they were ties he kept at a distance. He said he loved her, but it was a love that was set apart from the rest of his life—a part, not the whole.

She could not love him back in that same way, always holding a part of herself from him. Nor did she have the courage to love him wholeheartedly. She was not strong enough to accept the consequences of such inequality.

But, having been awakened to the joys of love, she also realized how much she was missing by choosing to live without it at all or by waiting for something that might never come.

She stood to lose all ways.

CHAPTER FIFTEEN

JOHN GRIPPED HIS COFFEE MUG with both hands as he blinked hard at Henry. "Could you run that by me again?"

"Melissa wants to relocate in Vancouver, closer to her mother, and she's found a group home that we can take over," Henry repeated patiently. "And I must admit that the prospect of a change of locale appeals to me. I've lived here my whole life—and my relations with my family don't seem to be getting any better."

"B-but isn't your decision rather sudden?"

"I've been thinking about it since I returned from Vancouver around the time of Brad's crisis. I just didn't want to say anything until all the plans were set and life settled down around here. But don't look so shocked. I'm not going anywhere until I'm convinced I'll be leaving Greenbank in good hands. I can't chance disrupting the lives of the boys more than is necessary. They'll all be here at least until they finish high school, which is another year yet."

"Which is why it would be ideal if I could stay on..." John murmured, his face lighting up at the prospect.

Henry waved a warning finger at him. "Don't get your hopes up. On a permanent basis the ministry would insist on having a married couple here—this place is licensed as a family-model home, and the boys were sent here because they needed that kind of environment."

The two men were sitting at one end of the heavy wooden kitchen table. Since it was past midnight, the boys were all sleeping upstairs. Henry had been tied up with official meetings all day, the nature of which he had not disclosed to John until now. John had spent the day with the group at Greenbank, temporarily shelving his pressing duties at the farm. But his most immediate concern was the change proposed by Henry.

"I'll do battle with the ministry," he insisted fiercely. "I'll convince them I can run the home on my own with the support of Margaret and Jessica."

Henry still looked skeptical. "What if the situation at the farm crops up again?"

"It won't. My sister is . . . supposedly marrying in October, and her husband will take my place. If that doesn't happen, other arrangements can be made. My own work has always been my priority. My family understands that— this summer is working out favorably for all concerned, but we all know it's a one-time affair."

"Look, I know you're good at what you do here, John— you've worked wonders with Brad, for example—but running this place properly is a full-time job for at least two people. Not just physically, to split the tasks, but emotionally, too. Plus, we may get a new resident or two any day now." He cleared his throat, sipped from his mug, then darted a look at his colleague. "What about Karin?"

"Karin?" John had never told Henry of his strong feelings for her, but his friend had obviously drawn his own conclusions.

"Yes, Karin. She relates well to teenagers—in fact, she's a natural with them. With some training, I bet she'd be accepted as a group parent, if you two are indeed serious."

"Wait a minute. . . ." John scraped his chair back in a sudden surge of restlessness. "Are you saying I should marry her just so I can stay on at Greenbank?"

As he pushed his glasses up the bridge of his nose, Henry leaned forward, then rested his elbows on the table. "I'm saying you should marry her if you love her and want to be with her," he said softly, not without discomfort at his presumptuous meddling. "*And* if she loves you. There're a lot of 'ifs' involved."

"There certainly are...."

"First, do you... love her?"

John drew a deep breath, then exhaled slowly. "Yes, but...I haven't let myself consider marriage." He swallowed. "My whole relationship with Karin is so iffy. I'm just zeroing in on what I want to do with my life, and having someone else share all its...quirks, the big ones and the little ones, seems impossible."

"Maybe you're afraid to try again. Our situations are different, granted, but I remember how terrified I was of marriage until I took the plunge with Melissa, and it was a plunge, believe me. But once I started *living* the commitment, day by day, it became the most natural thing in the world, for both of us. This past year has been difficult, but it's also made our love stronger than ever."

John had only met Melissa briefly when he'd first come to Greenbank and she'd flown home for a visit. She had the same high energy and serious manner as Henry, and he'd thought at the time how perfectly in tune they were with each other. He compared that compatibility to the rare moments of harmony he'd shared with Karin during their discordant months together. Both had seemed to crave the intimacy they had found in each other, but they were each determined to keep absolute control over their lives. His last sight of her tearful, rain-soaked face rose up before his eyes.

"Karin's leaving," he said bluntly, making a supreme effort to mask his pain. "Apparently she has a leave of absence from the club, and she's flying off to Australia. She's never stayed in any one place long enough to put down roots. Why would she change now? Who's to say she can change?''

Henry stared at him for several long seconds. "I don't know Karin very well, but the night we dropped her off after the ball game, she looked so deflated as she stood in front of her apartment building. She didn't seem to want to go in. People like Karin, who make such an effort to prove they don't need anyone, probably seek stability more than they'll ever admit."

John remembered her impassioned determination to leave the city and to sever her ties with him. She hadn't looked back. "Karin has made up her mind. I can't force her to stay."

"Melissa and I have proven that you can't always *be* with the person you love. Sometimes other important parts of your life, such as your job or your family, pull you in other directions. But what has helped us survive this temporary separation is our love for each other, and that has to be strong enough to survive all the tests that life can dole out, and those can get awfully tough...."

"For reasons of her own, Karin has resisted loving me...with all her might," John admitted with great difficulty.

After a time Henry said gently, "Then maybe it's best you move on, alone, to a new home, after all."

John's head was swimming, but he could not give up on his original plan so easily. "I still want to try running Greenbank on my own—I can make it work. I know it. But I'll need your support when I approach the ministry, Henry. Can I count on you?"

"I think we should both sleep on this," Henry answered in a quiet, noncommittal voice. "We'll talk about it again in a day or two, okay?"

John agreed wearily.

THE NEXT DAY, as planned, John drove the familiar route to the farm with Brad and Karl. The bruised-looking sky threatened rain, so they were on the road at seven o'clock to try to cut as much of the field of mixed grain as possible before the probable downpour.

Karl stayed to tend the animals in the barn, while the other two drove off in the tractor, the rusted binder trailing noisily behind.

They had only been working about an hour when the clouds broke. Hoping that the storm would blow over, they ran for the nearest shelter—a grove of tall, canopylike cedars on the far edge of the property by the maple bush.

"What do you think?" John asked, staring up at the wide gray expanse overhead.

Brad didn't even bother looking up. "We're going to be here a while. At least it's not a lightning storm."

"Yeah. You cold or anything?" He eyed the youth's rain-splattered clothes. Only a few drops were escaping from the protection of the thick cedars above them. "We can always head back."

"We'll get drenched that way for sure. Let's eat our lunch." He reached into the bag of sandwiches they'd quickly packed that morning and salvaged from the rain.

"But it's only eight-thirty. We just ate breakfast."

"Minor detail. Tuna or peanut butter and jam? Or do you want one of each?"

John made a face. "No, thanks. I'll take a pass right now. You go ahead, though." He constantly marveled at the boy's phenomenal appetite.

Brad chose the peanut butter and jam. Leaning against a relatively dry trunk, he devoured the concoction in a few bites. "That wasn't bad," he finally pronounced. "A soggy PJ sandwich just wouldn't have been the same."

"No, I guess not...."

"I heard you talking to Henry last night."

Brad's sudden statement caused John to glance at him sharply. "How much of it?"

"Practically the whole thing. I came down for a bowl of cereal but decided not to interrupt. I know I shouldn't have listened, but I couldn't help it."

"Did you tell any of the others?"

"No, of course not." He jumped back from a flood of rain that spilled through the overhanging boughs as the wind picked up.

"Well, I prefer that you don't say anything, not until everything's resolved."

Brad nodded, his brow troubled. "I don't think you should let a neat lady like Karin get away." His light hazel eyes met the darkness of John's in a hesitant challenge.

"And why not?" John said quickly, taken aback by Brad's unexpected comment.

"She's the one who told me that anything that's worth having is worth fighting for."

"She said that?"

"Yeah—why do you look so surprised?"

"Why? Because she's the first one to run away when things get tough," he said swiftly, then regretted it. He ran a hand through his hair in agitation. Discussing Karin with Henry had been difficult enough, but it was even harder with someone as young as Brad. "Look, I don't think I should be telling you all this—"

"Maybe she doesn't *want* to run away," the youth cut in with growing boldness. "Maybe she's just mixed-up. Or scared. Or—or needing help... only she doesn't know it."

John was thrown into silence, and he was thinking how much Brad had changed during the summer. He seemed older, somehow, more self-assured.

"I'm glad you stuck it out with me," Brad went on. "It helped. It really did."

"But you were ready to help yourself, too, and I admire you for that, because I know it wasn't easy. But Karin's a grown woman. She doesn't want anyone trying to take over her life. She's free to make her own decisions—and I respect that."

"But how can she make up her mind if she doesn't know all the facts... about Greenbank, about being your partner? I think you're afraid to ask because you're afraid she might say yes."

"It's more than just a business partnership—a lot more—and I just don't know anymore...."

For a long interval, Brad stared at the moving mass of gray clouds. Finally he spoke again. "There's a lot I have to make up to you... like all those rotten things I said about you being lousy at your job. They weren't true. I don't even know why I said them, 'cept that I was mad at everybody. I hope you didn't listen to a guy who just liked to shoot off his mouth."

"Well... you did cause me to take a good hard look at myself and the job I'd chosen. But you helped me realize I wanted to stay with it, even though I still had a lot to learn."

"See!" Brad smiled, a rare winning smile. "Somehow I did something right, even when I was all messed up. So think what good I can do when I know what I'm talking about."

John could not resist a grin at the boy's logic. "Match-making, you mean?"

Brad's smile faded and he didn't answer right away. "No, keeping you at Greenbank," he said with the utmost seriousness. "I don't want to lose you. Just when..." He stopped, began again. "Karin's my... our only hope. Unless you really want to work at a new home... with better kids...."

Moved by the teenager's words in ways he did not stop to examine, John replied without hesitation, "No, Brad, what I want most is to stay at Greenbank. With the other guys and especially you, too. I'll never find a better chess partner, for one thing."

Brad refused to be swayed by the attempt at lightness. "What about Karin? Will you ask her?"

But John could not give him the answer he needed to hear.

THE TORRENT SHOWED NO SIGN of letting up, so they soon decided they had no choice but to return to the farmhouse. As they rode back, their shirts, coveralls and straw hats absorbed the rain like sponges, and even though the temperature was warm, both were becoming chilled from the dampness.

At the yard, they jumped off the tractor and immediately headed for the shelter of the barn. They burst through the door to find Karl standing there, his arms around Mary.

The two jumped apart and faced the intruders with startled, flushed faces. Through the shaft of anger that pierced him, John saw that Karl appeared to be only mildly guilty. His stance was defensive, his eyes rebellious, his mouth twisted in self-righteousness. Mary, though, was horrified. With her cheeks burning in shame, her fists tightened around the skirt of her pink frock and she brushed past them, out the door, running through the rain toward the house.

John let her go. "What do you think you're doing?" he ground out to Karl in a deadly bass voice.

"It was just an innocent kiss," Karl retorted defiantly. "She came out here to ask if I wanted some fresh-baked cookies or something and . . . and it just happened."

John continued to glare at him. "Mary's not like other girls, Karl. She's lived here all her life, and she hasn't met many outsiders. You have no right to take advantage of her. She's just a kid."

"Who's getting married in a few months. I think she stopped being a kid long ago, but you just won't admit it."

John took a step toward him, but Brad held out a restraining arm. Willing himself to freeze, John stared at Karl as if he wanted to tear his limbs apart.

"Hey, settle down. I wasn't going to *do it* with her or anything. She's been looking at me funny all summer, and I think she's pretty, so I just wanted to kiss her. That's all. Maybe it was a test, too, to see if she'd let me, to see if she really cared about that wimp Joshua. . . ."

"If you so much as touch her again, I'll—"

"You'll what?" Karl flung at him menacingly, giving John a rare glimpse into the hardened core beneath his outwardly deceptive charm.

"J-just let it go," Brad said quietly to both of them.

Finally, without saying another word, John swung around and marched across the muddy yard to the kitchen door.

Anna Martin took one look at him, and her plump face creased in concern. She immediately took over. "You're soaked through to the skin, John. Here's a towel. Step into the privy, dry off, and I'll bring you some of your father's clothes."

"Get some for Brad, too," he mumbled, wiping his head with the cloth and kicking off his boots as he glanced around. "Where's Mary?"

"Said she wasn't feeling well. She's up in her room."

"I'll be back to change in a minute." He took the stairs two at a time, oblivious to the curious stares of his parents and grandfather.

Mary was sitting by the window, staring out listlessly.

"Are you all right?" John asked awkwardly, closing the door behind him, then perching on the small bed, not noticing the damp stain he was imprinting there.

"Yes." She turned to look at him, and John saw that she had been crying. "Don't be angry with Karl. It's not his fault. It's mine. I wanted him to kiss me."

"Why?"

"I don't know. I just did. No one but Joshua has ever kissed me. Maybe I wanted to see if it was different . . . with someone else."

"And was it?"

A soft look crossed her face. "Yes . . . ."

"Mary . . . it's not too late. You don't have to marry Joshua, if you're not sure."

"But I *am* going to marry him. There was never any question of that. Maybe it was wrong to let Karl kiss me, and I wish you hadn't seen, but I'm glad I did it. For *my* sake. I will always remember it," she added, smiling with a quick show of whimsy.

"But, why? Why are you marrying Joshua, if you have these other feelings?"

"Because I am a Mennonite . . . and I will always be one. I will marry another Mennonite . . . Joshua, because the time is right for me to marry him." Her voice was calm, insistent.

A strong unwavering loyalty shone in her eyes, and John knew that she would indeed carry through with her promise to marry the boy who would ease the burden of farm work off her ailing father's shoulders. Even if it meant tempering her own happiness. She did not see her decision as self-sacrificing, though. She was perfectly at home in the Mennonite world with its set parameters, and she was prepared to settle for contentment within that world. He could not fault her for that, if it was what she wanted. In his own way he shared her single-mindedness, but his was directed to his new life of freedom.

"Everything has been arranged," she went on matter-of-factly. "Father went over his books with Joshua a little while ago. We will make less money this year because of the falling price of wheat, for one thing. If we get a loan for another tractor, Joshua will have to help out by getting an extra job in the winter, but he doesn't mind. He will be working in his brother's furniture-making shop. Everything is going to be fine."

"And what if I had stayed, Mary? Would you still have married Joshua then?" John had to ask.

"That is not a fair question—to either of us."

"Just answer it."

She spoke slowly, carefully. "I would have married Joshua or someone like Joshua—a good man, a Mennonite . . . eventually. But don't worry, I am ready now." She smiled reassuringly at him, her hands folded in her lap like the petals of a flower.

John stood and approached her, dropping to his knees by her side. He kissed her cheek, then his arms encircled her. "You're a special woman, Mary," he said, his voice hoarse as he fought to accept her choice.

A HEAVY RAIN CONTINUED, making outdoor work impossible, so John drove Karl and Brad back to Greenbank. He did not mention the incident with Mary again. The protective anger he'd felt had gone out of his heart, and the boys sensed it. Each of them was preoccupied with their own thoughts during the journey, though. The only sound in the car came from the whirring of the windshield wipers.

At the house, Henry, Jordan and Phil were draped over chairs and couches watching the horror movie they'd rented. The three of them burst out laughing when their eyes alighted on John's and Brad's makeshift outfits.

"Going to a fashion show?" Phil asked dryly.

"Stuff it!" Brad retorted, tossing his bundle of wet clothes to John, who took them to the laundry room.

"Mother Nature give you all the afternoon off?" Henry murmured, his attention back on the grotesque creature filling the TV screen.

Karl flopped down beside Jordan. "Yeah. Watcha watching?"

"The Thing," Jordan answered, without the stutter that was appearing less and less.

"I'm going to check on a few things at my apartment and pick up some fresh clothes," John said from the doorway. "I'll be back shortly, then maybe we could have that little chat, Henry?"

Brad looked at him sharply, but John ignored him.

"Why don't you take the rest of the day off?" Henry said casually. "You haven't had a moment to yourself for weeks, and the six hours of sleep you grab at night don't count."

"That won't be necessary," John immediately protested. "I—"

"We'll be fine on our own, won't we, fellas? Phil chose a supposedly more educational film to see next. It's about prehistoric times—*Clan of the Cave Bear*."

Brad made a face. "He just wants to see Daryl Hannah wearing nothing but a few fur skins."

"Is that so?" Henry darted a suspicious look Phil's way.

"I'd really like to talk to you, Henry." But his colleague would not meet John's eyes.

"And I say there's no rush. Take some time off...."

In front of the others, John had no choice but to give in to what was a thinly veiled order. "I'll see you tomorrow," he said brusquely, then left.

ALONE AT HIS APARTMENT, where he'd spent little time during the past several weeks, John stood at the window, his body such a reservoir of tension that he felt his skin could burst at any moment.

He started to pace, but the room was too confining. With a sound of frustration, he grabbed his umbrella and jacket and, wearing his own clothes once more, headed out to the rainy street. He didn't know where he was going. He just needed to walk.

He soon found himself in an air-conditioned, multi-leveled mall. He bought an ice-cream cone, baffled by the variety of flavors. He chose an old favorite, chocolate. He tried to interest himself in the many specialty shops, thinking he would buy a gift for someone. A wedding gift for Mary? No, *she* might think she was ready for marriage, but *he* hadn't accepted her decision fully. Brad? The teenager's simple admission that he didn't want John to leave Greenbank had touched him deeply; it had also unwittingly opened up his own deeply buried urges to know a parent's bond to his own child, he finally admitted. But any present would fall short of what he wanted it to convey.

Besides, such favoritism was not advisable. Maybe he should get all the boys a little something. But what?

His steps slowed as he suddenly asked himself what would happen if his plan fell through. What if the ministry wouldn't let him run Greenbank on his own? Would Henry and Melissa decide to stay on, after all? No, he didn't think so. Henry had seemed eager for a change. Perhaps there had been hints of that off and on, but John had been too absorbed in his own problems to notice. If Henry left and John's request was refused, he had no doubt that eventually the ministry would find another qualified couple to take over. And he would have to adjust to a new job somewhere else. In fact, back at his apartment sat a letter from a staff-operated home in Peterborough, requesting an interview with him. They needed someone as soon as possible....

John passed a travel agency, and he was drawn to the rack of colorful booklets. He reached for one on Australia. Leafing through it, he tried to see it all through Karin's eyes.

"Are you interested in Australia?" a young blond agent asked.

Disoriented, he stared at her blue eyes. "Oh ... just indirectly. A friend of mine is going there."

"It's a popular destination this year. Definitely one of the in places to escape from it all." She smiled at him. "You haven't got the travel bug?"

"No," he mumbled, stuffing the brochure back into its slot. "Thank you...."

He exited the suddenly claustrophobic mall, feeling a headache coming on, perhaps from the unaccustomed glare of the many fluorescent lights. He started walking again, carrying his umbrella, and only after several blocks did he realize that the rain had stopped.

He came to an antique shop. Dominating the window was the biggest rocking chair he'd ever seen. No, maybe it wasn't *the* biggest, after all. He remembered another that could possibly rival it for size. The one he was staring at was more burnished, though, that was for certain. Someone had taken great care in staining and polishing it. But, still, it looked so familiar....

He studied it for a long time, then finally pushed open the door of the shop. Tiny bells announced his arrival, echoing the sudden levity in his heart as he realized what he wanted to do.

CHAPTER SIXTEEN

KARIN HAD NOT HAD TIME to study all the signatures on the giant card her staff had given her earlier that evening during the surprise farewell party they'd thrown for her. So the first thing she did when she got home was to flop down on the couch to decipher the scrawls, the card propped on her knees, her short denim skirt rising even higher.

On the front of the card was a cartoonlike kangaroo, followed inside by the printed words, "We hate to see you hopping along." She'd groaned in delight as she'd read it, and Cindy had sheepishly admitted it was the best they could come up with. Then Karin had been presented with a multipocketed traveling vest, and it had finally hit her that she was really leaving. She'd been in a kind of daze as she made a brief thank-you speech, wished Cindy well in her new position, then fielded all the questions from her own well-wishers, including many club members who'd shown up for the wine-and-cheese affair.

Even though soft music came from the radio, her apartment seemed especially quiet after the boisterous good cheer of the party. As she read all the sentiments expressed in the card, Karin knew she would miss many of the friends she'd made, but she comforted herself with the knowledge that if she hadn't left her *last* job, she wouldn't have met all the wonderful people she now had to leave behind. She had to look ahead, not backward. Nevertheless, her eyes were glistening with a delayed, private show of emotion. No one had known that today was her thirtieth birthday, either, but she couldn't think of a nicer gift than the congenial card.

Suddenly she remembered that tomorrow she had to see the travel agent to sign over full payment for the plane trip. She had made up her mind so late about her date of departure and stopovers that she'd missed out on the advance-booking discount. She'd finally heard from Satch, who'd informed her that unfortunately he had not been able to juggle his schedule to accommodate her stopover in Vancouver. She'd been disappointed, but to her surprise Satch had sounded even more upset that their plans were once more being thwarted. His call had left her in good spirits....

As she reached for her purse, the card dropped to the floor. She found her bankbook and was soon absorbed in some final mental tallying of her upcoming expenses.

The apartment buzzer honked insistently. She turned down the music to hear a muffled voice on the intercom informing her of a delivery. A spiral of hope ran through her. Maybe her father had remembered her birthday after all and was sending her something to make amends for not being able to meet her in Vancouver.... She pushed the button that opened the lobby door, then quickly tucked in the escaped tails of her white cotton shirt and rerolled the sleeves.

Filled with anticipation, she forgot to look through the peephole when the knock sounded. She flung the door open, and her heart turned over.

John Martin was standing there, smiling crookedly, and she ached with loss to see him. Stunned, she watched as he carried an enormous rocking chair into the room and sat it beside her own. The two were not identical—his was maple, hers was oak—but the size and shape of each were almost a perfect match.

Karin's eyes were drawn like magnets to the darkly striking man she'd thought she'd never see again. "W-what on earth?" she sputtered, tearing her gaze from him back to the set of chairs.

"A gift. I couldn't resist her—she seemed a perfect mate for Rocky."

"'She'?" Karin smiled in spite of herself. "But I can't accept such a—a going away gift, no matter how...sweet. I—"

"It's not a going away gift," he said quietly, and her eyes flew to his questioningly.

"But how did you know—" She stopped, in case she'd misinterpreted his meaning.

"Know what?"

"Oh, just that today's my birthday. My thirtieth." She laughed, a tiny tinkling sound that sounded false to her own ears. "But I've been too busy getting ready for the trip to hardly notice it myself."

"Well, happy birthday, Karin. I'm doubly glad I showed up tonight, after all."

"But why *did* you show up? I mean, no one just buys a rocking chair at whim. And even if I kept it, which I can't possibly, where would I keep it? I've just rented enough storage space to keep what I have, and that's going to be a tight squeeze as it is...." She knew she was babbling, but she had to keep talking to immunize herself from the heated way he was staring at her, as if he'd just made love to her.

"I was hoping the two could live together...possibly at Greenbank."

Overwhelmed by his unexpected presence, his strange behavior and the aftereffects of the party earlier, she sat down hard on Rocky, chastising herself once more for not investing in a cushion. "I—I don't understand."

He sat beside her, on the new chair, and taking her hand in both of his, willed her eyes to meet his. "I'm saying this all wrong. I love you, Karin."

"We've been through all this, John. I'm very touched, really, and I'm sorry I behaved like such a child before, but—"

"Just hear me out." His hands became a warm restraint that penetrated through to the rest of her, and she let him speak.... "I-I'm not the same man who walked off the farm to begin a new life for myself. I've changed, without realizing how much...until today. I was standing at a shop window and I saw the chair and it was like something muddled inside me just...became clear. I finally heard what everyone has been trying to tell me. What I've been ignoring in myself all along. Or maybe I wasn't ready to acknowledge it."

His voice thickened as his hands tightened over hers. "I realized I would never be completely happy without you by my side, Karin, sharing my dreams, my disappointments—everything—the past, the present, the future. I need you in my life, not only as my friend and lover, but as my wife, too. Especially as my wife. I can't bear the thought of losing you."

Karin's senses and brain were on overload. Disentangling her hands from his, she stood and slowly walked over to the window, trying to assimilate it all, to sort out the exhilaration and chaos at war inside her.

"I'll give you all the time you need to consider this, Karin—I know it's a lot at once. But if you don't make up your mind soon, you may be responsible for driving a man desperately in love crazy."

She turned to face him and saw the stark nakedness of a man who had given everything and was terrified of receiving nothing in return. "What did you mean when you mentioned the chairs . . . being at Greenbank?" she asked, amazed that she could piece together a coherent sentence.

"Henry wants to move on . . . and we—you and I—can take his and Melissa's place as group parents . . . permanently. I know you could do it, but ultimately the choice is yours."

"And if that's not what I want?"

He tried to hide his deep disappointment, but failed. "Then I could fight to run the home on my own, but realistically I know my chances are slim, especially when we get new residents. . . ."

"So if you were refused . . . ?"

"I'd have to give up one dream and find another. But that's no different than asking you to give up Australia, your career plans, for . . . me, for this chance. But, Karin, trust me. I know it can work. *We* can work, if you want us to. . . ."

She stared out the window as a group of children raced by on their bicycles, dodging passersby. "John, I can't help but think that you came to this conclusion . . . about us . . . only because you need me at Greenbank so you can stay on. You are making a decision based on present need, not as a true commitment, a lifelong pact. . . ."

She heard the chair creak, and then he was behind her, his arms forming a solid band of warmth around her. "I know that's how it appears, but you have to believe me when I say that everything fell into place at once. I love you, Karin, and I want to be with you, always, and if there's a way we can be together, both working toward the same goals in the same place, both fulfilled, then we have to act on it."

"What about *you*, John?" She turned to face him, and her arms had nowhere to go but around his waist, because he would not release his hold on her. She pressed backward as much as she could. "You fought your love for me—you fought it hard. How can I believe that you've really changed? I think you've convinced yourself you've changed in order to keep everything Greenbank is to you. But what will happen when you realize you've made a huge mistake in involving me? 'Sorry, Karin,'" she mimicked, her voice rising in pitch, "'but it's time we go our separate ways again....'"

He grasped her by the shoulders, his intensity as strong and sweeping as a rainstorm breaking over a still lake. "Karin—all I can tell you is that everything that eluded me became so simple. You were right before when you said that love is not enough, that two people have to share *living*, to be two parts of one whole. I see that now, and more.... I see that loving is only the first step on the path toward commitment. I want to marry you, Karin. I want to be true to you and only you. I want to be father to our children. I am ready to promise all that I am and all that I have to you."

"But what about your fears, mine? How can they just vanish?" Her voice was part of the storm, too, but quiet, pained, almost lost in its fury.

"Making such a commitment requires the greatest courage of all, my love, and courage can be stronger than fear. All I can hope is that in time, you'll return my love, that you'll trust in it...."

"I haven't trusted anyone in that sense for a long, long time," she whispered, dry tears tightening her throat as his eyes compelled her to go on. "I *know* I'm afraid of being split into little broken pieces of self—as I was when my parents divorced, as I could have been if I'd given *everything* to someone like Eric. But I don't know how to get rid of that fear—it's always there, no matter how hard I pretend otherwise." She swallowed, trying to ease the parched ache. "Love always has the upper hand—the power to cause pain, to destroy. To me, marriage, even with the best of intentions, is that power multiplied a hundred times over."

"But love... and marriage also have the power to bring joy, to heal pain. Together we can be strong. We're right for each other, Karin. I feel it in my heart, and you must, too."

"'Right' is such an elusive quality," she countered on an explosive breath, past the choking sensation in her throat. "What's right today may not be right tomorrow or next month or next year or—"

"That's where trust comes in. By trusting in love, by trusting in an opportunity, such as the one at Greenbank that can make us a team in every sense of the word...."

As soon as he'd spoken, he realized his error in judgment. His juxtaposition of love and work was unfortunate, considering the accusations she'd hurled at him about his own motivation. He should be dealing with her feelings on each issue separately, but it was too late. Her face was already deeply creased in distress. He plunged on. "First, could you see yourself working as a group parent at Greenbank?" In the split second that he'd reasoned with himself before asking the question, he'd known that he could deal with her ambivalence about such a major career change, but he was not ready to face her possible refusal to marry him.

"Is it an either/or situation, John? Is it you and Greenbank or nothing at all? What if I choose to do something else, instead? Do you still want me as your wife?" She pulled away as she hurled the challenge at him and waited for the answer she needed to hear.

But he did not hesitate. "Above all, I want you to be happy, Karin. Our commitment to each other will be what binds us, not the fact of our working together."

"Even if it means you may lose Greenbank?"

"I'll fight to stay there, with or without you," he answered slowly, "and if I lose the fight, then that is what must be. I can't deny that I'll take such a loss very hard. But we—I—will find a way for everything to work out."

"And if I choose to move on . . . alone?"

He did not reply immediately, and when he did it was with great difficulty. "Then I must let you go." In direct contradiction to his words, his need to reach for her, to hold her, was suddenly overwhelming. Everything in him revolted against losing her when he'd come so close to having her. But he also knew that it was imperative that he not push her. With a supreme effort, he willed himself not to touch her despite the passion burning in his soul. "Just tell me what you truly want, Karin. That's all I ask."

"I—I feel as if I'm riding on an emotional roller coaster," she answered, trying to explain the strange combination of numbness and hyperactivity she was experiencing. "I don't know if I can properly separate my...wants from yours, right now. Please, I know it's not fair to you, but I need more time...."

He saw her disorientation and exhaustion, but he could not walk away from her at this critical stage. He knew with an uncanny certainty that by abandoning her, she was bound to run from herself, from him again, and too much was at stake for him to accept defeat so easily.

"Let me stay with you tonight," he said deep into the sky-blue eyes he loved. "I promise I'll just hold you. For the last time, if that's what you wish...."

Long moments passed before she nodded wordlessly. He took her hand and led her to the bed, where he stretched beside her, and she slipped into his arms as naturally as if she did so every night.

Darkness crept around them, and at some indeterminate point, Karin's breathing took on the soft rhythm of sleep. Only then did John stop fighting his own fatigue.

UPON WAKING, Karin's first impression was of the room's brightness. Vaguely she realized she must have forgotten to pull down the blind last night, but it was so pleasant to be greeted by sunshine pouring through the window. She rolled onto her back and encountered the long, sleeping form of John Martin, fully clothed. The events of yesterday trickled back....

Unconsciously his arm wrapped around her and his cheek pressed into the curve of her shoulder, oblivious to the wrinkled shirt she still wore. Her skirt was curled up around her thighs. The sheets had been kicked out of sight.

In sleep, there was nothing threatening about John Martin—there was only strength and integrity and trustworthiness. So why had she felt so threatened by everything he'd told her last night, by his presence in her life since she'd met him? *Because I love him,* a voice inside answered as clearly as if she'd spoken aloud.

Tears filled her eyes as she finally admitted the truth to herself, and for a moment she despised her own weakness in loving him. But distantly she knew that that weakness was strength, that the pride and fear that kept her from acting on her love were not strengths.

But did she have the courage to face the riskiest proposition of all—to commit herself to him for all time, thus making herself vulnerable to the power such all-encompassing love would hold over her?

John maintained that he had found that courage. He was ready to put himself on the line for her, whether she shared his desire to work at Greenbank or not. He *had* changed, she finally realized. A new unselfishness and a willingness

to compromise had become part of his love, part of the life
he was offering her. One thing had not changed, though.
John Martin had always understood her on a level that even
she had been reluctant to probe. He had known that for
her, love was a matter of profound trust....

Trust: an affirmation, whitewashed pure but tinged with
the knowledge of darker moments, solid but abstract—
terrifying paradoxes. Involving a giant leap of faith. Not
just for one night of passion or a finite time, but forever.
John was willing to make the leap for her. She wanted to
believe in him. She wanted to believe that the vows of marriage would ultimately seal the trust between them. She
wanted to believe that love could survive whatever had
pulled her own parents apart. Most of all, she wanted to live
her passion for John Martin so, so much....

She studied his face, memorizing every pore, watching
every breath he took. Her fingers touched the arm encircling her, as if it belonged there. And she faced the simple
indisputable truth—she could no longer walk away from
the happiness he was promising her. She belonged with
him.

But if she stayed, it had to be on new terms; she would
not let the stifling fear of love control her—*she* would control it. She had never wanted anything as much as she
wanted that.

As if a wonderful tapestry were unfolding before her
eyes, she looked at what her future could hold if she willed
herself to act courageously. The prospect of working in the
group home with John truly thrilled her. To build a home,
a real home, with the man she cherished as much as life itself, and to help extend that home into a sanctuary for
others who were homeless, filled her with excitement at a
gut level. Nothing else could ever accomplish that in the
same way, she suddenly realized. Not Australia. Nor the

world of health clubs. And surely she could never trust or love anyone as much as she trusted and loved John Martin.

Beside her, John stirred, burrowing closer. To wake every day in his loving arms would be sweet paradise on earth.... His eyes opened to find her looking at him, smiling softly.

"Yes," she said simply. "Yes."

He was instantly awake, his comprehension just as rapid. One side of his face pressed against hers until their lips met for a deep lingering kiss of confirmation.

"But is that all?" he asked incredulously at last. "Just yes?"

"That's it—yes to you, Greenbank, everything. Somehow, thanks to you and my own determination, I'm not afraid anymore." The unadorned words sounded like a song bursting from her heart.

"I don't have to beg you on my knees to marry me? I don't have to run through the list of your credentials as to why I know you'd be perfect at Greenbank or anywhere else, as long as it's close to me? I don't have to convince you over and over that I'll never leave you, that I'll love you forever?"

She propped herself up on her elbow to look down at him and said playfully, "Well, come to think of it, I'm listening...."

"Later," he growled in a low velvety voice as his lips were drawn to the soft hollow of her throat. Suddenly he stopped and nudged her head down to the pillow again so that her eyes were close enough for him to scrutinize every nuance. "What about your trip, opening a new club? I don't want you to have any regrets."

Her fingers traced the outline of his furrowed brow, then tried, unsuccessfully, to pat down a tuft of his sleep-tousled hair, the familiarity of the gesture filling her with a deep tenderness. "Everything I really want is right here," she said with all the conviction of her newfound trust. "I love you, John. I may have been slow in recognizing it, but I guarantee I'll make up for lost time. We're going to make an indomitable team." She felt a boundless surge of joy at the rich play of lights that shone from his eyes at her words.

"To think how close we came to letting each other go...."

Between an exchange of light kisses, she murmured, "I probably would have come to my senses somewhere in the middle of the Pacific Ocean."

"Ah, but I'm glad it happened in your bed." His hands traveled on a journey of their own, following the line of her hip and thigh beneath her bunched-up skirt. "We do have one more very pressing problem, though...."

"And what's that?"

"We seem to be overdressed for this fine occasion."

"Hmm—so far we're in perfect agreement."

And with each other's full cooperation, they continued their celebration of love....

EPILOGUE

THE GRAND OLD MAPLE at the center of the Martin lawn wore a crown of gold—a festive greeting to the many visitors to the farm on the clear October Tuesday of Mary and Joshua Brubacher's wedding.

Topless black buggies lined the driveway and yard; waiting horses were hitched to every available fence post. One car joined the rest at midafternoon. A group of children who were playing in a pile of raked leaves stared curiously at the vehicle. When the occupants, a man and a woman, did not immediately emerge, they went back to their game.

"Nervous?" John asked, his hand closing over his wife's. Sunlight streamed through the car window and caught the shiny new gold of their wedding bands.

"A little," Karin answered. "How many people do you figure are here?"

"Who knows? Most of the relatives from both families. Some friends of Mary and Joshua. A few neighbors. Why are you looking so concerned? It's not *your* wedding."

Karin sighed. "I almost feel as if it is. Maybe because I'll be meeting most of your relatives for the first time as your wife. Your immediate family have been wonderful in accepting me—us—but I don't know these other people. Are you sure our presence here won't offend anyone? I don't want to be shunned publicly, embarrass your family and spoil Mary's special day."

"Is that what's been on your mind? Don't worry. They are all good people. If my parents have accepted us, so will they, out of respect for our family. Under the circumstances, I thought that attending the ceremony itself might cause some...discomfort, which is why I didn't suggest we come earlier, as much as I would have liked to have been there for Mary's sake. But this celebration afterward is a different matter. Come, you will see." He squeezed her hand reassuringly before stepping out of the car.

Karin clutched an unwrapped box, adorned only with a sprig of baby's breath, and inhaled deeply as she, too, exited from the car. She and John had debated long about what to give the bride and groom. They'd finally chosen a simple wood carving of two morning doves, purchased at one of the SELFHELP Craft Shops, operated by the Mennonite Central Committee. All profits were sent to help Third World countries.

As soon as they entered the crowded house, they sought out the newlyweds. Karin had wondered whether Mary and Joshua would approve of an ornament as a gift, no matter how plain. But to her relief, Mary's face broke into delight as she opened the package. "It's lovely!" she said, holding up the carving for her husband. "See, Joshua.... I'll put it in our room. We will always have birds with us."

Joshua smiled indulgently at her. "Does this mean we can cut down on bird feed this winter?" he asked in his soft voice, knowing Mary's penchant for keeping the local bird population well provided for.

"Of course not! How could I disappoint all my little friends?"

"Women!" Joshua exaggerated the word, rolling his eyes for emphasis, and Mary looked a little surprised, and pleased, at his uncharacteristic outgoingness.

"I hope we won't be responsible for your first marital spat," Karin said lightly, her eyes warmly resting on the young couple.

"Don't worry about that," Joshua said, shyly slipping his arm around Mary's waist, but holding it there boldly. He looked down at her briefly, and she blushed as she returned his gaze.

Neither seemed inclined to pull away until John broke the intimacy. "My deepest congratulations to you both," he said, extending his hand to his new brother-in-law and firmly shaking it.

"Thank you . . . John."

For the first time, Karin noticed, he had not addressed her own husband as "sir." In fact, Joshua radiated a fresh confidence. His new dark suit fitted him to perfection, making him seem dignified, more mature. His face glowed with pride every time he looked at his pretty wife, her dark coiled hair and natural rosy cheeks complementing her simple white hand-sewn dress. In turn, Mary's eyes were bright with excitement . . . and something else, ever so subtle—a heightened awareness of Joshua that had not been there before. Perhaps Karin was sensitive to the attraction because of her similar feelings whenever she was near her own new husband.

Despite John's earlier concerns, Karin knew that the couple's quiet fondness, budding sexuality and deep sense of loyalty would give them a foundation for a good marriage. She caught John's gaze and knew that he was thinking the same thing, not to mention suddenly remembering how they themselves had spent a great part of the previous night.

When the bride and groom's attention was caught by a family who were about to depart, John took Karin by the hand and slowly introduced her around. In her classic navy skirt and jacket with a white blouse, she had already drawn attention among the printed smocks and chin-strapped prayer veils worn by the Mennonite women. But just as her concerns about whether Mary and Joshua would like her gift had dissipated, so did Karin's worries about her reception by the various wedding guests.

True, she was aware of some overtly curious stares, but everyone made an effort to be courteous to both her and John. She sensed that the family occasion was more difficult for him than he had admitted, because it was so visibly apparent that he had left the Old Order to lead a different life. Instead of the traditional Mennonite clothing, he wore a tweed jacket, a fashionable shirt with a button-down collar and brown pleated pants. Particularly among John's elderly aunts and uncles, the polite conversation was strained, even awkward at times, but it was still clear to Karin that even those folks were trying hard to accept John's decision and his new non-Mennonite wife.

Karin had met only about half of the fifty or so guests who were smilingly bumping shoulders in all of the lower rooms of the house, when John was called away by his mother to fetch more firewood. A seemingly never-ending supply of aromatic food was being heated on the old wood stove to fill platters on the long kitchen table beside her, as well as on another table set against one wall of the parlor. Karin surveyed the assortment of meats, vegetables, breads, preserves and desserts, and decided she would wait no longer to sample them. Then she felt a tap on her elbow and turned to see a stooped Erwin Martin, who seemed to have shrunk even more in size. But his dark, buttonlike eyes were more lively than ever.

"Anna has sent me over to order you to eat," he began in his no-nonsense way. "She thinks we'll run out, the way everyone's been going back for seconds and thirds."

"I don't think a shortage is likely. . . ."

"I agree. Mainly I just wanted to see how you're getting along. A lot of folks here wanted to meet you, though they'd never admit it. They all want to have formed their own opinion when the subject of John and his new wife comes up in the future, as I'm sure it will. People like to talk—you know that. But I hope they've all been very. . . kindly to you, no matter how they feel about what John has done."

Once more Karin marveled at this wizened man's perception and tolerance for his grandson's choices. "Yes, everyone has been pleasant. John had faith that they would."

Erwin nodded. "His dedication this summer and fall while his father was ill did not pass unnoticed. People no longer feel that John has deserted his family—to the same degree."

Karin thought of John's conscientiousness in making sure all the tasks at the farm were looked after, either by himself or Mennonite volunteers, until Joshua could take over. Even before her approval as a group parent had been finalized, she had unofficially spent most of her time filling in for John at Greenbank when necessary, but somehow he had managed to juggle his time so that he was always where he was needed most.

"John cares very much about all of you," Karin said softly, "even if he can't always be here, what with his duties at Greenbank and looking after the gang there."

"'Bout time he gave some of that love to his own children, too," Erwin prodded with a friendly sternness.

"Oh . . . we'll see." She felt a rise in coloring, because lately she had been giving some thought to the subject herself.

"You and John shouldn't wait too long, or you'll never get to meddle in your grandchildren's lives, like some of us are wont to do. . . ."

Karin laughed. "You have a point there—I'll give the matter serious consideration someday." He raised an eyebrow at her. "Soon." He nodded in satisfaction.

Suddenly Anna Martin was in front of them, her flushed face ready to scold. "You two can talk later, but first Karin must eat. We have enough good food for everybody—I hope. *Everybody* came—even those who thought they might be too busy with harvesting. We are so pleased." She was talking so quickly that Karin had difficulty following her. "See, it was not such a bad thing having Mary's wedding earlier than usual so Joshua could be nearby, no matter what *some* folks were whispering. But enough talk. You must eat, Karin. . . ."

"I was just about to try some," Karin reassured her, amused by her uncustomary flustered manner.

"And I was telling John's wife that I am getting impatient to see my great-grandchild," Erwin added.

Anna's expression immediately lighted up as she looked at him. "Well, then, I can forgive you for keeping Karin from the food." She turned to her son's new wife. "Family is good. You'll see." She handed Karin a plate. Leaning toward her, she whispered in her ear conspiratorially, "They might forget you're not Mennonite if they see you enjoying food as much as we do. And you must take home some for the boys," she added, her mind busily skimming all the different matters that needed seeing to. "How are Karl and Brad?"

"Fine. Brad is still quite keen about studying agriculture. This year he plans to apply to several universities offering courses in that field, but first he has to improve his marks so that he will be accepted."

"Ah, he is a smart boy. A good boy. If he wants to be." And then she noticed a plate emptied of cabbage rolls, which prompted her to hastily leave her daughter-in-law's side.

Karin had no trouble filling her plate with the inviting country cooking. She'd already put on a few pounds since leaving the club, but John assured her that he liked her more pronounced curves. And she didn't really worry about gaining too much weight—the demands of her new job, especially her morning jog with the boys, kept her reasonably fit.

She thought back to the day Gary Fries had finally told her she'd been accepted as a group parent, after she'd filled out form after form, attended countless interviews—and prayed a lot. She'd actually cried, so great had been her jubilation at hearing the news. John and Henry had assured her she'd had nothing to worry about from the start, but once she'd made up her mind, her approval had taken on momentous importance, and she'd dared not even think of what she would do if she had been refused.

Thankfully, she hadn't been. The past month at Greenbank had turned out to be the most fulfilling of her entire life, everything she'd hoped for in such an occupation and more. The best part of all was that her day-to-day dealings with the boys, the follow-up meetings with the support personnel, her household and administrative duties and all the other challenging aspects didn't seem like a job at all, but a satisfying way of life. She didn't feel as if she'd traded one dream for another by giving up her trip and the chance to manage a new club in Toronto. No, she felt as if she'd finally found what she had been searching for her whole life. And at the center of it all was her new husband....

She looked around, but didn't spot him. Erwin Martin had wandered off, too. Needing to steal a few quiet moments away from the roomful of near strangers, she headed toward the front of the house, careful not to spill the mountainlike pile on her plate as she maneuvered her way around the many groups. She pushed open the door of the porch and stepped outside into the welcome coolness. Her suit jacket provided adequate insulation against the bite in the air.

Leaning against the wooden rail, she nibbled at her food while gazing out at the many hues of autumn—the blazing crimsons, oranges and golds of the changing leaves, the pale yellow corn stalks ripe for harvesting, the rich brown soil of the overturned garden, the fading blue sweep of the prewinter sky.

She thought how her own life had changed as naturally as the seasons blended into each other, and she marveled at how easily the transformation had taken place once she had learned to trust in love....

Suddenly the door behind her opened. She didn't mind at all that her solitude had been invaded when her eyes met the beloved dark lights of John's.

He slipped beside her on the railing and slid his arm behind her, pulling her close. "Cold?" he murmured.

"Hmm, very." She put down her plate and snuggled against him.

"Liar. Sorry I had to desert you."

"Don't worry. I had a cozy little chat with your grandfather. He put in some very unsubtle hints about seeing some Martin offspring. Your mother seconded the motion."

"Must be a conspiracy. My father and a few other interested parties made the same pointed suggestion."

"And what did you tell them?" Karin inclined her head to watch his face.

His expression was blank, maddeningly so. "I told them to be patient. Then they wanted to know how patient."

"And?"

"And I wanted to tell them that my wife has recently adapted to many changes in her life—and quite admirably, I might add. Until she is ready for more changes, everyone should mind their own business. Meanwhile, I am taking immense pleasure in having her all to myself—or more accurately, to sharing her with only four... sorry, five other housemates, counting Tyler, our latest addition."

Karin eyed him warily. "But you didn't really say all that?"

He smiled. "No, of course not. I left them all in suspense."

"And what if I am ready to, ah, cooperate in that department?"

Anticipation flickered deep in his eyes, but he shook it away. "Karin—it's too soon for you. I don't expect you to... I mean, there's lots of time. Don't pay mind to a few interfering relatives."

She looked squarely at him and said softly, "I can think of nothing I'd love more than to have our child, to add to our brood—if we could find the room, that is." Already she fondly thought of the teenagers at Greenbank as part of her own family.

John's face was tight with unspoken emotion. Finally he said, "We could *make* room if we had to, but just think about this longer to make sure it's what you want."

"I already have," she replied with heartfelt sincerity. "Actually... I'm well past the intellectual stage."

"Don't look at me like that, or we'll have to make a hasty exit," he warned, his eyes sending an equally sensuous message.

"That would make us just as unpopular as staying out here too long. Should we go in?"

"In a minute." His free hand reached for hers and stroked it with the eroticism and affection that was always between them. "We shall pursue the, ah, delightful matter we were discussing in... finer detail, later."

"I can hardly wait," she murmured, feeling the familiar racing effect he always had on her cardiovascular system, definitely more pleasant than any aerobics workout.

"Good... but first I want to ask you something. When you see all these people gathered in Mary and Joshua's honor, do you regret that our own wedding was so quiet?"

"I have absolutely no regrets. Our wedding was the most beautiful day in my life," she immediately answered, the memory of it as clear as if it had happened yesterday instead of six weeks ago.

The simple but intimate ceremony had been held at Greenbank, performed by a minister, with Henry and Cindy as witnesses. Afterward, amid champagne toasts, to everyone's delight the boys had crashed the party. Apparently they had grown suspicious of being taken to dinner and a movie by Jessica and Margaret, when they *knew* Karin was applying to join the staff at Greenbank and when they'd seen how gushy John and Karin had been acting around each other. So they'd wrangled the truth out of their flustered chaperons, neither of whom were having an easy time keeping such a secret, and persuaded the women to let them all forgo the movie for some real-life drama and fun back home.

The two highly apologetic women had not stayed long, but the youths had added a memorable heartiness to the small gathering. Henry had supervised the teenagers at Greenbank that night while John and Karin had left for a brief honeymoon—one night at the elegant Walper Terrace Hotel in downtown Kitchener. A few days later, the boys had surprised the newlyweds with a framed print of a winter river scene by Peter Etril Snyder, famous for his vivid reproductions of Waterloo County. They'd discovered that Karin and John had met by the Conestogo River....

Henry's admiration for the artist had been apparent to all during the presentation. So when it was time for him to make his move to Vancouver, Karin and John had bought another Snyder print for him on behalf of all the remaining members of Greenbank. Henry had been deeply touched by the sight of the Mennonite buggy on a country road, saying it would always remind him of his roots while he was resettling on the West Coast.

Karin had sent a marriage announcement to a more established resident of western Canada—her father. She hadn't really expected him to receive it for many months, but the timing must have been right. A beautiful bouquet of roses with a note of congratulations had arrived at John's apartment, where she and John had been staying until Henry moved out. And the next night, Satch had called to extend a profusion of good wishes. He had talked to her for more than an hour and had even asked to speak to John. He'd *promised* to visit them both at Christmas, and he'd bought a ticket to cement his intentions, swearing he'd refuse even the queen if she asked for a private jazz performance. Karin was sensible enough to prepare herself for a last-minute cancellation, because with Satch, as she well knew, anything could happen, but this time she just had a feeling that he would make it. He'd kept saying how good it would be to see her again, before he was a dotty old man, and he'd kept insisting he ought to give his blessing to the marriage in person—after all, wasn't that what fathers, even largely absent ones, were supposed to do...?

"No, I have absolutely no regrets," Karin repeated, smiling fully at the man with whom she'd shared so many precious moments, both before and after their marriage. "But what about you? When you see your family all together, do you wish some of the closest ones had been there with us on our wedding day?"

"Maybe a little," he admitted, "but you were the only one I really needed to see there. I was terrified that you might change your mind, that I'd rushed you by showing up on your doorstep with a marriage proposal on my lips and a rocking chair in my arms...."

"For both of those, I'll be eternally touched and grateful."

"And I'll be forever in debt to your travel urge, safely redirected for the time being, I hope. To someone like me who's lived such a stationary life, Australia seemed to sit at the far corners of the earth...." He kissed her lightly, as if to reassure himself of her nearness.

Karin's heart was bursting with the happiness that her commitment to him had brought her. It now seemed inconceivable to her that she had been so afraid to risk loving him. The opposite had become true. She would risk anything to keep their growing love intact.

The clouds were streaked with the soft lavender tint of the slowly setting sun. Arms linked, the couple lingered on the porch a few minutes longer, mesmerized by the late-afternoon sky and its changing play of light and color.

And both reflected that just as surely as tomorrow would witness a new dawn, there would be more joy ahead, more avenues to explore together... because of the ever-awakening, boundless love they gave each other....

Six exciting series
for you every month...
from Harlequin

Harlequin Romance·
The series that started it all

Tender, captivating and heartwarming...
love stories that sweep you off to faraway places
and delight you with the magic of love.

◆

Harlequin Presents·
Powerful contemporary love
stories...as individual as the
women who read them

The No. 1 romance series...
exciting love stories for you, the woman of today...
a rare blend of passion and dramatic realism.

◆

Harlequin Superromance®
It's more than romance...
it's Harlequin Superromance

A sophisticated, contemporary romance-fiction
series, providing you with a longer,
more involving read...a richer mix of complex plots,
realism and adventure.

Harlequin
American Romance™
Harlequin celebrates the American woman...

...by offering you romance stories written about American women, by American women for American women. This series offers you contemporary romances uniquely North American in flavor and appeal.

◆

Harlequin Temptation™
Passionate stories for today's woman

An exciting series of sensual, mature stories of love...dilemmas, choices, resolutions... all contemporary issues dealt with in a true-to-life fashion by some of your favorite authors.

◆

Harlequin Intrigue™
Because romance can be quite an adventure

Harlequin Intrigue, an innovative series that blends the romance you expect... with the unexpected. Each story has an added element of intrigue that provides a new twist to the Harlequin tradition of romance excellence.

Harlequin Books®

PROD-A-2

What the press says about Harlequin romance fiction...

"When it comes to romantic novels...
Harlequin is the indisputable king."
—New York Times

"...always with an upbeat, happy ending."
—San Francisco Chronicle

"Women have come to trust these
stories about contemporary people,
set in exciting foreign places."
—Best Sellers, New York

"The most popular reading matter of
American women today."
—Detroit News

"...a work of art."
—Globe & Mail, Toronto